75¢

"GREY'S SHOT TOM! HE'S DEAD!"

"Tom's down, but he ain't dead," said another voice, hidden among the rocks. "Get up there and give him a hand."

"Give him a hand yourself! You see how that Grey can shoot!"

I could have laughed at that, but all desire for laughter was wiped out of me by the pain in my leg. Then, with a hammer blow, I was hit in the right shoulder—the gun arm!

Through a haze of pain, I saw half a dozen men start up from the rocks around me. I propped my rifle against my shoulder and fired with my numb hand. A man dropped. Then another shouted, his voice filled with rage, "Is one damned brat going to stop the whole lot of us? *Get him out—and eat him raw!*"

Books by Max Brand

Published by POCKET BOOKS

Max Brand

DEAD OR ALIVE

PUBLISHED BY POCKET BOOKS NEW YORK

POCKET BOOKS, a Simon & Schuster division of
GULF & WESTERN CORPORATION
1230 Avenue of the Americas, New York, N.Y. 10020

ISBN: 0-671-81754-X

First Pocket Books printing February, 1979

10 9 8 7 6 5 4 3 2 1

CONTENTS

1

A SHADOWED RANCH

The day that "Lanky" arrived sticks in my mind partly because of the story that he told a few minutes after he reached the bunk house, and partly because of the events that happened afterward. There were so many of them, that before the wind-up you'll understand why everything connected with Lanky is printed in my mind with red ink.

We had finished for the day. Even the roustabout was finished, which meant me, because I was the youngest of the outfit. I was twenty-two, at that, but being the youngest and the greenest hand, of course all the mean jobs came my way. However, I hardly minded that. The Porson outfit was one of the best on the range. They worked the men hard, but when the lean times came in winter, they always found some sort of an excuse for keeping on every good man. The bums and the loafers got their walking papers when the cold weather began in earnest, but every honest puncher could be sure of wintering with the Porson people. Sometimes the extra men got half pay. Sometimes they only got their chuck; but as soon as there was a ghost of an excuse for starting the work full blast in the spring, every man went back on full pay. Of course no one minds working for an outfit like that.

For my part, intending to spend my entire life either working cattle, or owning them, or both, I was happy to learn from old Jeff Porson. He was one of the hardest men on the range, but he was about the squarest, and he knew cows! He knew them so well that if he saw a yearling throwing its head and tail on a sky line, he could tell you within ten the number of flies that were bothering it. At least, that was what the hands all said about him! His son, Dan Porson, bossed the outfit, when the old man was away, and he was a good boss, too, very keen, and a little too fond of working up a fight, now and then, but on the whole a good boss, with lots of understanding.

What's a good boss? Well, a good boss is a fellow who knows his job in the first place and his men in the second place. He knows when you've done your best and when you haven't. The first week I was on the place, I broke a bad-acting four-year-old for the outfit. It took me the whole week, and it was a question whether I would break the horse or the horse would break me. In the end, I had given that gelding nearly all the bad habits that a horse can pick up in a lifetime, but young Dan Porson let me keep on working away at the gelding. I found out, afterward, that when one of the fellows complained about the way I was mishandling that horse just through ignorance, Dan said that an educated cowboy meant more on the place than a well-educated horse, any day, and that I never would learn any younger, and that I never would have a better teacher than experience.

I dwell on this, and on Dan Porson, because about the time that Lanky arrived, there was a good deal of trouble on deck because Dan had gone to town with the bunch, a few weeks before, and lost his temper in a saloon brawl. The brawl didn't amount to much. It was just whisky talk. But it led to a gun play, and being a fast man and a straight man with a gun, Dan dropped his man.

The bullet hit Josh Acker just inside the right hip bone and came out the small of his back. They put Josh to bed in a back room of the saloon, and of course Dan Porson paid the doctor bills, and all of us hoped that Josh would pull through, partly because it was tough for a kid of his age to be bumped off, and partly because he had a brother drifting in some part of the range who would be sure to come and ring the front doorbell of Dan Porson if Josh went West. That brother was Tom Acker. He was a natural gunman. He fought partly because he loved fighting so much, and partly because he was so good at it. For his killings he had been tried half a dozen times, I suppose, but every time he had been freed on the excuse of self-defense.

This was the way that things were standing, when along came

a letter scribbled by Josh Acker containing the money to pay back Dan Porson for everything that Dan had spent on doctor bills and keep since the shooting, and also mentioning that it was his brother, Tom, who was supplying the coin, now, and that Tom Acker said he was hitting the trail for the Porson place as soon as his hands were free.

He wanted to talk to Dan Porson, said the letter, and any half-wit could have foretold that the only conversation at that meeting would be words spoken by Judge Colt!

So a shadow gathered over the ranch. The laugh went out of the supper time, and the hands were frowning all day long. We knew Dan's faults, but we liked him, and we hated to think that he was getting so close to planting time.

This was the layout, and the reason that we were sitting around in front of the bunk house with mighty little conversation, when a rider jogged his horse over the hill and pulled up in front of us. He was the real cow-puncher style—built long and lean, with a goodish pair of shoulders and arms set on top. He had an ugly face but a good-natured one. He had a big, crooked nose, and a big, crooked mouth that smiled on the same side that the nose leaned toward. He had the look of a fellow who had spent his life with the wind blowing always on one side of him, like a timber-line tree.

He slowly slid off his horse, when he pulled up in front of the bunk house.

We could see that his clothes were all in tatters. His horse was a lump of a roach-backed mustang, that dropped its head, as though a weight were hung on it. Yes, they made a sloppy pair. Most punchers like to make a snappy stop, and jump out of the saddle as though they had some life in them, but this stranger simply half stepped and half fell out, and got to the ground the easiest way.

"Hello, boys," he said. "Any chuck left in the kitchen, over yonder?"

Dan Porson was sitting with us. He said:

"Put up your horse, stranger. Then go inside and tell the cook to give you a hand-out. Tell him to give you an extra pair of blankets, too. There's a spare bunk for you, in here."

"I'll put up the horse if I can get him to the barn," said the tall fellow, "but he makes hard leading."

"What is he? A downhill horse?" asked some one.

"This horse? No, sir, this is a bear horse," said the stranger.

He went off toward the barn, dragging the roach-backed mustang behind him; then we saw him head toward the house.

"What does he mean by a bear horse?" asked Dan Porson.

"He looks like a tramp, and he walks like rheumatism," said "Lefty" Guiness. "I hope he don't stay long."

It was the end of spring, when the days are at their longest, and there was still rosy light when the stranger came back from the house, carrying a blanket over his shoulder, and smoking a cigarette. He stepped slow and short, as though he had sore feet and a cramp in his stomach.

Dan Porson was a good-mannered fellow. He came out and shook hands.

"You know this outfit?" he asked.

"No," said the stranger. "It just looked handy as I was sailing by."

"It's the Porson place," said Dan. "And I'm Dan Porson. Roll down your blanket inside and make yourself at home."

"Thanks," said the other. "I'm by name of Lanky, usually. I'm glad to know you, Porson."

He gave the blanket a fold and made a cushion of it; then he sat down, cross-legged, with a groan.

"What's a bear horse, brother?" asked Dan.

"A bear horse?" said Lanky. "Don't you know what a bear horse is, Porson?"

"No," said Dan, "I don't. Never heard of one called that before to-day."

"Well," said Lanky, "now I come to think of it, maybe you haven't, and maybe I haven't myself, before the other day."

He paused, and in the pause his long, lazy fingers made a fresh cigarette, that he lighted from the butt of the one that he had just been smoking.

By the silence that held on until he had the new smoke going, he could see that we were all waiting for his explanation, which came like this:

"Few days back, I was loping my pony along and damning him, now and then, though you shouldn't talk harsh to a gift horse. But he's all wrong in front, and bad behind, and he hasn't any middle piece. He trots with his hind legs and walks with his front legs, and he's always getting crooked, like cows going downhill. He's broken-winded, and nearsighted, and the only strength he has he burns up every morning pitching to get himself warm for the trail. His gait is so hard that he fills me with aches from my heels to my Adam's apple, if you know that kind of a horse. Every time he puts a foot down, I can hear my brains rattle in my skull like dried peas in a tin pan."

"Yeah, I know that kind of a horse," said Dan Porson.

The rest of us sat tight, because it was clear that the long, lean stranger knew how to spin a yarn. He went on:

"I was getting hungry. The eating was few and far between, and the vibrations of that mustang sure worked up the appetite, when I get a flash of a gang of white-tailed deer. I get down, tie the mustang on a long lead to a willow, and sneak over the hill. I get a shot and have the luck to drop a young buck. I go up and cut off all the meat that I can use, and I come packing it back through the brush to load on the mustang.

"Just then out of the shadows a grizzly rises up and stands so high that his nose is pressed against the sky. The biggest grizzly that I ever saw, bar none; not even the kind that they tell about in the barroom, after the third drink. He was so near that when he grunted, he blew my hat off. I dropped the meat I was carrying, picked my hat out of the air, and started for the horse, and the bear started after me.

"I climbed that mustang, and put my spurs into him as far as they would reach, and he started for the north pole like a hawk. You see, I'd forgotten all about that long line I'd tied to the willow, but when we come to the end of it, the mustang dives on his head, and I keep on sailing till I hit a bunch of thorn bushes, and crash into it, and it claws me from head to foot. That's what's the matter with my clothes.

"When my brains stop spinning, I sit up, and see that the mustang is climbing back to his feet, and the bear has just about made up his mind that he'll eat horse that day.

"So he comes charging in. There's rope slack hanging under the neck of the broncho, but he don't take it up. He knows all about that rope by this time, and he's not taking any chances with it. So when the bear moves in, he moves back a little, and puts his head down to take aim, and swings his hind hoofs a couple of yards past his ears, and then slams the bear right on the end of the nose.

"That bear was so big that there was a lodging place for both of those hoofs on the end of his nose. He rolled over backward, and the noise he made seemed to come out of the middle of the earth. Then he stood up, and put forth forepaws to his face to find out what's left of it, and when he finds that he still has part of it left, he decides that he'll get out of there pronto before he loses the rest of it.

"So he starts galloping away on three legs, with one paw held up to his nose by way of comforting it.

"And that's how he goes over the rim of the sky line and drops out of sight.

"So I collect the mustang, and pick up the meat and the rifle

I've dropped, and ride along. But every now and then, the horse remembers the rope, and stops dead, and shakes his head a while. And every now and then, he puts down his head to see if the bear's coming at him from behind again.

"And that's why I call him a bear horse."

He stopped, as he reached this point in his story, rose with pain, and groaned again.

"Those briars," said he, "clawed me to pieces."

Then he went inside the bunk house, and the fellows were still chuckling.

"A bear horse!" said Dan Porson.

We all laughed together.

"I'll tell you what he is, this fellow Lanky," said Porson. "He's a talking fool!"

2

THE ENTERTAINER

We expected that Lanky would be with us for no more than the night, but it was three weeks before there was anything as important as that to report about him. During those three weeks, we expected every day that he would pull up stakes and leave us, and we hated the idea, because he was one of the most amusing men in the world. "A talking fool," he had been called by our boss, not to indicate that he was a half-wit, but just as one would use the expression, "fighting fool," or "working fool."

Certainly he was not a great worker. For a few days, he was so stiff and sore from the cuts of the briers and thorns into which he had fallen from the back of his horse—at least, according to his queer story—that it was obviously painful for him to move. But after that, it was equally plain that no matter what his condition might be, he was never in shape for work. No matter what it was, so long as there was a physical effort connected, he was troubled.

He used to make all sorts of bargains with us. He had tricks up his sleeve like a stage conjurer, and we very quickly found out what he was interested in. He would never bet you a dollar that you could not find the right card, but he would bet the repairing of his bridle, or the new stirrup leather that he needed, or something like that. He would bet you the currying and brushing

13

of his mustang—which the brute didn't need at all—against fifty cents, that he could pull a jack rabbit out of your coat. He did that to me, and when he reached his hand into the bosom of my coat, presently I felt a wriggling and a kicking that frightened me half to death, and there he was, holding the rabbit by the nape of the neck.

Everybody whooped and laughed at the sight of it. Lanky kept his sober face, as he said:

"It's not everybody that I can get a rabbit out of. It takes an open heart and a confiding nature to let a rabbit get inside him. But you see that Nelly Grey is full of rabbits!"

And, by thunder, he seemed to pull another jack out of my coat in the same way, and it went streaking off into the twilight just like the first one.

I have to explain that my name is Nelson Grey, which was usually shortened down to "Nels," but it was Lanky who called me "Nelly" for the first time; and that name never left me, to my very great disgust.

Tricks like that were worth a good deal, at the end of a day of riding the range. Instead of being the gloomiest place on the range, because of what was hanging over the head of our boss, the bunk house used to be a cheerful spot in the evening.

Dan Porson made it a practice, now, to come out and sit for an hour or so after supper, listening to the lingo of Lanky. And when he started a story, we all piped down and waited and listened for it. Dan told him, one evening, that it was worth the pay of two good cowhands to have one entertainer on the place, and he offered to pay Lanky for the time he spent talking!

"I was a hired talker once, and believe me, I'll never be one again," said Lanky.

"When was that, you were a hired talker?" I asked.

And that started Lanky on a new story. Almost anything would start him on a story. He began:

"I was working on a brig that had a mean pair of mates on board of her. They were feeding out the belaying-pin soup all the way down the Pacific, and just when we were sliding into port one evening in the Solomon Islands, the pair of them started handing me a ladleful of the same brew."

"Did you lick 'em both, Lanky?" asked Porson.

"I'm not a fighting man," said Lanky. "I'm too long and thin to be any good in a fight. But when they came at me, I remembered that I'd drawn most of my pay to use at poker, and lost it, and there was nothing much to tie me to that ship, anyway, so I dived overboard and swam ashore."

"No sharks bother you?" I asked. "Those waters are full of sharks, aren't they?"

"Now that you remind me of it, they are," said Lanky. "There's nothing like a well-read boy to keep a gent reminded of what he might forget. Yes, there were a lot of sharks, but I noticed years before that sharks never took a liking to me. That evening, they were so thick in the water that I was kicking them out of the way all the time. But I got ashore minus the beating that the first and second were going to give me, and I walked right inland till I found a camp fire, and smelled roast pork. And when I followed up the scent, I ran right into the king. He had a whole lot of villages under his thumb, and when he found out that I spoke English, he was pleased, because he'd learned a little English himself, and he wanted to hear more of it. I sat around the fire that evening, and spun some yarns, and he was so pleased with 'em that he gave me a hut all to myself that night—a sort of hut of honor, you might call it. And the next morning, when I woke up, there were a couple of blackfaces sent over to wait on me and ask me to breakfast with his majesty.

"I sauntered back over, and had breakfast with him; and all day long, off and on, I ate his food—he was feeding his face a few spoonfuls every half hour—and drank his liquor, which tasted like smoke up the nose—and yarned with him. That is, he sat and smoked and drank and listened, and I sat and smoked and drank and talked. It was one of the best days that I ever had. And at the end of it, the king said that I was all right, and he wanted me to stay there to be his top sergeant, or head chief, or vizier, or whatever you please.

"I didn't mind. That life was better than belaying-pin soup, you can see for yourself. So he gave me a bolt of calico for a present and sent me home for the evening.

"When I woke up the next morning, besides the two servants that he'd already given me, I found that he'd sent me a wife and two pigs. I had the pigs roasted, but I sent the wife back to him because I like peace around my home, even if it's only a hut.

"The king was surprised when I refused a bride. When I went to see him, that day, he ordered in a dozen of the little beauties, all oiled up, and with their lip rings on. I told him I was tickled to death with the honor, but that there was a magic curse laid on me, and that the minute I got married, I would never be able to tell another story. When he heard that, he ran the whole herd out of the palace, and I sat down to do some more yarning.

"That kept up for six months, and all that time I lived on the fat of the land, and had everything that I wanted to eat and to drink. I got presents every day, too, from pigs to bolts of cloth, and beads, and guns, and ammunition, and I got a whole war canoe for one present, and a first-rate handful of pearls for another. But the trouble was that I had to talk every day. There was one little war came along, with a neighbor, but that only lasted for a week before our enemies got tired of kicking us around through the woods, and peace was declared, and I had to go back to talking again. I had to talk that king to sleep and talk him awake, too.

"I used up all the stories that I'd ever heard; I used all the ones that I could make up. I retold all the lies that I ever had told, which was several barnfuls, and then I started retelling all of the stories that I ever had read in books, and all of those stories I made twice as long and twice as mixed up as they really were. But even then, I could feel the words running lower and lower in me, and finally I knew that the time was coming when I'd be talked out. And, by thunder, that time came. I couldn't believe it. But it did come. And I opened my mouth to speak another word, and there was no word to come! Not one. I couldn't even say 'The next day,' or 'As I was saying before,' or 'And now to go back to Bill, whom we left at the edge of the forest waiting for the pirates.' No, I couldn't say anything, because I was talked out! The king asked me what was the matter, and I said that somebody must have turned on the tap when I wasn't looking and left it running for a few nights before, because all the words had gone out of me.

"When the king heard that, he opened his eyes and stared. Then he opened his mouth and growled. He said that I was a damned pretender and not a real first-rate medicine man at all, and he called in his guards and told them to cut me up small and fry me for the pigs, because I was too skinny and mean and worthless for them to eat me raw. But I managed to dive between the legs of the chief guard, and when he fell down, he blocked the door of the palace long enough to get me out of spear shot. And with a start like that and so many reasons to make me light, I gained on the soldiers all the way to the beach.

"I saw a ship anchored in the harbor, close in shore, and I took to the water like a duck, and swam out to her. They threw me a rope, and I climbed up that rope, and when I got to the deck, what do you think that I saw?"

"What did you see?" I asked.

"I saw the same pair of hard-boiled mates that I'd dived overboard to get away from, six months before. They'd come right around in a circle in their trading voyage, and there they were waiting, and each one had a bigger grin than the other, they were so glad to see me."

"What did they do to you?"

"Well," said Lanky, "I'm not a fighting man, so we won't talk about what happened, because I haven't the right sort of words. But that's why I never take a job as a hired talker."

That was typical of the way that Lanky talked. It was mostly made up, but you never could tell what part was true, and there was always a feeling that a part of it *was* true. Which part you couldn't make out. We used to put our heads together, after he'd finished yarning, and try to get the straight of it, but we always disagreed. All we could agree on was that Lanky was the best natural, and self-made, and hand-tooled liar that ever had ridden onto our range.

Things were going like this when "Old Man" Jeff Porson, Dan's father, rode out to the ranch and started to spoil everything. For almost the first thing that he did, when he saw Lanky sitting in the door of the bunk house, and the sun not yet down, was to say:

"Are you taking a day off? Or are you fired and waiting for a lift to town?"

3

THE GUNMAN

Lanky might have guessed from Jeff Porson's habit of talk that he was somebody important on the ranch, but when Lanky saw the funny clothes and the slovenly air of Porson, as he told me afterwards, it never occurred to him that this was the owner, so he said:

"I'm holding down my regular job right now, stranger."

"What's your regular job, eh?" asked Porson.

"Doing the thinking for this whole gang," said Lanky.

"Oh, you're a thinker, are you?" asked Old Man Porson.

"Same as a medicine man," said Lanky. "I could tell you a story about a medicine man that used to make rain for the Sioux—"

"How long you been working here like this?" asked Jeff Porson.

"Nigh onto three weeks, brother," said Lanky.

"I'm damn sorry that you've come to the last one of them weeks," said old Jeff. "Go roll your blankets!"

"Who might you be, brother?"

"I might be Jeff Porson," said he. "Vamoose! Get out! I'll medicine man you!"

"You're Jeff Porson, are you?" asked Lanky.

"Start moving," said Jeff.

"The way it looks to me," said Lanky, "I don't see how I can move along till to-morrow morning."

"Maybe you could be persuaded, though," said Jeff through his teeth, for the old man was a fighter from way back.

"I'm always open to argument," said Lanky. "But you can see how it is."

"How is it?" said Jeff. "The only way I see it is, is for you to start moving."

"Why," said Lanky, "I'm asking you if you'd let a man testify in a law court before he's proved his identity?"

"What's that got to do with this business?" asked Jeff Porson.

"It's got this to do," said Lanky. "I'd like to go to oblige you, but I can't do that till I know that you're Jeff Porson, the owner of this ranch."

"Go ask the cook, you blockhead," said Jeff Porson.

"Ah, that settles it for me, partner," said Lanky. "You're not Jeff Porson. You can't be. You can't be the father of that fine fellow, that real gentleman, his son. The father of Dan Porson couldn't call harmless strangers blockheads. No, sir, whatever you are, you're not the father of Dan Porson, and therefore I'll have to wait till Dan comes in off the range."

Jeff Porson was in a rage. He ran to the house and got a rifle, but the cook saw him and dissuaded him, and said a lot of favorable things about Lanky. Yet when Dan and the rest of us came in off the range just before sunset of that long day, old Jeff was at a red heat. His whole face was crimson, and he lighted right into poor Dan. He wanted to know what he meant by having bums and loafers hanging around the place; and he pointed out Lanky and told him to run that man off the place on the double.

To make this worse, it was said right in front of Lanky, who sat in the door of the bunk house and whittled at a stick, and smiled and nodded to us one by one, like the lazy good-natured vagabond that he was, and paid no attention to the heat of Jeff Porson.

Dan Porson frowned and shook his head and tried to take this order from his father, but couldn't quite manage it. Not when the order was so peremptory, and given right in front of Lanky.

"Look here, father," he said, "this is Lanky—and every last one of us would rather lose three hard-working men than Lanky. He's kept us cheered up for weeks!"

"You need cheering up, do you?" yelled old Jeff Porson. "I'll cheer you up. I'll send a minstrel show out here to keep these here boys entertained. But you—Dan, you throw that worthless hound off of the place—or get off yourself!"

Bang! It just came out like that. The Porsons were famous for their bad tempers, and Dan's temper was just as short as his father's.

He flared up right away, and threw his hat on the ground.

"If I get off the ranch, I'll *stay* off," said he.

"Stay off and be damned, for all I care," said his father.

"I will," said Dan.

"Hold on, Mr. Porson," said Lanky, "don't you be fool enough to let your son get off the place on account of me. I'll slide out of here in no time at all."

"If you go, Lanky, I'm riding with you," said Dan Porson, getting more and more ugly.

"I don't want you to stay!" shouted his father at him. "I'd rather have you gone. I'd rather have a *man* running my place for me."

"And I'd rather *work* for a man than for you," said his son.

It was a mean situation, and every one of us wanted to break it up, but there was no way of handling those two firebrands. Then, over the rim of the hill, a Mexican youngster came riding down on us, and he sang out:

"Hai! Gringos!"

That nearly jumped us out of our skins. It's all right for the Mexes to call Americans gringos when they're by themselves, or in their own country; but for a Mexican kid to waltz up to a whole gang of us and call us "gringos" took the breath of all of us.

Lefty Guiness pulled off his hat and gives a bow to the kid, who had reined up his mustang beside us.

"What'll you have, señor?" said Lefty.

"Is there a Dan Porson around here?" asked the sassy kid, who had reined up his mustang beside us.

"I'm Dan Porson," said Dan. "What can I do for you?"

"I don't want you," said the Mex, "but there's a man on the other side of the hill that wants you, and wants you bad; his name is Tom Acker, and he wants to see you alone!"

Things were happening and happening fast. First the scrap between Dan and his father, and now comes man-eating Tom Acker to finish off Dan.

And still, what could we do? We couldn't go out in a body and chase Acker off the place—no, because that would look as though Dan Porson had showed the white feather, which would be enough to ruin the rest of his life.

There was nothing for all of us to do, willing and eager as we all were, except to stand aside and let Dan Porson handle the job for himself.

One thing was accomplished, at any rate, I'm glad to say. I mean, the foolish wrangle between the father and the son was stopped on the spot.

Jeff Porson said: "Now, my son, there ain't a man in the world that'll blame you if you tell a professional gun fighter like that killer, that Tom Acker, to go to the devil."

And Dan Porson answered: "Maybe nobody would blame me, but I'd blame myself. I'm going over the hill to meet him."

His father grinned suddenly. It was a queer thing to see the white sickness in his face, and the pleasure that was there, also, when he saw that his son was dead game. We all felt about the same way, over the thing. We knew that Acker would kill poor young Dan as sure as anything. But we knew that we wanted Dan to go out and play the man.

Just then, we heard Lanky saying: "It's not altogether fair, though, that you should have to go over the hill. Why shouldn't Tom Acker come halfway? He doesn't have to come clear over on this side, but neither do you have to go clear over on that side. There's a halfway place— and that's the crest of the hill."

The Mexican youngster was already scampering his horse back over the ridge to tell his boss that Dan was coming, and when I looked up, I could imagine the two of them sitting their horses face to face on the ridge, and then the whipping of the guns, and the shooting, and Dan pitching sidewise out of his saddle, a dead man.

It made me weak; it made me shake.

I could see that he knew there was no help. He was as gray as ashes. Gray as stone, I'd better say, because he was as firm and steady as stone, too.

"You stay here one minute, Dan," said Lanky, "and I'll walk over the hill and see if I can talk Acker into meeting you halfway."

With that, he stepped up the hill, and when he was standing against the gold of the sky, he stopped, and made himself a cigarette, and lighted it, and walked down out of sight, again with the smoke blowing back over his shoulders.

We waited. The silence grew so heavy and so grim that Lefty began to talk about the hard job he'd had tailing a cow out of a mud hole, that day, and we all pretended to listen, because anything was better than that silence.

Then, like a hammer stroke on the brain, we heard a gun go *bang!* And an instant later, there was another explosion, and then the drumming of the hoofs of a horse going off at full speed!

4

ACKER'S ACCIDENT

All of us were sick and silent, I can tell you. Then young Dan Porson put what we were all feeling into words. He said:

"If Lanky has stepped in ahead of me and taken my medicine—"

That was all he said, and he said it through his teeth, and we knew what he meant. If anything had really happened to Lanky from that two-handed murderer, Tom Acker, Dan would be on the trail of Acker and riding hard!

Dan took three steps from the bunk house, and then over the brow of the hill came one of the queerest sights that I ever saw the great Tom Acker himself, riding a slim-legged, dancing gray thoroughbred with four stockings of black silk, and a sooty black muzzle, and a black tip to its tail, the daintiest horse that you could put an eye on in a year's riding on the range.

He was guiding it with his knees, and holding his right hand high and to the side, gripping it at the wrist with his left. And behind him stalked Lanky with a long, lazy stride, and as they came over the hill and down the side of it, it seemed to me like a picture of a lean-ribbed old range bull driving in a great mountain lion—there was so much suggestion of speed, and grace, and dangerous strength about Tom Acker.

We could see that Lanky was shaking his head, as though in

wonder, and when he was still at a little distance, he called out:

"Acker's had an accident and hurt himself. There's not going to be any trouble, Dan. One of you boys hustle over to the house and unlimber the medicine kit. There's gotta be some bandaging done!"

Old Jeff Porson himself jogged to the house, and as the great Tom Acker went by, he sat as proud as a king in the saddle, and kept his fine, dark, handsome face turned straight before him, and he didn't seem to see any of the rest of us at all.

We trooped along behind, not saying very much but looking a good deal at one another. When we got up to the house, Acker already had gone inside to have his hand bandaged, and Dan Porson went in behind him, but Lanky stayed out with the rest of us and told us what had happened.

"The dog-gonedest thing that I ever saw," said Lanky, shaking his head, and his eyes popping a little. "When I got over the hill, there, I saw the Mex lad talking to Tom Acker, and Acker shrugging his shoulders and looking very proud and fine. And when I came up, I just said: 'Well, Tom, why not ride up on top of the hill and let the show take place there, where people can all see what's happening?'

"At that, he turned on me a little in his saddle, and he snapped out: 'Who thinks that I've got a double cross up my sleeve? D'you?' And as he said that, he made a play with his gun, just to dazzle and scare me, and he whipped out that gun like a flash of light. You never saw anything like it. Why, I couldn't 'a' blinked my eyelids as fast as he moved that big Colt. It was a neat play, but the luck was against him, and the gun caught, somehow, in the sleeve of his coat—one of those things that'll happen once in ten million times to the best of 'em—and as it caught, it exploded, and the force of the explosion knocked the gun back, and the hammer ripped into the flesh at the wrist and made a pretty bad, ugly rip, I can tell you! And the gun flipped out of his grip and hit the ground a good ways off, and went *blam* again, it's such a hair-trigger devil of a Colt, d'you see?"

As Lanky reached the end of this queer tale, we fired a lot of questions at him, and he was still answering them, about as fast as we could ask them, when the door of the house opened, and out came the two Porsons and the great Tom Acker.

It was a grand thing to see that fellow Acker at such close range. I mean to say, he was so slim-bodied, and strong-shouldered, and he had his head fitted with such a fine balance on the round of his neck. And his step was as light as willows springing in the wind. I admired him a good deal, but it seemed that he was not admiring himself. All about his lips was a white streak, he'd compressed them so hard, and there was a burning spark in each eye, the sort of fire that can burn up a whole human life in a flash, once it's turned loose.

He walked up to the gray beauty, and touched the withers of the mare with his left hand, and floated up into the saddle like a feather, and his toes found their way into the stirrups as though he had eyes and mind in his very feet.

He looked us over, as he gathered up the reins, and the mare turned its head, and told him with its eyes that it loved him, and that it would rather carry him on its back than all the kings in the world!

Acker seemed to be noting down our faces, one by one, with that deadly look of his.

His right hand and wrist were thoroughly bandaged. He held that hand close to his chest. But having a wound in one hand didn't incapacitate the great Tom Acker, if what one heard about him was all true. The fact was that he was supposed to be as fast and as accurate with his left hand as with his right!

Whatever the truth might be about his ability with his left hand, he did not talk of using it this evening. He spoke to Dan Porson:

"You're Dan Porson, aren't you?"

"Yes," said Dan.

"I'm Tom Acker," said the gunman. "The play goes against me to-day, but I'll be back on your trail, Porson. I want to tell you that before I start."

He turned before Dan could answer, and pointed the forefinger of his left hand, suddenly, at Lanky. Then he said: "I'd like to have a coupla words with you, Lanky."

"Sure," said Lanky amiably, and he started off, striding beside the horse of Tom Acker as it took Acker up the hill, with no other word of good-by to any of us, and no thanks for the decent treatment he'd had in the house, in the care taken of his wound.

They went thirty or forty steps away, and there Acker stopped his horse and said a few words to Lanky. He was leaning from his saddle, and talking rapidly, and Lanky, from his gestures and the shrugs of his shoulders, seemed to be apologizing.

Then Acker touched his mare with the spurs, and off it carried him like the wind, its mane and tail blowing straight back with the speed of its gallop, and Acker sitting the animal as only one man in ten thousand is ever born to sit a horse.

Old Jeff Porson came out of the house just then, and muttered:

"What did that worthless tramp of a Lanky do to Acker?"

"Why, it was just an accident," said Dan Porson, looking very grave, with the memory of what he had heard from Acker still clearly in his mind. "Acker tried to scare Lanky, and his gun caught, and went off. The hammer cut his hand. That's all."

"Is that all?" exclaimed his father. "Are you dead sure that that's all?"

He added, with a strange grin: "What happened was enough to make the little sassy Mexican brat ride for his life. Accidents don't scare boys like that out of a year's growth!"

That was putting it in a new way, and I saw some of the older men nodding and looking wisely at one another.

Then Lanky came back, with his ugly face twisted more to one side than ever.

"Take these man-eaters," said Lanky, as he came up, "and you never can tell when they'll get so hot that all their blood'll start boiling. Whatcha think that he wanted to say to me, over yonder?"

We asked what it was, and Lanky went on:

"Why, just because I was there when the bad luck came on him, just because of that, he's putting the blame on me, dog-gone him, and he says that he'll have a reckoning with me. With *me!* Why, what harm'd I ever do him?"

Lefty spoke up suddenly, saying: "Where'd he learn your name so good and quick, Lanky?"

"I introduced myself to him," said Lanky. "When I went over the hill, the first thing that I did was to introduce myself. It's always the safest plan, when you meet up with a gunman. It keeps you from getting killed by mistake, for one thing. But I guess the thing for me to do is to pull up my stakes and get along before he comes back and calls for me, with both guns working red hot. I'm going to go out and roll my blanket now. No, dog-gone it, I ain't got a blanket. I'll just go and grab my mustang, and slope."

"You go out to the bunk house and roll the blankets that you've been using, Lanky," said Dan Porson. "You might as well have 'em as the next man. And why make your start at night? Why start at all? You're luck for us here, Lanky. We'd miss you a lot."

"That's a kind thing to say," said Lanky.

He turned and looked at old Jeff Porson.

Jeff said, with his head bent a little: "You go out there and roll up them blankets. They're yours, like Dan says. But I dunno about your staying on. Maybe you attract more trouble than you'd shoo away."

"What might you mean by that, partner?" drawled Lanky.

"You figger it all out," said Jeff Porson. "I'm not explaining."

Lanky went off through the dusk toward the bunk house at that. And as he neared it, the cook came out and clattered the big bell that called to chuck.

Jeff Porson said: "Some of you boys, if you wanta see some fun, come along with me. But step soft—step soft. Pull your boots off, if you wanta have a chance to see something. Hey, doctor," he added to the cook, "keep raising a clatter with that bell, will you?"

As he said this, and as the cook kept on banging and clanging with the bell, away goes old Jeff Porson toward the bunk house, and the rest of us sneaking along behind him.

We got outside the door of the bunk house, and looking into the dimness inside, we could mark the tall figure of Lanky bending and rolling up the blankets that had been given to him.

Jeff Porson waved us back a little from the door, and called out:

"Hands up, damn you!"

And as he yelled, he jumped for cover.

Something else moved, in the shadows inside the bunk house. It was Lanky. I've said that he was one of the most slow-moving men in the world, and so he was, ordinarily. It was simply that he had turned into a big, long-legged mountain lion, when he heard the yell of Jeff Porson. He bounded clear across the width of the narrow room, and landed flat on his face, as it seemed to me. But before he landed, while he was still falling through the air, his gun spoke, and a bullet came whistling through the doorway. It missed my own head by a fraction of an inch, and I still duck and dodge, when I even think of it!

We all gaped at one another in amazement. The infernal clangoring of the dinner bell stopped as the gun exploded; and then I saw old Jeff Porson nodding and wagging his head, as though he were very satisfied with something.

5

NIGHT ENCOUNTER

He had reason to lose some of his satisfaction, a moment later, because out of the door of the bunk house came a long figure with a bound, and reached to me, and grabbed me by both arms at the elbows, and the face of Lanky came near to mine, all drawn with pain and fear.

"Did that bullet tag you, son?" asked Lanky.

"It fanned my cheek, all right," said I, with the shivers still going through me, "but it didn't do any harm."

"Thank Heaven!" said Lanky. He let go of me, and put a hand up to his forehead. "I thought for a minute—"

Then he turned around, and his voice was ringing like iron against iron.

"Who yelled out: 'Hands up?'" he demanded.

The rest of us were silent. There were no grins, either, you can bet. Then Jeff Porson said:

"Why, partner, I did that myself."

"You did, did you?" said Lanky.

He walked over to Jeff Porson and stood tall and straight and alert before him. All the clumsiness had gone out of his step, and even his voice was something that none of us had ever heard before.

"That reminds me of a story," he said, "but the story would be a pile too long to tell—it's about a lot of fools, and the biggest fool of the lot was the oldest man!"

Straight talk? Yes, talk such as old Jeff Porson had not heard, you can bet, for a long time. He had no answer on the tip of his tongue, either, but simply shrugged his shoulders and said nothing.

Lanky turned on his heel and stepped out for the barn. The rest of us went back for the house, to have supper, and not a soul spoke on the way.

We were washing our hands and faces around the pump, when Lanky jogged his old bear horse, as he called it, back to us from the barn, and slid out of the saddle. He went around and shook hands with all of us, and said good-by. I asked him if he wouldn't stay to supper with us all, and he shook his head.

"Somebody walked over my grave, a while back," he said.

All the smile was gone from him. When he came to Jeff Porson, he left the old man out of the handshaking.

Jeff spoke up like a man, and for that matter, he had reason enough to speak.

"I was wrong, Lanky," he said. "I was dead wrong, and I ask pardon, man."

"That's all right," said Lanky. "But it wouldn't be so right if Grey were lying on his face with a hole through his brains."

Dan Porson made a last bid to make him stay with us, but Lanky wouldn't be held—not even for supper. He said that he had to hit the trail, and in another ten seconds, he was on it, and the old mustang stumbled away with him uphill, into the dimness of the evening.

When we sat in around the long dining table, the talk warmed up again, after everybody had had a first plate or so of fried beef and potatoes.

And all of that talk was about Lanky.

Jeff Porson said: "It sort of jumped through my brain that he was a lot more than he seemed—that he was even man enough to stand up against Tom Acker. I thought that I'd try him out, and you all stood by and saw what happened. I guessed that there was a lot of powder in him, but I didn't guess how much, or how little spark it needed to set off the lot. Maybe it was a fool play that I made—but least-wise, it showed how Tom Acker got hurt in the hand—and *might* have got hurt in the head, too!"

Everybody agreed with Jeff Porson. And the men were grave about it. For my part, I ate supper in a haze—that bullet had come so close to my head, and more than that, I kept seeing the queer play among the shadows—the sudden change of long

Lanky into a wild cat, bounding to the side, and shooting while he was still in the air, shooting so straight that the hum of the bullet was still singing in my brain.

I dreamed about the affair all over again, that night, and for three or four days, after this, there was nothing much talked about, except Lanky, and the possibilities of who he really was, because it seemed certain that he was a fellow with a past and a long one. Nobody learns to use a gun the way we all had seen Lanky use his, unless he has practiced, and practiced a lot, and with the knowledge that his life depended upon his skill with the gun, and his speed and accuracy.

I made up my mind that, from that minute forward, I would never dare to judge a man on appearances.

Well, it was about four nights after Lanky had left us that I had a little adventure of my own that's worth telling about. I had been riding a pinto mustang all day, a high-headed little devil of a bunch of energy that had been written down as a bad actor by the other fellows. I tried it myself, because I guessed that it was not really bad, but just filled with too much nerve energy. It could not help shying and dodging, and the boys had kept on straightening the little gelding out with the curb and the spurs, until it was as uneasy as a cat walking on a hot stove whenever a saddle was on its back. So I tried my hand with it, and found that I had a hard day's work ahead of me, but just the same, I made some progress. I got two pretty bad falls, that day, because I was only an average hand in the saddle, but I had a lot of sympathy for horseflesh, and gradually I managed to get results. After all, I always have figured that what you learn about your horse is as important as what you teach your horse about yourself.

As I say, it had been a hard day's work, and when I got the gelding in at the end of it, it was so sweating and trembling with exhaustion, that I put it in the barn instead of turning it out to pasture. And after I'd laid around after supper with the rest of the boys, as they were turning in, I remembered that poor little frightened, jumpy rat of a horse, and went out to the barn, and gave the gelding a rub-down. It was still sweating, when I got there—cold sweat, which takes it out of the soul, where hot sweat takes it out of the fat. I rubbed it dry, and the poor pinto, when it made out that I was simply trying to comfort it and not punish it for wrongdoings that it never had understood from the first, was the most surprised little horse in the world. It was always putting its head around, and snuffing at me, and even went so far as to take a nibble at my hair!

There it had been standing without touching its hay or

barley, but before I left, it was at work on the grain, and when I went away, it whinnied after me, to call me back.

I went on toward the bunk house, feeling happy and sad, all at the same time, for it makes a fellow glum to think how much misery we're always distributing around us, and how much happiness we could make with half the effort. I don't mean to say that I was growing philosophical, but I was swearing to myself that I would give every horse a better chance, on account of the pinto, when I got near to the bunk house, and was aware, all at once, that something had dropped down out of sight behind a fallen log.

It might have been a mountain lion, or a wolf. And I was scared to death, because in spite of its size it seemed to me that it was *not* either of those animals, but a man.

I was afraid to go near that log, and yet I had to go, or else I would have another black mark chalked up against my secret record of myself. There were a lot of those black marks already down, and if a few more were marked, I would know that I was a plain out-and-out coward!

So I steeled myself, and got out the Colt, and waited till it had steadied in my hand. Then I walked straight over to the log. As I got to it, a voice said softly:

"Don't shoot, kid!"

The sound of the whisper shot electric sparks of horror through me; then I realized that the words had been simple and easy enough.

Up stood a tall silhouette with very broad shoulders against the stars.

"Lanky!" I muttered.

He came to me and touched my arm.

"I'm sorry for this, Nels," he said. "I'm dog-gone sorry that you spotted me out here. All I wanta tell you is that I'm not here to do any harm."

"Oh, I'd know that, Lanky," said I. "I'm not such a fool that I wouldn't know that."

"You're a good kid, Nels," he said. "Step back here far from the bunk house with me, will you?"

I went along with him. I was prickling all over with curiosity sharper than electric needles stabbing into the brain.

I had caught Lanky out, and in a peculiar way. And a sort of awe and terror of him came over me—that is to say, when I thought of the man sneaking around like a wolf in the cold and the darkness of the night.

We got to a broad-shouldered stump, and there he sat down,

and the swing of his hand told me to sit down beside him. I did that.

"Smoke?" he asked.

"No," said I. "I'm too nervous to roll one."

He chuckled, and I heard the tobacco sift into the paper, and then the light dry crunch and rattle of the thing in the making.

"What are you nervous about, brother?" asked Lanky.

"Why, about you—about you standing around in the night, this way," said I. "It's a scary thing, to me!"

"You've got plenty of nerve, Nelly," he said, chuckling again as he brought out that confounded nickname which he had given to me. "You've got plenty of nerve or you wouldn't *admit* that you've been scared. It's the fear that's held up inside of a fellow that finally freezes his soul, and makes it all brittle for him!"

I thought this over. He lighted his cigarette, and I noticed that hardly a spark, hardly a ray of light got away from the perfect shield that he made of his hands. There was only one glimpse of his face, through the mist of the smoke that he was breathing out.

That long, lean, twisted, crooked face—what could a fellow make out of him, he was so ugly? He might be all right. But I guessed at all sorts of strange and terrible things in his past, and always blood—yes, somehow, there was always blood connected with him, in my mind.

"I wanta talk to you a little while, kid," he began. "You mind?"

"No, Lanky," said I. "I'll talk to you, all right."

"I wanta know," he said, "how things have been going around here?"

"Why, they're going all right," said I. "Why should they be going wrong?"

He broke out: "Don't the lot of you know that all hell is due to—" He stopped himself. I heard the click of his teeth.

"Well," he said, "I'm glad that everything is going on all right."

"Tell me what's likely to happen?" I said.

"If I exactly knew," said Lanky, "would I be crawling around here through the dark? Tell me about Jeff Porson. Has he been off his feed any, lately?"

"No, not so's I've been able to notice," said I. "He always eats twice as much as the biggest man on his place, and he always does twice as much work as anybody else, too."

"Then he doesn't know or suspect anything, I suppose," said Lanky. "And that's all right, too."

Suddenly he stood up.

"Will you do something for me, kid?" he asked.

"Why, I think I will, Lanky," said I. "I'd like to, as a matter of fact."

"You say that everything seems to be going along all right?"

"Yes, as far as I can see."

"Then do something that'll help *keep* things going along all right, will you?"

"Tell me what."

"Forget that you've seen me out here. Never say a word to a soul about bumping into old Lanky out here in the night. Is that a go?"

I thought for a second.

"I'll shake on that," said I.

"I always knew you were a good kid," said the voice of Lanky in my ear. "Now I'm dead sure of it. And I'll trust you, is what I'll do!"

I turned around to say something more, but he was already almost out of sight among some poplar saplings, and he quickly disappeared.

6

AN INVITATION

This last little meeting that I had with Lanky may not seem to have been important enough to write down, but there was something about it that got me on edge and kept me there. It was the mystery behind Lanky—that was what burned me up!

By this time, old Jeff Porson had been making inquiries everywhere. He'd been to town, and talked to the sheriff. He'd sent out the picture that one of the fellows happened to get of Lanky in the crowd, and that picture had been looked over by a whole lot of marshals and frontier police of one sort or another, but not a word came back about Lanky. He had not been spotted anywhere! No, he had not once been connected with any sort of a past. Although three separate reports came back to say that the writers thought that they had seen Lanky somewhere before—his was not a face to forget, and three of the people thought that they had met that strange, twisted face somewhere.

But there we were, just where we started, almost. We knew, now, that our long, lazy liar of a camp entertainer was as a matter of fact a cunning devil with a gun, and a fellow who knew how to fight for his life. We more than suspected that he actually had shot a gun out of the hand of the great Tom Acker, and Jeff Porson went so far as to suggest that Acker must have known

Lanky before, and that Lanky must have met him. There had
not been very much time for talk before the gun play started, on
the day when the pair met behind the rim of the hill!

"Where would Tom Acker have met him?" Jeff Porson used
to groan. "Where's Acker been, except up and down the range?"

But there was another closed door. For Acker was one of
those fellows who gave himself a long leave of absence, every
now and again. He might pop up at one end of the range or the
other. Stories about him drifted down to us from Canada, and
up to us from Mexico. There were even yarns from Chile and the
Argentine!

"There was still fight in Tom Acker," old Jeff was fond of
saying. "He's a two-gun man, and he'd lost only one gun, but
when he seen that Lanky had the edge on him, he give up the ship
right pronto. Yeah, boys, take it from me, this Lanky oughta be
worth knowing better! The facts that he could tell might be a
dog-gone sight better than the yarns that he spins to you-all!"

I nearly bit out my tongue, two or three times, when I was on
the verge of telling about my meeting with Lanky in the dark of
the night near the bunk house. But I managed to keep still.
Imagine what a chill of excitement would have gone through
every one if they'd heard about that meeting!

As for me, it made me sleep light at night, and keep my eyes
open in the daytime.

During those weeks, I burned up I don't know how many
dollars' worth of ammunition. I practically wore my old Colt out
a size larger. And when I wasn't shooting at a tree stump as I
trotted the horse by it, I was practising quick draws, until I
nearly rubbed the skin off the ends of my fingers.

But I hadn't the gift for the game. I was a good second-rate
shot, and that was all. But if I got too fast, I was sure to miss the
target, or just chip it. For center shooting, I had to have a breath
of time, and that breath of time is just what a man is not apt to
get when a gun fight starts in the West. The target is likely to be
close, and the winner is the fellow who has the quicker hand
even although it's only a thousandth of a second the faster.

However, in those days, I was always burning up with a
feeling that some tremendous thing was in the air, and that I'd
better get myself in good shape for the handling of it. So I kept
on burning up gunpowder and plastering lead all over the
landscape.

Then trouble came and sat at the lunch table with us, and
everybody on the ranch knew the face of it in a flash. The mail
came out in the morning, and we generally sent down somebody

to the mail boxes that were nailed to the fence at the crossroads, three miles below the ranch. That was as far as the mail carrier went, and though most of us got hardly three letters a year, still the idea of mail kept our heads up a little all morning, and made them drop again a trifle when there was nothing for us.

This lunch time, a letter came for Dan Porson, and he opened it, according to our custom, at the table. I remember he turned it over and looked at the postmark first, and then said:

"This comes from Cat Hill!"

That remark lowered our temperatures a lot, you can bet, because Cat Hill was the name of the village where the Ackers hung out.

Dan read the letter over to himself, frowning, and then he read it out loud. It went something like this:

"DEAR DAN PORSON: The other day, a few weeks back, I tried to call on you, and got interfered with. Now I'm wondering if you wouldn't like to drop over and call on us.

"I'm not the only one that would be plumb tickled to see you. My brother's up and about, these days, and I hear him mention you pretty frequent.

"Wednesday night, there's a big dance, over here. Maybe you'd like to come then. The fellows would all be glad to have a look at you, and so would the girls.

"As long as there's two of us on the entertainment committee, why don't you bring along a friend? Lanky would be my suggestion, but get anybody you please!

"Yours truly,
"THOMAS ACKER."

When he had finished this letter, Dan Porson looked down to his plate and began to crumble some bread that lay beside it.

And the rest of us looked back and forth at one another.

"If Lanky were here, I *would* ask him to go along with me," said Dan. "But Lanky's gone."

He went on crumbling bread again. I saw a couple of forks frozen in the air, wanting to deliver what was on them, but not able to move, because the handlers of those forks were all afraid that *they* might be asked to share the invitation that Dan had just received!

I wasn't bothered much about that. I was the youngest man of the lot, and yet even the idea of the danger that was lying ahead for somebody gave me the chills and fever up the spinal marrow, I can tell you!

Then Dan said: "Well, somebody will come along with me, I suppose. How about it, Nels?"

I squeezed down in my chair so that my collar came up to my ears.

Big Lefty was right across the table from me, and I saw him grin, but more in sympathy, I thought, than in disgust.

"Aw, it's all right, Nels," said Dan Porson. "I wouldn't be dragging you along to a show like that."

It was another case, I told myself, of finding the final test right under my eyes, and this time, I vowed, I would have to meet it. No doubt I'd get there to that party and make a fool and a coward of myself. But still, I simply had to say something, and I dragged myself upright in the chair.

"Look here, Dan," I said. "I don't pretend to be any hero. I don't pretend that I'm the right man for you to take along with you—but, if you're really wanting me to go, I'll go."

Dan didn't look at me, but he said: "Well, the rest of these fellows don't look as though they waste much time dancing. Dancing a whisky glass on the edge of a bar is about the best that they can do at a party, but you're pretty slick with your feet, Nels. You come along with me, and we can pretend that we've gone expecting to have a good time."

He pushed back his chair, and laughed, and that laughter was as brittle as frost.

"That letter's enough lunch for me," he said. "I'm going out where the air's better."

He got up and stalked out of the dining room. But I went on with my meal. I steeled myself not to think of what was ahead; I tried to pretend that I was hungry.

But pretty soon I found myself with my hands frozen on my knife and fork, and looking straight ahead into an emptiness that was thinly filled up with phantom music, and with the rustling and the whispering feet of a big dance, and out of that pleasant mist I could see Tom Acker coming with a leveled gun!

That was only a daydream, but it was a great deal more real than day, to me.

Out of the haze of it, I saw Lefty looking at me with popping eyes, fascinated.

"I know, kid. It's hell!" said Lefty.

"You bet it is!" said I. And I said it from the bottom of my heart!

7

AT CAT HILL

Wednesday came, and I expected that Dan Porson or his father would suggest that he and I should take a part of that day off to clean up ourselves and our guns for the dance. But there was nothing like that. The Porsons, you would say, took a shooting scrape as a matter of course—took it in their stride, so to speak. What did they care if the shooting Ackers had made up their minds to get young Dan Porson and the fellow he picked out to go with him?

No, they didn't seem to care at all. Only, in the dawn of that Wednesday, Dan Porson came to me and said:

"Look here, Nels. You know you don't have to go with me to-night if you don't want to. You know that, don't you?"

"Miss a party like that?" I said to him. "Get away from a chance to see a whole flock of pretty little Colts flashing and winking smoke? Why, Dan, what d'you think I am? Of course I wouldn't stay away from that party. I guess that I can eat my share of lead as well as the next man. Only, Dan, you realize that I haven't any reputation behind me that'll stop a fight, and once in it, I'm no lightning-draw artist. I'm not one of the boys that can knock quarters out of the air as fast as you can spin 'em up."

Dan considered me for a moment, and I had a half hope that he would change his mind and try out one of the other fellows.

But finally he shook his head, and answered: "You're no speed burner with a gun, maybe, but what you shoot at is going to go down and stay down. I've noticed that!"

I knew what he was thinking about. We were riding out together, one day, and all at once a little sand-colored devil of a coyote jumped up and started off as fast as it could pelt, snaking in and out through the rocks and the brush. Dan had his rifle at his shoulder pumping lead in a second. I didn't have a rifle along, but I unlimbered my revolver and tried one of those foolish, long-distance shots. It wasn't so foolish, either. I was feeling confident, and I thought I rated that coyote exactly right, and that I had him dead to rights.

And then, as Dan jerked up his gun, and swore, I let drive, and broke that coyote's back. It was a good bit over a hundred yards. Dan insisted on pacing off the distance. He didn't say much about it, at the time, but when he looked at me on this Saturday and shook his head, I knew mighty well that I never had a chance of getting off. That fool of a lucky shot had bagged me for him. He wanted nobody else on the ranch!

We worked right on through that day, and we prepared for that dance the same as for any other dance. That is, half an hour before supper time, we each pumped some water into a galvanized-iron laundry tub, and then climbed in and scrubbed down with yellow laundry soap. It certainly did a good job in taking off the dirt. It made one feel like nice new, clean leather; it made one smell the same way, too!

Then we dressed up in our best clothes, which were specially gay and slick, and all the time I was dressing, I remembered that I was saying to my sick heart: "Heavens, I'm going to die in these clothes!" And as I buttoned up my coat, I told myself that the bullet would probably crash through the coat on the left side, and leave a small hole, with the blood just gradually oozing out.

I tried to take my mind off the thought of the guns. But I couldn't. I hoped that I would die fast, because I could remember seeing poor Terry Williams die, and how he kicked himself around in a circle on the floor, horribly like a chicken with its head off, and gasped, and choked, and how his eyes stood out of his head, and how he begged one of us to kill him and put him out of his misery.

Poor Terry Williams! Well, he was a bigger and probably a much braver man than I, but he had screamed and begged when the agony was on him.

Then it all had ended for him. He was up on his hands and knees when he stopped yelling, and his face looked surprised, and rather amused, and he fell over on his side in a loose slump. That was the way he died. I never could stop thinking about Terry Williams. Not from the beginning to the end of that evening could I stop thinking about Terry Williams, and hoping that I would have a faster death than he had had!

I hated to go in to the supper table. Usually, when just a couple of fellows went to a dance and the rest stayed home, they were guyed and kidded a good deal at the table; and I wanted to talk about anywhere except where I was going.

But it turned out different, though worse than my expectation. For when we went in and sat down at supper, you would have thought that none of the fellows had any idea where we were going, or that such a family as the Acker tribe ever had existed, or that there was such a town as Cat Hill, or that a dance was being held there!

That was a great deal worse, because it showed what all the fellows were thinking about.

About the end of the meal, old Jeff Porson, who had been staring down at the table, saying not a word, suddenly banged his hand hard on the table. It was a noise as loud as a gunshot, and the sound hit me like a bullet. I fairly gasped.

While the tableware was still dancing and jiggling around, old Jeff bawled out:

"Great guns, is this the first time that a pair of fellows ever stepped out to face the guns and the music they make? A degenerate lot of half-bred puppies, that's what the youngsters are, to-day. There ain't the making of a real man in ten gross of 'em! You make me sick. You all make me sick! Sitting around here like mourners at a funeral! What does it matter if they go out and get a dash of lead in the face? What does it matter if they get their brains blasted out, and their hearts smashed? It don't make no difference. They're only two brats. The world'll roll right along, just the same! There ain't any nerve left—you kids are all a bunch of putty. The real men are old or dead, in this here world!"

He jumped to his feet, picked up his chair, slammed it back against the wall, and then tramped out of the room.

As for me, I couldn't eat any more. I was too sick. After that speech, I was nearly dead on my feet. I knew my face was white and that perspiration as cold as water was beginning to run down my forehead. I just threw up the sponge, left the table, and went outside. But Dan Porson had more manhood in him than that, and he stayed inside and faced the music right through till the third cup of coffee. I heard him talking, and I admired his nerve. But I couldn't have gone back in there to join him.

I went out and saddled his horse, and I took for mine that same pinto which I had been gentling for the past few weeks. It knew me, by this time, and it was about all that you would ask from a horse. It didn't have enough length of legs to be a sprinter, but it would run all day and never say no, no matter how much you asked.

When I brought the horses back to the house, Dan Porson came out and joined me.

"How are you, Nelly?" he asked.

It made me mad to hear him use that name; it warmed me up a good bit, and I said:

"Oh, I'm not so well. But when the pinch comes maybe I'll be able to do something besides talk about it."

He gave me no answer to that, and we headed right across country until we hit the main trail for Cat Hill.

It was a good long ride. It was a quarter past ten when we got there. We were tired. And a cold wind that came with the sunset never let up, but grew stronger and stronger, and now and then it dusted us with a chill, misting rain, and the moan of it was always somewhere behind us, or beside us, talking about the end of the world.

I thought about summer days, and warmth, and sunshine, and my mother and father, when I had nothing to do but play and somebody else would shoulder all the big burdens for me. Yes, I was pretty sick, and I thought that Dan Porson had taken a good deal on himself to invite me along on such a ride. Why, he never had been much of a chum of mine on the ranch. If there were mean jobs to do, he always had picked on me for more than my share, as a matter of fact.

So, half sick, full of resentment, sullen, down-hearted, I saw the lights of Cat Hill appear, and widen out into a broad armful in the dim half circle of Cat Creek.

We got down into the town, and put our horses at the livery stable, which was already crowded. A fellow with a patch of dirty leather over one eye took our horses.

"Say, one of you fellows might be Dan Porson, eh?" he asked.

"I'm Dan Porson," said Dan. "What of it?"

"What of it? Why, nothing at all," said the fellow with the one eye. "It don't make no difference at all—to *me!*"

And he walked away from us, leading the two horses toward the stalls.

Oh, we knew what he meant, all right, and Dan stood for a minute looking after him.

"That means that they're ready for us," he said. Then he turned and walked quickly out into the street, and with me trailing a step behind, he led on toward the dance hall.

It had been an old barn. A lot of old wagons and other junk, including a combination harvester, was stored in the lower part of it, now, but the haymow above, where the floor had been polished for many years by the rubbing of the hay, was used for a dance hall, or for town meetings of one sort or another.

There was a flimsy, long stairway that ran up the side of the building to get to the dance room, and it seemed to me that I was taking a long climb to get to a scaffold, as I trudged up the steps, along with Dan Porson.

We were almost to the top, when he paused for a minute, and lifted his head, and looked around at the night.

"What's the matter, Dan?" I gasped, because I was afraid that he was losing heart all at the last minute.

"There's nothing the matter," said Dan, under his breath. "I was only thinking— "

He went on climbing again, without finishing his words. He didn't need to finish them, because I knew what was in his mind. He was just taking a last look around at the world. That was all! And I suppose that the stars looked pretty fine to him, just as they looked ten times bigger and more wonderful than ever, to me. I wondered why I had never paid more attention to them before. I would have been glad to lie flat on my back whole nights at a time, now, and admire them, and study them, and learn their names and their faces.

As I got up to the door, I saw the swirl of lights, and I heard Dan Porson asking:

"Are the Acker brothers anywhere around here?"

And like a voice from heaven, the ticket seller said:

"No, Josh and Tom are not at the dance!"

8

BOBBIE MEADE

Yes, that was a voice from heaven. I could hardly believe my ears. I had to look down at the floor, to keep from shouting.

I saw that Dan was buying the tickets, just the same. I wondered why. We'd come here; we'd asked for the Ackers. Then why not let a good thing go, without running it into the ground?

"Hold on," I heard the ticket seller saying. "You two boys come from the Porson place?"

"Yes," said Dan. "I'm Daniel Porson."

"Why," said the other, "I've been hearing that Tom Acker thought that you might come over. It won't take long to send around word, and maybe he'll drop in here to see you. Come right on in!"

He nearly dragged us through the door and into the room. And while the lights were still flashing at our faces, and I saw the colored streamers that had been hung among the rafters, and the lanterns burning all around, and the floor shining like water, except that it wouldn't take an image very clearly—in the middle of all that, I heard the ticket seller saying:

"Here comes the best girl in town, fellows, and maybe she'll entertain you till your friends, the Ackers, come in."

Up, then, came a slim young girl, eighteen or nineteen, and if

43

all of her had been hidden except her wrists and her throat, you could have told that she was a beauty. While she was still a little distance away, so that you couldn't make out her features very clearly, you could tell that she was a lovely thing.

The ticket man had called her the best girl in town, and it was true. I would have known that without telling. Because, in every town, no matter how big, no matter how small, there is always one girl who is the "best." She's prettier than the rest, she's braver, gentler, truer, stronger, kinder, cleverer. She shines by her own light. She's the kind that a middle-aged man would want for a daughter and a younger man for his wife, and even a boy would want her for a friend.

That's the sort of a girl that walked across the floor with a thinnish young man, and as she came up, she said:

"Hurry along, Slim. Hurry as fast as your legs will go, will you?"

"You bet I will," said Slim, and ducked out through the door.

Then that girl sashayed right up to me, and gave me a smile. It was one of those deliberate, one of those intentional smiles that a girl uses with malice aforethought and when she means to make trouble.

"Are you Dan Porson?" she asked.

"No," said I, "but—"

I started to turn to Dan, and believe me, he was ready to be turned to. But she said:

"That's all right. I wanted to meet one of you. My name is Roberta Meade. People call me Bobbie, in Cat Hill."

"My name's Nelson Grey," I said. "People call me Nelly Grey, on the range."

She started, and looked at me again, and suddenly her smile was a little less bright and a great deal more real.

I introduced her to Dan, and she shook hands with him. And she carted us right on and introduced us to half a dozen other people. Everybody looked at us with eyes that either narrowed sharp and hard, or opened with a pop.

Dan Porson asked her to dance.

"I can't," she said. "Your friend was just a step before you, Mr. Porson."

The music was up on a low stage at an end of the room. It was a slide trombone, a cornet, and a violin, with drums; and there was an old upright piano that sounded like tin pans being beaten. But there was a good rhythm to that music, and I danced away with the girl, and we were almost the first on the floor, the others pausing, and staring at us.

"You should have danced with Dan," I said. "He knows how to step."

"You dance all right," said she, a little impatiently. "What are you two fellows up to, here to-night?"

"Well," said I, "we're just here. We were invited to come, you might say."

"You mean," she said, "that Tom Acker invited you?"

I didn't want to incriminate any one. So I simply shrugged my shoulders. She filled in a few gaps, thinking aloud.

"Tom wants to meet Dan Porson again. His brother's up and about again now. And Dan asked you to come along with him. Isn't that it?"

I looked down at her.

"I can't keep time when you talk like this," I said.

"Pull up over here," she said. "I'd rather talk than dance, anyway."

I stopped in a corner of the room, and she went on:

"You were brought along because you're a good bet in a pinch. Isn't that it? You don't back up when the shooting starts, Nelson Grey?"

I thought of the ice that had been in my heart and my brain ever since I knew I had come to this place, and all at once I was able to laugh, which did me a lot of good.

"Look here," said I, "I'm so scared that I'm weak. I never shot at a man in my life, and I don't know what it means to be shot at. You seem to know a lot or to guess a lot. But everything that you guess about me is all wrong. I was just asked in."

She continued to watch me, half frowning, as though she wanted to read behind my words, but finally she shook her head.

"You're not a proud fellow," she remarked.

I had to say, frankly: "I've got nothing to be proud about. I'm just an ordinary puncher, and I'm only beginning to know my job, at that. You think that I'm a regular hell-bender, coming over here with a chip on my shoulder, and ready to shoot it out with the Ackers. But the fact is that Tom Acker could eat me, and I know it. I'm just here; don't ask me why."

She seemed to be both more puzzled and more pleased.

"You mean it," she said. "You're not just being modest. Then you'll be glad to know that I think I've smoothed things over for this evening. That is, if the sheriff can do it! I've sent for Loren Mays."

I knew that name. Everybody in our part of the world *did* know it, in that time. He was one of those heroes who stand head and shoulders above the crowd of ordinary men.

"Great heavens," says the girl, a minute later. "Slim is taking ages, and there comes Josh Acker, already!"

He stepped through the doorway, just then, a very fine-looking young fellow, much bigger than his brother Tom, and just as handsome, but without that electric touch about him that makes the world know when he's around.

I looked at him with a queer mixture of horror and admiration. This was the fellow that Dan Porson had shot down in the unlucky saloon brawl. My respect for Dan mounted. I, for one, would not have liked to stand against such a man.

"Tom will be here in a moment," said Roberta Meade, her voice quick with excitement. "And then the trouble will start! Where's Slim? Where's the sheriff?"

I watched young Acker by the door, hailing one friend, and then another. He limped a good deal when he walked, but I guessed that there would be no limp in his right arm, once he started his hand for a gun.

Then in came a middle-sized man with a burly pair of shoulders, and on his head a sombrero which he did not take off in honor of the dance and the ladies. He looked rather soft, and blond, and his face was as sunburned as a tenderfoot's after his first week on the range.

"Thank heavens, there's Loren Mays!" said the girl beside me.

She squeezed my arm, in her excitement and her pleasure. "Are you glad?" she whispered.

"You bet your boots I'm glad," said I, heaving a great breath.

Tom Acker came in through the door, just then, stepping light, like the wild cat that he was. The sheriff, reaching around, caught his arm, and then made a step or two, and caught the arm of his brother.

The music came to a stop with a wrangling jar. And then as the buzzing voices went out, like a light, we all could hear the voice of the sheriff saying:

"I'm going to bind you two to keep the peace. You hear me, Tom? You hear me, Josh? I've heard about this shenanigan. And it won't work. Not while I'm wearing a badge in this town and trying to keep law and order. It won't work at all!"

He let go of their arms, and slapped his hands together.

"You don't have to shout," said Tom Acker. "I can hear you without being shouted at."

"Is that so, my fine young man?" said the sheriff. "I'll tell you what you may hear, one of these days, and that may be the voice of a judge saying that you're condemned to be hanged by the neck till you're dead. But no judge is going to have to say that while I'm on the job in this county, I hope. Tom—Josh—I know the devilment or worse that you're up to. Mind me, now—I mean what I say. I bind you over to keep the peace; and if you won't give me your word, I'll slam the pair of you in jail, by thunder!"

He was worked up, and he meant what he said. For my part, I never heard any talk that was such pleasant music to me! I could have cheered the great Loren Mays, and with a loud voice, too.

And then, bawling up the outer stairs, and through the door, so that the whole dance crowd could hear him, someone shouted: "Where's Loren Mays? Where's the sheriff?"

"Up here, at the dance," we could hear voices at the door answering.

The other, panting as he ran, yelled: "A fine time for the sheriff to be at a dance, when Rudie Clark has killed two men already, and has gone after his wife and his kid to kill them, too."

I saw the sheriff throw his arms above his head, and I heard his groan. He didn't wait for the voice of the messenger to come into the doorway, but charged straight out through it, and his heels made a rapid thunder on the stairs outside.

"Who's this Rudie Clark?" I asked the girl.

"He's a poor, good-natured fellow," said she, "who goes on a tear once a year, and then he's likely to make trouble. But I don't like the sound of this. I don't believe that Rudie would ever get crazy enough to do more than threaten. I think it's only a dodge."

"For what?" I asked.

"To get the sheriff away," said the girl, "and to get you and poor Dan Porson closer to a killing!"

9

GUN PLAY

I'm coming close to a thing that needs some believing, and I'd even hesitate to write it down, except that so many people saw it and can bear testimony about it.

How the lights went out at Cat Hill I'm about to tell—all the lights in the dance hall, and in the anterooms that were built around the dance floor. All of that big place went dark—all the electric lanterns that were burning around the walls, and from the ceilings. All of them went out—and a queer thing happened in the darkness.

What led up to it was like this:

I was still with Bobbie Meade after the sheriff ran out of the place, and straight across the floor to me came Josh Acker, and stood in front of me, about to speak, his face dark with a scowl.

The girl beside me said: "You keep away from dirty work, Josh, and try to go straight."

He looked at her, and I saw the shock of her words go through him. Everybody in that part of the world felt her influence, and that was very clear.

Well, what she said nearly put Josh Acker off balance, but he blinked and said:

"This is my business, Bobbie, not your game at all!" To me he added: "You're with Dan Porson, I guess?"

"I'm with Porson," I said feebly.

"Will you step over to the coatroom?" invited young Acker.

"Sure," I said.

"Wait a minute!" exclaimed the girl.

She caught me by the arm, and seeing that, Josh turned on his heel. He just threw over his shoulder:

"We'll be waiting in there for you, stranger!"

I was ready to follow, but I was only trying half-heartedly to get away, and Bobbie Meade had a strong grip.

"You don't belong in this party. You go home," she urged.

"I can't do that," I said.

"Why can't you?"

"Honor—" I began.

"Honor!" cried Bobbie Meade. "Oh, I'm sick of that word. Every crooked and shadowy and mean thing in the world has that word 'honor' tacked onto it, one way or another. 'Honor!' Every murder has 'honor' behind it. I think the people that use the word ought to be horse-whipped back into their better senses. You stay right here. Don't try to make a hero or a gun fighter out of yourself, because you simply can't. You're not the makings of the type. You're green around the gills right now. You stay here, before you make a fool of yourself before the whole world!"

That was sure stating it pretty strongly. What gave me strength was her remark about the color of my face.

I said to myself that if I were the same seasick color outside that matched the seasick feeling inside, I couldn't possibly be more ashamed, except by running away, and that the only thing for me to do was to haul off and get into some sort of violent action. When soldiers charge, the bullets will kill the cowards along with the brave men, and nobody can tell which is which, after they've been tagged. So I decided to charge.

I brushed her hand away.

"It's all right, Bobbie," I said. "But I'm going over and take my share of trouble!"

I started away from her, and heard her saying:

"You blessed idiot, come back here! I wish I were a man—I'd step in and stop this murdering nonsense!"

I got to the door of the coat-and-hat room, which was just a partition standing out into the floor in a corner near the doorway. And I heard Bobbie Meade calling out behind me:

"They're going in there to fight like rats in a trap. It's murder! Harry—Joe—Willie Stacey—Jack—Marvin—are you boys going to let this thing go on?"

I heard a murmur of the crowd behind me, a deep murmur of men's voices, and the sharp voices of women; and one of the latter cried out on a high, piercing note that unnerved me completely, as I stepped in. I was shaking from head to foot, so I set my jaws and scowled as blackly as I could manage it.

I slammed the door behind me—that much I can testify to. And though it's barely possible that some one may have been standing all the while behind the long overcoats and slickers that hung from the pegs along the wall, I could almost swear that the shanks of the hidden man would have been in view.

When I stepped inside and slammed the door, the other three were already there—I mean Dan Porson, and Josh, and his famous brother, Tom Acker.

Dan Porson, looking as gray as though he had been covered with dust, stood at one end of the little room, with his head thrown back and his chin in the air, and a faint smile frozen on his mouth. Josh Acker was at the opposite end, standing beside his brother, and it was plain that Josh was not afraid of Dan, no matter what had happened at their first meeting. He stood with his head thrust forward, slightly crouched, and he looked ready to leap forward and put his big hands on Dan's throat.

There was a mighty ugly look about his eyes and mouth, a cruel, hard look, and I knew by that glance that no matter what men might say about Tom Acker, he could never be quite the brutal savage that his younger brother was. As for Tom himself, he was the only one who remained calm and at ease. Only the muscles at the base of his jaw were continually working, playing in and out, and there was a glittering about his eyes. No wonder he looked contented, for I knew, as I stared at him, that he had enough magic at his command to face Dan and me alone, and finish us off before anybody could say Jack Robinson. Josh was just thrown in for extra measure—and because the quarrel had been the quarrel of Josh in the beginning.

I stepped over and stood beside Dan. He turned his eyes toward me, without moving his head, and I saw in those eyes the gratitude that you get from a dumb beast when it's in agony.

Tom Acker said: "I went over to your place, Porson, to have a talk with you about what you did to my brother—blood's thicker than water, in my family. And what happened to me was a damned trick, and a low trick. I asked you back here—and you've been fool enough to come. I say you've been fool enough, because I'm going to clean you up—you and the green-faced brat that you brought along with you. If you have a second chance to come into Cat Hill—which you ain't going to have—you oughta bring a real man with you."

He ended with a snap of his fingers that made me start, and I saw poor Dan Porson jump a little where he stood beside me.

"Let's start," Josh said. "We've talked enough. They're going to break in on us, in another minute. We've got the fool of a sheriff out of the way—and what more d'you want, boys? Come on, Danny, fill your hand!"

As he invited Dan to make the first move, I heard the rising murmur of protest in the room outside. And there was the voice of Bobbie Meade, pleading, ordering, threatening the men, unless they attempted to do something to justify their existence and their claim to the *title* of men.

She was getting a response, too, and there was a rising tide of sound of voices, and the movement of feet toward us, when Dan Porson answered:

"Make your own first play. I'll fill my hand fast enough to suit the pair of you—you rats!"

He was trying to talk himself into a fighting heat, but his voice was pretty shaky, as I noted with a sick heart. I made up my mind that Tom Acker would have to be my goal—that I would get the gun out as fast as I could, but that I would save all for a sure sight, and a steady pull on the trigger. He might knock me down with a bullet, but I'd try to get him before I died, shooting from the floor, lying on my side, my back, no matter how I fell. Slow and sure would have to be my motto.

Well, just as we stood in this way, at the final tension, with death a tenth of a second away from all of us, the lights snapped out.

They snapped out with a groan that came from every person on the dance floor, and then there was a screech from a dozen women at once, and a rush of feet that sounded just like the stamping of a frightened herd.

Well, it was pretty awful, at that, to have a crowd keyed up to murder, and then to have that deep, thick blackness spread over the eyes. But, for my part, as I stood there with my gun in my hand, I was thanking God with every breath I drew, and in between.

Then, through the blackness, I distinctly heard a voice say in the room, close to me:

"If you act up, Tom, I'm going to run this knife through you. Come along quiet, you damn sheep killer!"

The sound of that voice was a balm to me—I recognized the speech of Lanky!

How he got in there, I don't know, but I could swear that I recognized his way of talking—it was printed too deeply in my memory!

A moment later, in the midst of the turmoil, the lights snapped on again, and I looked around for the rest of them, with Lanky added to the group. But I was amazed to see the door open, and Tom Acker, and Lanky, and Dan Porson, all three of them gone.

There remained only Josh Acker in front of me, his gun in his hand, as mine was in mine.

I began to put up the Colt, but Josh Acker was in a frenzy. He had come there to kill or to be killed, and he wanted to go on with the horrible business. I never saw a face like his, as the lights flashed on again.

"Damn you!" he yelled at me. "I'll get one of the pair of you, anyway!"

And he fired as he spoke.

I know what saved me. It was being on tenterhooks, every nerve and muscle tight, so that merely the sound of his voice made me literally jump to the side, and that dodge made his bullet streak through the air beside my face.

As I jumped, I stumbled, and dropped on my knees and one hand.

"Take that—and that!" he yelled, as he shot again. And his lips curled back wolfishly from his teeth as he sent a second bullet through my hair.

I fired upward, wondering at the way my nerves remained steady and thanking God and my hand as I pulled the trigger. And with the boom of the gun in my ears, I distinctly heard the thud of the bullet striking his body.

I knew that I had killed a man!

10

A DYING MAN

You people who hear about gun fights, and about men who have killed a dozen or a score, and who pass the thing up as nothing—well, I want to tell you the truth about what it was like.

How I felt when I heard the horror of that bullet striking on flesh, human flesh, that I can't describe at all, and that was the worst of all—everything that followed was easy in comparison.

Then, as I got slowly to my feet—slowly because my knees were weak—I saw the shining gun drop out of the hands of big Josh Acker as he spread his fingers over his breast.

"You," he whispered, staring at me, "you've gone and killed me!"

He was a big fellow, and a strong fellow, mind you, as I said before, and within two seconds he had been looking like a devil bent on eating me. But now he turned at a touch into a frightened child, and as he spoke, I saw a thin, red trickle break out through his fingers.

He felt it, and put out his hands and looked down at the crimson that was dripping from them.

"You've gone and killed me!" he whispered again.

You would have said that the idea struck him with more physical weight than the actual lump of lead with the drive of the explosion behind it, for all at once he wilted to the floor and hit it with a soft, loose thump that I can still remember, and feel in my mind as if with the sense of touch.

People were pouring into the room, now; they stood packed all around, with their hands hanging helplessly. I ran over and dropped down on my knees beside Josh Acker.

He had both hands over his breast; the blood was oozing fast through the fingers; his face was white and strained, and his eyes were closed.

He opened them, saw me, and threw up his hands, with a screech.

"Take him away!" he yelled. "He's murdered me! Take him away! He's murdered me!"

And, at the same time, his hands thrust against my face, and I felt the wet, thick moisture of the blood that was on them!

That yell of his had an effect on the others as well as on me. Hands grabbed me by the shoulders and yanked me forcibly away, so forcibly that I came to my feet and went staggering back until my shoulders struck against the wall of the partition with a crash. Ugly faces turned and glared at me in a way that meant trouble, before long.

I tell you, I wanted to get out of that place, but somehow my feet stuck to the floor; I couldn't run before Josh was actually dead.

Now, I wish that I had, because it might have avoided nearly everything that followed. Not altogether everything, because I think that the devil was already walking the earth and taking pleasure in putting poison into the minds of men in that part of the range. But the greater part would have been avoided, perhaps, if I had followed my first instinct, and bolted.

However, I stayed there, and the crowd thickened about Josh so that I could not see what was happening to him. Everybody was telling everybody else to get back and give the man air, and nobody moved, except to crowd closer and tell the *others* to get back, and so it went.

I was getting my first real introduction to the workings of the mind of a crowd. I was to get more knowledge of that before many more days came!

A doctor came in, and they hauled him through the press. I heard poor Josh whimpering: "Oh, doc, he went and murdered me! He went and murdered me!"

"You're going to be all right, my boy," said the doctor in a clear, strong voice. "I *hope* you're going to be all right!"

How I liked the sound of that voice! The strength and the clearness and the good enunciation all meant a man of education, I felt, and in this age of miracles perhaps Josh could be brought back from the edge of the long night into which I felt he was drifting.

Some one shook my arm. I looked down, and there I saw Bobbie Meade standing beside me.

"Get out of here!" she muttered, close to my ear. "Get out of here, and get fast."

"I can't go, till I know what's happened," I said.

"You'll know that when there's a rope fitted around your neck," she answered me.

Her face was tense. There was a savage, angry look about her. I could see that she was the sort of a person whose mind worked properly in an emergency, but just the same I could not go. My feet were still stuck to the floor.

"It wouldn't be square for me to go," I said.

"Will it be square," she asked, "for the rest of 'em to lynch you? Is that any better?"

I heard the word "lynch" well enough, but I could not make head or tail of her meaning. It had been a fair fight, if there *is* such a thing as a fair fight. There must have been witnesses. Some of the people who looked through that door must have known that two shots were fired at me before I used my gun. So what could this talk of a lynching be?

Well, I was to do some more learning about mobs and how they use their brains, before long!

I heard the voice of the doctor, speaking as clearly as before but more solemnly. He said, while a sudden hush ran coldly through the crowd:

"Josh, it's a sad duty to me to tell you that you may not have many minutes to live. Have you anything that you wish done—have you anything to say that—"

The yell of Josh broke in on him.

"You lie, doc!" he screeched. "I ain't going to die. God wouldn't let me die. I'm too young. I've got a lot of strength left in me. God wouldn't let a sneaking skunk like that step in and murder me!"

A slight groan came from the crowd; every man, including myself, had caught his breath quickly and deeply. It was that word murder, coming into nearly every phrase that Josh spoke, that rang like a bell in my ears, and no doubt in the ears of the others.

My arm was shaken again.

"Will you go now, Nelly Grey?" demanded the girl.

I was in such a state of mind that I could hardly hear her, let alone act on her excellent advice. There was a gray mist before me. Through it the chief thing I felt was that I must be justified. I wanted to say something. I wanted to tell them that it was self-defense. I wanted to yell the words in their ears. Then I heard the doctor saying:

"Josh, no matter how strong you may feel now, I warn you that in a few minutes you will be dead. It's my duty to tell you so."

"Damn you—damn you and your duty," gasped Josh. "Oh, I knew that he'd murdered me. He went and murdered me! I wanta see him. I wanta see his face!"

That crowd parted like magic. Men turned to me with faces of iron—with hands of iron that caught hold of me and dragged me suddenly before Josh.

He had changed frightfully in the minute or so that had come between. His face was still whiter than before, while the whole front of his body, which had been bared, was crimson. But the most horrible part was the pinching in of his cheeks, and the thrusting out of his eyes as he recognized me.

He started up on one elbow—I wish that I could forget that memory of him!—and he shook his fist in my face.

"You dog, you dog!" yelled Josh. "You sneaked in and murdered me! You killed me! You done it! I'm going to put a curse on you. I'm going to curse the water you drink, and what you eat, and the air you breathe, it'll choke you. I'm cursing—"

He broke off short in the midst of the shouting. I can't tell you how those words got hold of me and trembled in my heart. They were not the sort of words you'd expect from a puncher like Josh, a rough chap, a regular cowhand. He might damn me black and white and bring in some fine strong language to do his damning with, for that matter, but this business of putting a curse on me was horrible, and more horrible because it was strange, and because it came from the lips of a dying man.

I felt, at that moment, a choking coldness in my throat, as though I was breathing fog that had no air in it, and were suddenly throttling.

But now his speech was taken from him.

He dropped suddenly back into several pairs of arms that supported him. They were no kin of his that were upholding him. His brother was not there, for one thing. He had not reappeared. When he came again, no doubt I should know it by the impact of bullets on my own body.

So Josh lay back in the hands of the townsmen, and gasped. And then he snatched up his legs until his knees were almost at his chin, and straightened them out again with a jerk that made him half sit up again,

The most horrible part of all came then.

He seemed to have a last touch of strength, and began to point at me, and shake his hand at me, and he nodded his head this way and that, while his lips moved, and he had the appearance of a man shouting at the top of his voice terrible threats, but the only sound that came was a frightful bubbling, and then a pale crimson bubble burst on his lips.

His face swelled and grew blacker. His eyes started out more than ever.

And so he fell over on his side, threw his arms wildly over his head, and died like that, with his body all extended, as though he were nailed on a cross.

That was a picture that would be painted to my disadvantage, before very long!

He lay still. His eyes were half closed, and no longer staring. I knew that this was death. Josh was there, and he was not there. That thing on the floor was no more, really, than the boards on which it was lying. It was only so many pounds of matter, and all that had made it think and speak was gone!

"He's dead," said some one quietly.

"He's dead," said another solemnly. "Poor Josh is dead."

A man kneeled down and closed the eyes. He took the out-flung arms and crossed them on the breast of the dead man.

"Don't touch nothing," said another man. "Not till the sheriff gets here."

"That don't matter, now," said the other. "We know who killed Josh Acker!"

11

MOB SPIRIT

It was the end, then, of Josh Acker. And I started for the door of the little room feeling that I would be dead, too, unless I got quickly to open air.

As I started to leave, I saw Bobbie Meade standing outside it, with her arms folded and her head dropped a little, looking up at me with an expression partly curious and partly sardonic.

At the same time, some one bellowed: "We know who murdered poor Josh Acker, and we've got him here!"

"We've got him for the taking!" yelled another.

Suddenly, between me and the door, flooded a mass of figures, one jammed against the other.

I retreated. There was nothing to be done. I looked vainly over my shoulder at the partition, but I could not jump that. It was ten feet high!

Still, I had hope. I was in the right, if there can be any right for a man who has taken the life of another man. If only I could put the plain facts before the crowd—

But it gave me a chill when I looked at them. I had seen the same expression, years before, when I was a small boy sent to a new school, and at the first recess found myself matched against the bully of the lot, with a circle of the other boys standing about. For there was in most of these faces the same cruel brutality, the same enjoyment of pain to come that I had seen in the faces of the youngsters that long time ago. Only it was worse, here—much worse, because these were men, not boys.

And when a man throws away all spiritual responsibility and gives himself up to brute instincts, he looks and is a great deal worse than any beast.

No one had laid hands on me, as yet, but I could see by the glare in many eyes that they were ready, or almost ready, to tear me to bits.

"Look here, men," I said. "You've a wrong idea. The game was started by the Ackers. They were looking for trouble. And when—"

"Shut him up," said a loud voice.

Instantly a fist landed on my mouth, and jammed my head back against the partition, and half stunned me.

A wild chorus of howling roused me again. It came from every throat; I looked out through the cloud of unconsciousness and found a raving mob all about me, with the grimmest eyes that a man could imagine.

He who had spoken before was speaking again. He was a big fellow who seemed to have come into the dance hall from the street—at least, he had a high-crowned black hat with a great wide brim on his head. And he had a long, narrow, pale face. He looked like a minister. He talked like a minister, too, with a deep voice, intoning his words. And he made gestures like a minister, slowly, sweeping his thin hands about solemnly.

"I guess, brothers," he was saying, "that this here is a time when we don't need to wait for no law. Law costs time. Law costs money. Where from? From us taxpayers and honest citizens. All of us that vote, we got the cost of prosecuting the rascals, like this one. But now I tell you, if I had my way, while this here poor boy is lying on his back, looking up to heaven—this lad that has lost his ma and his pa, and his brother that loved him, this here boy that we seen playing about our streets, and growing up into a fine manhood—while this here dead man, Josh Acker, is lying here, I'd take his murderer and hang him as high as one of the rafters in that dance room, yonder. And there I'd leave him swinging to and fro, sir, if I had my way about it. Because to hell he's going to go, sooner or later, and to hell he might as well go, right now!"

It was a pretty convincing speech, it seemed. It took no account of right or wrong. It argued no points of the case. I've noticed that most clever talkers never do those things. They never let the audience think. They never argue. They simply take it for granted that all right-minded men agree with them. If there are any fools and rascals in the audience, then it's as well for them to keep silent! At any rate, it was clear from the start that the tall man with the black hat had the entire group with him at once, and to a man.

Great Scott, how I looked around them, hungrily, from face to face, and hunted for a single man who looked dubious, or pitying, or disgusted. But I found not a single one. The mob is a beast with a thousand bodies, but with only one brain, and that brain is pretty sure to be the lowest in the mob.

It's the lowest common denominator!

Well, there was a growl, and a surge, and a dozen pairs of hands grabbed me. I was bruised to the bone by the grips that fell on me, and the force of their arms lifted me clean off the floor.

I was whirled out of that anteroom and into the dance hall in a jiffy, and in another jiffy, a large rope was flung over a central rafter.

"Up with him, boys!" shouted the man in the black hat. At the same moment, he had the noose around my neck, and his hands were touching my throat as he pulled up the slack, and I saw the horrible joy that shuddered and flickered like a candle flame in his eyes!

He looked me up and down, with a hideous recognition and delight in the wretched death that I was to die, and then he drew back again, grinning.

I was going to die. I knew I was going to die. I felt that as a man I ought to resist, as a cord was used to tie my hands behind me, but I could not move. I could only look blankly before me.

I many times have heard of people who, at the moment of death, see the entire course of their lives flow before them. But it was not that way here. All that I saw was a huddle of ideas, faces, terrors, sorrows, regrets, entangled in a fog, like forms struggling together, but none of them really clear.

"Up with him!" shouted a voice.

Suddenly there was the girl, there was Bobbie Meade standing in front of me, with one of her hands hooked into the rope that went around my neck. And her shoulders were against my breast, and as she spoke, I felt the tremor of the effort, and the catch of her breath.

"Cat Hill's the wrong name for this town," she said. "It ought to be Rat Hill. You're a lot of wretched rats. I'm ashamed to look at you fellows I've known all my life men I've respected. What's the matter with you? Are you brain-sick? Here's a poor fellow comes with his friend, because his friend begs him to come in the bad time that he needs help. He comes with Dan Porson riding into Cat Hill, because the two Ackers have invited them to come, after Josh Acker was dropped by young Porson, and after Tom Acker was beaten and sent home from the Porson ranch.

"These two ride in, like men, and they expect that they'll find men in the place, to treat them like men. And instead of that, they find murderers!"

"*He's* the murderer!" said the man with the big black hat, and the long, pale face. "He's the murderer, Bobbie Meade!"

"You fools," said the girl, overlooking the man in the black hat. "You're letting a seller of patent medicines, a sleight-of-hand artist, a cheap crook—you're letting him walk into your town and run your affairs for you, and shame you forever! A fine lot you are!"

"Take her away!" called a voice from the rear of the crowd.

"I recognize your voice, Lem Walters!" she answered instantly. "And if this man is lynched, then *you'll* be known and accused, I can promise you. I'll mortgage my life and soul to get the money to run you down, every man jack of you. And who says that this boy murdered poor Josh Acker? Everybody knows that the Ackers came here expecting trouble. And they got it. If it was murder, where is Tom Acker now? Where is Dan Porson? Why not find them and ask *them* what was happening? Who dares to say that he saw this man take advantage of Josh Acker, when they fought?"

Now, that was a speech that I could appreciate, and through my faintly chattering teeth, I managed to gasp:

"God bless you, Bobbie."

The man with the black hat and the long white face stood biting his lips and twisting his ugly mouth, as the girl talked. I tell you, he looked to me like the devil walking the earth, as he stood there, snarling and sneering silently. And when he saw that she really had snatched from the crowd all of the momentum that he had given it toward a killing, he spoke again, and grandly:

"Brothers, there's not a man of us that doesn't pity a poor girl pleading for her sweetheart. I say it's right for us to stand and listen like gentlemen, while she has her whole say, but after that, I say that it's a good time to start moving, brothers. It ain't a pleasant thing that we got before us. But we wouldn't leave garbage standing in the open street. And we wouldn't leave this here man to walk alive in our town. No, brothers, we wouldn't do that and still be able to call ourselves men!"

"Tommy Clark—Red Malvern—Ben—Vince—are you going to let that scoundrel hypnotize you?" exclaimed the girl, hooking her other hand inside the noose of the rope that circled my neck.

She was the only woman who had had the courage to stay. She was the only woman in the world, anyway, it seemed to me.

And still the fine, brave courage of that act comes over me with a sweep—she was so small, I mean, and there were so many against her.

"As for the girl," said the man of the black hat, "it ain't a pleasant thing to do, but we gotta put her aside, and sadly, not gladly, we gotta go ahead with our duty, remembering the face of the poor boy in the next room, yonder, where he was shot down by a sneak, remembering his face as he lay choking to death, not able to speak out the accusations that he had started but he didn't need to finish 'em, because there's men here in Cat Hill that are ready to see justice done, and quick justice!"

He had them caught up in the palm of his hand, by that. They came with a sweep, and tried to pull the girl away. She clung to the rope, and screamed out at them, wildly, her whole body vibrating as if with electricity.

I saw fellows reach for her, and then hold her hands. It was the man with the pale face and the black, wide hat that tore her suddenly away, and got his claws on the rope that was to strangle me, and then I saw Sheriff Loren Mays come into the room red and puffing, and fairly snorting steam, like a bull.

He fired three shots into the air, and that gang of lynchers melted away right and left. The law came marching up to me, and I was the gladdest man in the world to be legally arrested for murder!

12

THE LAW

The sheriff was in the hottest sort of a rage. As he clapped me on the shoulder with one hand and arrested me in the name of the law, with the other hand he tore off the noose which was around my neck.

"This is a fine bit of work," said Loren Mays. "This here is a gaudy, neat bit of good work, I gotta say. I'm going to get at the bottom of it, is what I'm going to do. The time's come when a man can't be hanged by the law in Cat Hill, has it? The law's gotta be helped by a gang of thugs and cheap skates and worthless tramps like you gents, does it? You can make a fool of me, can you? I'll show you who's a fool in the long run! Back up, the lot of you, or by the living image of an army mule, I'm going to drill some half-inch holes in you. Back up and gimme air!"

They backed up, fast enough. And among them all, I remember the face of the man in the black hat, and the rage, disgust, and venom that still twisted it this way and that.

His voice came sounding through the tumult that followed the sheriff's speech.

"Can one man go and take him away from all of us? Can any one man slap the whole of Cat Hill in the face like that?"

The sheriff left me standing there—and I felt like a derelict adrift, let me tell you, and adrift in a storm—while he lunged through the mob. He got to the man in the black hat and caught him by the shoulder and shook him.

"Who are you, you long-faced undertaker?" asked the sheriff.

The man in the black hat was calm and steady enough.

"Take your hand away from a law-abiding citizen," he said. "My name is Reginald Channing Carter, sir."

He struck an attitude, as he said this.

"I'll Reginald Channing Carter you," said the sheriff, angrier than ever. "I'll take and slam you in jail, if I hear another word out of you. I'll—"

While he was going after that devil of a Carter, the rest of the crowd came milling in toward me. I remembered my revolver and felt that this might be a good time to flash it. Not that I intended to use it, but that I thought perhaps the sheriff might need a little help in getting me to the jail in safety. So I pulled my Colt and shouted something, I don't know what.

You would have thought that I had swung flaming fire in the faces of so many wild animals. They threw up their hands as though to shield their eyes from the flash of the gun, and they spilled back from me, stumbling over one another.

The sheriff had wheeled about with a wild yell, when he heard the commotion behind him. By the look of him, and the way he held his revolver, I'm sure that he was on the verge of pumping lead into some of them, but he saw that they were giving way, and he called out to me:

"Good boy! We've got 'em on the run, and we'll keep 'em running. We'll get to the jail as slick as silk!"

We had become partners, as it were, to get me to the Cat Hill jail!

The sheriff shifted his gun from his right hand to his left, where it seemed perfectly at home. Then he hooked his right arm through my left one, and bawled out at the top of his voice:

"Keep your gun out, brother, and the first flash of anything you see around you, if it ain't no more than a pocket handkerchief, you pull that trigger and shoot to kill. I'm going to teach these boys a lesson, if I gotta have it wrote in blood. That's the only kind of writing that they can read and remember!"

He led me first not out of the building, but into the anteroom where the dead man lay.

I looked no farther than the feet of poor Josh Acker.

"Well, here he is," said the sheriff quite cheerfully. "You done this job, Nelson Grey, didn't you?"

I rather wondered that he had picked up my name so quickly.

"He fired the first two shots," I said. "Then I let him have it. I call that self-defense."

"That's all right," the sheriff answered. "There he lies, and you're the one that put him there. That's all I wanta know. You come to jail, and the judge and the jury'll settle the rest of it!"

He turned about.

"Any of you gents see this here shooting?" he demanded. Instantly came the booming voice of Reginald Channing Carter.

"I was standing close to the door," he said. "I seen the lights come on, and I seen that this here gent had a gun in his hand and that Josh Acker didn't have none. I seen this gent raise his gun and shoot—and as Acker fell, I seen poor Josh pull his gun and fire a coupla times, wild!"

As he told this lie, in order to make his speech more impressive, he stepped toward me, and brandished his forefinger under my nose. Then he cried out:

"Take a look at his face! Ain't that the look of a guilty man, all right?"

As a matter of fact, the strength and the greatness of the lie had simply overwhelmed me, and I was gaping like an idiot as the scoundrel threatened me with his finger.

The sheriff knocked down the long arm of Channing Carter.

"That's all right," he said. "The judge and the jury may be glad to hear you, but we don't want no speeches made tonight. I don't like the looks of you, Carter, for my part. Come along, kid. You step right along with me, and I'll have you snug in the jail, in no time at all."

I started out of the room with him, and as we came to the door at the head of the stairs, there I saw Bobbie Meade. She gave me a smile and a wave of her hand. I reached out and grabbed her hand as she was waving it.

"I'd be choked by now, except for you," I told her.

And there was never anything truer than that!

"Keep your head up, Nelly," said she. "They can't kill you with lies—not while Loren Mays is around."

I went on down the outer stairs with the sheriff.

Behind me, I could hear Reginald Channing Carter beginning a stirring oration to the crowd that remained in the dance room. He was rousing them on my trail again, and I wondered what in the world could have started his malice against me. It was nothing that I ever had done to him—I never had laid eyes on him before this moment. And it was nothing that he could gain from me, except a little notoriety as the leader of the crowd. That must be it, I thought. Simply a savage desire to be the leader with all eyes fixed upon him!

I wondered at the crowd, too. At least half of them must have been thoroughly decent fellows, as good as any man, but they had been swept up in the blind, dark, vicious course of mob enthusiasm. Separately they were as good or better than you and me; together, they made a group of animals, cruel as wolves, and a lot more dangerous, but cowardly it seemed, too, when a real man like the sheriff stood up to them.

He took me right on down the steps, and as we got to the bottom of them, there came Dan Porson running across the street to meet us, with his hat off, and a wild look on his face.

"How's everything, Nels, and what's happened?" he gasped at me.

"Here's the sheriff, and I'm arrested for killing Josh Acker," said I, a little bitterly, for I couldn't help remembering how entirely this was Dan's party, from the beginning to the end.

He staggered and groaned.

"Is he down?" he asked. "Is Josh down again?"

"He's down for good," said the sheriff. "He's dead. You walk along with us, Porson—I suppose you're Dan Porson. But try no funny plays to get your partner loose. It wouldn't be any good. Even if I was down, look at the dogs that are ready to run at you rabbits!"

It was true. Behind us, twenty or thirty men were following, and their voices made a steady muttering. It gave me chills up the spine to think of all the guns that were there. One volley would wipe out all three of us—the sheriff, Dan, and me!

"I'm not trying to break the law," said Dan eagerly. "I'm inside of it. I want to stay inside of it the rest of my born days, too!"

"Yeah," said the sheriff, "that's the way everybody feels on the morning after."

I muttered to Dan: "Tell me, what happened? What became of you?"

"I'm sick, seeing you in like this," said Dan. "But I'll stand by you, partner. I'll stand by you if it means getting inside of the same rope they use to hang you! But it won't come to that. The finest lawyer that money can buy is the one that I'm going to get for you!"

"Thanks," said I, perhaps a little too dryly. "But what became of you and Tom Acker in the anteroom?"

"I heard a voice in the dark," said Dan, "just after the lights went out. I heard the voice, and straight off I thought that it was the voice of Lanky. And I was mighty glad to hear it, let me tell you. I was the gladdest man in the world! Then I heard him speaking to Acker—threatening him. And it seemed to me that the door of the anteroom was opened, though I couldn't see a thing in the blackness.

"But I stumbled toward the place where I supposed it to be, and found it, and pushed through, and thought that I could make out a dim silhouette as tall as Lanky. So I followed along into the crowd, but I lost the shape.

"Then I thought that Lanky, if he had Tom Acker in his hands, would surely go right outside the building with him, so I dove for the stairway, and fought my way through the crowd to it, through the darkness. And when I got to the head of the stairs, I saw two men, one very tall, toward the bottom of it. I raced down after them. They turned away into the shadows. I lost them again. I started running every which way to locate them.

"And finally I came back here, winded—and I find that you've been grabbed by the law. What happened?"

"What has happened?" I said. "Heaven knows—not I! I suppose that the Ackers arranged the false alarm about the fellow that was trying to kill somebody. Maybe Lanky arranged the putting out of the lights. And everything else is a tangle, in my mind. I only know that Josh Acker is dead, and that I'm most likely to hang for the killing of him!"

13

IN JAIL

Well, I was brought to the jail, and there, at the door of it, Dan Porson wrung my hand and swore that he and his father would stand by me while they had a penny in the world. I saw him go, and as the door was unlocked, the sheriff said to me:

"He's a good friend of yours, that Porson, is he?"

"He's all right," I said.

"Yeah, he's all right, I guess," said the sheriff. "But he talks a lot, is what I mean."

We went into the jail, and there I was duly written down as Nelson Grey, born of such and such parents, at such a date, in such a place. I was so high, weighed so much, had no distinguishing marks, had brown hair and gray eyes, and was average size. I seemed to be "average" all the way through the list.

"You're the kind that are hard to trail," the sheriff confessed to me. "It's a dog-gone good thing that more 'average' gents don't go in for crime, or we'd have a devil of a job holding up the law!"

Then the crime I was charged with was written down.

"Murder!"

I stood there, and saw the pen scratch out the word on the page, and it meant no more to me than any other word. I was

68

stunned, and nothing registered in my mind. The bell was being pressed, but the current was shut off and not a sound was made, so to speak.

They searched me, and took away my gun for the first time. I remember that the sheriff looked the gun over and complimented me on keeping it in such good order.

"A right good Colt will last a man a lifetime, if's took proper care of," said he, "but some of these young bloods that wear 'em for show, they let the rust eat out the heart of 'em, and they wouldn't hit the side of a barn inside of the first year. But now, this here gun is what I'd call a working gun, a gun that expects to do something in the course of the day, every time that it gets up in the morning—a gun that only closes one eye at night, because it dunno when it'll be called on in the dark."

I remember this speech through the haze of my mind, and then I was taken to a cell, and the sheriff locked me in. I was suddenly so tired that I could not move hand or foot. I slumped on the cot, and the sheriff paused one moment at the bars.

"I wish you luck, kid," he said. "Any friend of Bobbie Meade's is a friend of mine. Good night."

And I *had* a good night, at that, without a dream, without stirring hand or foot, and wakened in the morning with a sigh and a groan, and seemed to hear the bawling voice of the cook shouting: "Turn out! Turn out!"

No, it was not the voice of the cook, but some one shouting in the street.

I had a breakfast of ham and eggs and graham muffins and molasses and all the coffee that I wanted and an orange to finish off on.

I said to the Negro who brought me the chuck: "Why, George, if you feed everybody in the jail as well as all this, I wonder that the whole town doesn't try to get into the jail."

"We see quite a lot of the boys, one time or another, mister," he said to me, "but everybody ain't fed as good as you are. Everybody ain't *in* for what you're in for."

I understood what he meant. People accused of murder got a little better treatment as though the law wished to pay them some attention during the wretched remnant of their days. I remembered that men about to be executed, once put in the death house, were allowed to satisfy any whim of fancy or appetite.

My own appetite remained good, strange to say, even after the remark which the Negro had made. For now that the morning had come, and the coffee had cleared away the fatigue from my brain, I could remember the whole affair clearly, and sum it up.

According to my lights—and they were those of the whole range, I could have sworn—there was really nothing against me. A friend in need had called on me in a pinch. I went with him. Two men who had asked us then proceeded to corner us. And I killed one of those men in self-defense.

As for the lying testimony of Reginald Channing Carter—why, the fellow would never dare to open his mouth and repeat his lies in the broad daylight!

Besides, there was the wealth of the great Porson estate behind me, to secure the best sort of legal advice, so why should I care a rap? No, to me jail would simply be a resting place, and when I came out, perhaps people would look on me with a little more respect and feel that I had grown up; Old Man Porson might steer me into a job as straw boss. He might make things easy for me to get the small piece of land that I had dreamed about so many times—the land that would make my start as a cattleman with my own brand!

Sometimes I thought that when I saw that brand appear for the first time on the flank of a calf, I would lose my mind with joy. Half my daydreams were in the devising of that brand!

I was content enough in the jail, as I was saying; there was only the thought of the dead man that weighed on me, and now and again a frightful darkness and coldness passed through my brain and my body. I remembered, then, that I had killed a human being!

Several important things happened that day.

The first was the arrival of the reporter for the *Evening Bugle*. He was the reporter and the editor, both in one, and he had a whole pocketful of pencils, ready and sharpened, and a face like the face of a ferret, with very small, winking eyes, red-stained, and with pale eyelashes.

He wanted to know all about me, and how it felt to kill one's first man, and how many hours a day I practiced with a revolver, and had there been any gunmen in the family before me, and such rot. I told him that I didn't want to talk about myself. That I was no gunman; that there never had been a gunman in my family; that all I wanted in this world was a chance to lead the life of a hard-working cow-puncher and finally own my own brand.

He listened to me patiently, and then he said that he enjoyed hearing a man talk the way I did, but that I might as well come out with the truth, because the case was going to be pretty black against me. If I would tell the whole story to him, with as much color as possible, he would write it up in such a way that every big newspaper East and West would copy, and in a week, the famous reporters would be flooding into town for the trial, and I would be a national figure. Otherwise, I was apt to hang and nobody in the world know the difference!

I asked him what made the case so black against me. He tapped out the points on the palm of his hand. I had ridden into Cat Hill to have a gunfight, hadn't I? After getting there, I had deliberately waited for my man. When he came, I had gone straight to him. Furthermore, there was an eyewitness that I had shot down Josh Acker before he was ready with his gun!

That was the case against me!

Well, my brain began to spin, when I heard the story put like this. And then I remembered the horrible face of Reginald Channing Carter, like the face of a ghoul. All the chain of testimony against me would be worthless—if his single link of it could be broken! But that talented liar would love nothing so much as the witness stand. No cross-examining lawyer would ever be able to break down the smooth and telling flow of his words. I could see him rising to every occasion like a prophet of destruction.

Yes, R. Channing Carter would hang me as high as a kite!

I said briefly to the representative of the *Evening Bugle* that I had nothing to say—but a great deal to think about by myself. He got up slowly.

"You wanta talk to the boys from the big papers in the big towns, is that it?" he said. "I wanta warn you, Grey, that public opinion right here in this here town is what's going to hang you or set you free!"

I saw what he meant and lost my temper, and told him to go to the devil.

So he went, slowly, looking back at me over his shoulder.

Later in the morning, Bobbie Meade came in to see me, and she had her father with her, a big fellow, with a splendid pair of shoulders, and as straight a pair of blue eyes as ever looked at trouble without a wink. He shook hands with me through the bars. He said that his girl had told him about me and he believed that I had shot in self-defense.

But there was a lot of bad talk around the town, he said. Did I have a good lawyer? Did I have any funds to pay him after I got him?

Well, when I listened to the talk of that big-hearted man, I felt a lot better and more secure. Before, it had seemed that the men of Cat Hill were all a lot of coyotes. Now I felt that I could trust public opinion like a Dutch uncle.

Bobbie hardly said a word, but she stood by with a sympathetic smile, looking from her father to me, and back again. I told Mr. Meade what she had done, and I told it straight from the shoulder. There was no use exaggerating because nothing could have been finer than what she had actually done.

Meade said, as I finished, "It's an old story. Bobbie is always tearing to the storm centers. She loves trouble like an old fire horse."

They went away, and left me thanking God for such people on the face of this miserable earth.

Then I started in waiting for the arrival of word from the Porsons.

But no word came!

All morning, all afternoon, no word came. Then I figured that they were busy with a lawyer, and not coming to me until they had arranged things for me.

But, in the evening, in came a note for me. I tore it open, and read what was inside once, and twice, and then again.

The note went like this:

DEAR NELS: Let us know when we can do anything for you. I would like to ride in to see you, but the people in Cat Hill are pretty excited, and it wouldn't be safe for me to show my face in the streets of the town.

However, we're thinking about you all the time. If we can do anything to help, say the word.

It was too bad that you decided to take a crack at Josh Acker.

So long,
DAN PORSON.

I read it four times, five times. The last line was what choked me: "It was too bad that you decided to take a crack at Josh Acker!"

14

A SMART SHYSTER

As I thought the thing over, I remembered that I had heard many times in the past that rich men will take a fellow up and use him, and then drop him flat! I don't know why that should be so, except that the rich are used to being served by every one, and they pay 'em off at the end of the month and forget about 'em. Here was a case in point. They couldn't very well pay me off. So I was to go my own way, even if it took me to the gallows!

I remembered again that scene at the table at the ranch, when Dan Porson had picked me out to ride with him.

And then I remembered the last line in his letter—he was sorry that I had decided to take a crack at Josh Acker!

Well, for a time the people in that part of the range would have hard feelings against the Porsons. But after a while, the past is forgotten, particularly when the owner of that past has a big ranch and employs a lot of men. What man could refuse the friendship of the Porsons, and what girl would be silly enough to turn a cold shoulder on young Dan, with all his wealth before him?

I tried to persuade myself that it was chiefly the fault of old Porson, and not of his son; but the thought wouldn't stay in my mind. As far back as I could remember, I had always been the fellow to get the bad luck; now I was simply getting more of it.

Perhaps it was as well to be headed for the hangman's rope, now, before I had a chance to accumulate a whole pocketful of disappointments.

But something inside me—heart, or soul, or whatever you want to call it—was growing harder and colder, and harder and colder, every moment. I could feel a smile pulling at the corners of my mouth, and there was nothing pleasant about that smile, no humor that any one else would have appreciated.

That evening, I had something else to cheer me up. The Negro who worked in the jail brought me the evening paper.

"That *Bugle* man, he don't like you, boss," he said.

I took the paper and spread it out. The headline that ran across the top of the page was:

NELSON GREY REFUSES TO ANSWER ALL QUESTIONS

And the article under it ran like this:

Nelson Grey, confessed slayer of young Joshua Acker, was interviewed by a representative of this newspaper in his cell, today, and refused to answer any questions. Sitting with his eyes fixed on the floor, and his face set in sullen lines of defiance, he merely sneered at the reporter, and snarled a few brief and ugly words; he would not talk for publication. With calloused indifference, he shrugged his shoulders when the name of his unfortunate victim was mentioned, and merely hinted that no matter what happened, he would get off scot-free.

There was more to the same effect. A lot more, and in conclusion that hound of an editor said that the confidence of young Grey that he would escape from paying any penalty for his crime was probably based upon the report that the rich Porsons, and their money, would be lined up in his defense. But, said the editor, perhaps the time had come when wealthy men and their tools, their hired men, no longer could commit murder with impunity. An outraged citizenry would rise up en masse and see that justice was done!

You can imagine that that made a fine start for my evening.

Later on, there was a great yowling and shouting in the street, and the Negro came to give me some more information. He said that Reginald Channing Carter was getting to be a great man in Cat Hill, and that he had been making a lot of speeches against me, calling on the men of the town to take matters into their own hands, before the rich got in their licks on my behalf.

And now the men were making a parade, and they were going up and down the streets of the town carrying signs that said, "Justice Before Capital," and "Money Cannot Buy Murder," and things like that.

This disturbance went on for some time.

I lay down on my cot after supper and turned over on my side and went to sleep with the racket still going on. I made up my mind that it was only a question of time before I was killed. And in that case, the lynchers might as well break into the jail and take me out and hang me to the next tree—better that than to wait week after week with the honor always before me, around the corner.

That was my frame of mind when I went to sleep, and when I wakened the next morning, I found out from George, the Negro, all about the latest happenings, and how public temper was getting hotter and hotter against me.

I finished breakfast, and I was allowed to shave, and after that I had a visitor. It was a tall fellow with a dish-shaped face, and a wide, thin mouth, and no upper lip at all to speak of. He stood with his hat on the back of his head and his thumbs in his vest pockets and looked down his nose at me.

"Well, kid, you're in the soup, eh?" he said.

I stared at him, made a cigarette, lighted it, and snapped the match through the bars of the cell onto the floor of the aisle at his feet.

The jailer, a big fellow called Jenkins, was standing by, and from under his battered forehead, his expressionless eyes watched the pair of us.

"Run along, brother," said the stranger to the jailer. "This kid is talking to his lawyer, now, and he has a right to talk without a witness."

The jailer shrugged his shoulders and strolled away, jangling his bunch of keys, and whistling.

"You're hard-boiled, are you?" said the stranger to me. "But I tell you what, brother, in this part of the world the hardest-boiled eggs are the soonest cracked!"

"Who are you, and what do you want?" I asked.

He pushed his hat still farther to the back of his head.

"I'm the counsel for the defense," he said.

"Whose defense?" I asked.

"Yours."

"You're no counsel of mine," I said.

"Oh, I'm just that," he told me.

"Who asked you to be?" I demanded.

"I'm retained by the Porsons," he said.

I got hot in a moment, and disgusted, too. The Porsons were standing behind me to the extent of hiring this cheap skate of a lawyer on a case that would need real talent or none at all. That was their way of washing their hands of the job. They could swear, now, that they had done their best for me, and had hired a lawyer, and all.

And then I thought of this smart shyster standing up in front of a jury and attempting to get a man free!

However, it's only a fool who throws away every chance as soon as it comes to hand. A straw may make the difference between keeping your head above water and drowning. So I asked him:

"Well, what's the lookout for me, what's your name?"

"My name's Sidney Jones," he answered. "And don't be flip when you're talking to your own lawyer."

"You're no lawyer of my choosing," I said. "But if I can't get a horse, I'll have to let a mule carry me. And there you are!"

He jerked his hat forward on his head until there was a deep shadow over his eyes, and his look was pretty ugly, as he said:

"I can see that we're not going to get very far, but I've got to do my duty, even if you're insisting on being a fool!"

I let that go, and merely threw in: "What's your plan of campaign?"

"A confession," he answered.

"A confession of what?" I asked.

"That you killed Josh Acker."

"Everybody knows I killed him. Everybody with half a brain knows that he fired two shots before I nailed him."

"Bah!" said the lawyer. "There's an eyewitness that you killed him before he could draw his gun."

"That witness is a liar," said I. "That long-drawn-out patent-medicine dealer—"

Sidney Jones broke in: "Nobody's a liar, in this town, that's willing to witness against you. What the town thinks is what hangs you, and the town thinks that you're guilty."

"But," I began, "Porson was asked into town, and—"

"Aw, shut up," said Sidney Jones, the lawyer. "Are you going to argue with me, kid, or are you going to listen to sense?"

"Go on," I said.

"You're guilty because the town wants you to be guilty. I don't give a damn whether you're guilty or not. My job is to keep you from being hanged. The only way that I can do that is to make a bargain with the prosecuting attorney. The way things are fixed now, it may be hard to make a bargain. I don't know. But I could feel him out. If you make a confession, maybe he will recommend you to the mercy of the court—youth, first offense, and maybe some liquor under the belt then—"

"I didn't have a single drink on board," I said.

He stuck out his arm and shook a forefinger at me.

"You had on board exactly what I say you had on board," he said. "And if I work the job to suit myself, with a little money put exactly in the right spot, maybe I can get you off with a twelve- or fourteen-year sentence."

"A what?" I shouted.

"Keep hold of your voice," he said.

"You talking about twelve or fourteen years in prison?" I asked.

"It sounds a lot, because you're just a youngster, and time goes slow to kids. Good behavior would cut that down a lot. Maybe you'd be out in nine or ten years. Just long enough to season you and take out some of the green that you're so full of. The point is, the confession. You willing to make it?"

I glared at him.

"Will I make that confession under oath?" I asked.

"Yes, of course."

"Then," said I, "I'll tell the truth and the whole truth, and nothing but the truth, and you and all the smart lawyers in the world can go to—"

"Easy, easy!" he said.

"You can do one thing that'll be worth your weight in gold to me," I told him. "Go and tell the Porsons that they're a lot of cheap crooks, and that they dragged me into this mess and then threw in a five-cent lawyer to get me out. Go tell them that, and if I ever see your ugly mug again, I'll take a poke at it through the bars!"

15

MEADE'S OFFER

It was a lot of consolation to me, talking like that to a crook of a lawyer. He pulled his hat to one side, put his hands in his trouser pockets, and told me gently, and softly, and fluidly what he thought of me. I'd heard mule skinners turn loose with their best line of lingo on a fool of a near leader, that didn't know its job, but I never heard any language that was up to the sweet flow from the tongue of Sidney Jones.

When he had eased himself a good deal, he turned on his heel, and told me over his shoulder that I'd hang higher than the sky, and that he hoped he'd be there to see me trying to walk on the air. Then he was gone.

I sat there grinding my teeth, and every time I thought of the Porsons, I cursed.

I was beginning to have another idea, however, a little later, and to decide that perhaps I had thrown away the only possible life saver before jumping into the black water, when in came Mr. Meade.

The jailer was with him, too, but he kept back a little distance, and I just heard him say:

"You keep an arm's length from the bars, Mr. Meade. That's all that I got to ask from you."

Then he backed up, and Robert Meade stood there in front of

me with a smile that did not look quite genuine. He asked me how I was. I said that I felt the way a man in jail usually feels before he's hung.

"I've heard that you've refused the help of one lawyer. Will you refuse the help of another?" he asked.

"I threw out a cheap shyster called Sidney Jones," I answered. "That's all. He wanted me to sign a confession."

He blinked, but he went on: "Suppose that that's the only way to keep you from the rope?"

"Then I'll hang," I answered. "I'd rather hang and be done with it than lie myself into prison."

"You insist that you didn't do this thing?" he asked me.

"I killed Acker," I said. "I killed him after he'd fired twice at me. There's where one of his bullets shaved away some hair."

"I can't notice any difference in the place you point to," said Meade crisply.

"All right," I said. "I'm telling the truth. That's all. There must be twenty people who heard Acker cursing me, before he started shooting. Does that sound as though I took him by surprise?"

Meade shrugged his shoulders again.

"Everybody's testimony has been taken the testimony of everybody who was at the dance. There's not a word in your favor—except from my daughter. And she saw nothing that will help you. It's only her thinking about you that's favorable, and thinking doesn't keep a man from a death sentence."

I nodded.

"The point is," said he, "that we must do what we can to save you from the rope. You see, we have to arrange it in the most diplomatic way."

"I see," said I, beginning to turn sour.

"I don't blame you for not placing confidence in Sidney Jones, but I know the finest lawyer in Denver, and I'm going to get him down here to defend you," went on Meade.

I blinked at that. The finest lawyer in Denver would cost a mint of money, if he were brought clear down here, away from all his other practice. I shrugged my shoulders, and I was about to speak when he went on:

"But the first thing we must do is to be frank with one another—perfectly frank."

"That's what I want to be," I said.

"Are you going to insist that young Acker fired at you first, and missed you—not once, but twice—at that distance, and Acker a fine shot?"

I saw what was in his mind, and it put my teeth on edge.

I explained, controlling myself: "When he threw his gun on me, I jumped and stumbled; his first bullet missed me as I was jumping, and his second went by me as I dropped to the floor. That's the only reason that he missed. I nailed him while I was on one knee. He thought it was his first bullet that had knocked me down."

Those broad, capable shoulders jerked up and fell again slowly.

"You think I'm lying, don't you?" I snapped.

"I want to do what I can for you," he said, "but I think that we ought to speak with perfect frankness to one another. After all, there is an eyewitness who saw you shoot first   "

"That lying hound of a Carter?" I cried.

He looked steadily at me.

Then I said, for I was in torment to think that such a fine man should really think me a murderer: "You've thought from the first that I was a guilty crook; it's your daughter who got you to come down here!"

He nodded. "I don't know that you're guilty, young man, but I don't deny that Roberta got me to come here. She's an excitable person, and I dare say you were able to see, long ago, that she'd made you into a hero. Now, my lad, I want to make a hard and fast bargain with you."

My anger was coming higher and higher, and a sort of despair, along with it. "Well, what is the bargain?" I asked.

"Whether you really took advantage of Josh Acker or not," he said, "what matters to me is that Bobbie's interested. I'm going to do my best—I've promised her that I would do my best—to get you free. And I'll live up to my promise. It won't be easy. Because I'm afraid that there may not be time to fight the matter through a long legal process. The man Carter, whom you call a bare-faced liar, is working up a powerful sentiment against you. But I might see if the sheriff would consider transferring you to—"

He paused. I immediately filled in the pause.

"Before the mob breaks in the doors of the jail and takes me out and hangs me to a tree?"

"Yes, exactly that," he said. "I'm glad to see that you can look facts in the face. Now, then, I want you to look some more facts in the face, if you will."

"Go on," I said.

He remained perfectly calm. There was nothing aggressive or insolent about him, but I could see that it was frightfully distasteful to him to be in that jail, and talking to me. I knew, then and there, that he believed in the testimony of Carter that devil of a lying Carter.

"My bargain is this," he said. "I support you in every way I can to combat public opinion, because I have some influence in this—directly and particularly through having some control of the newspaper. In addition, I bring down the lawyer I spoke of from Denver. You understand? I'll be glad to do these things, and I'll hope from the first that you'll be freed from the charge or else given a very light sentence. If you *are* freed from the charge, then I want to ask a promise from you—to fill your part of the bargain."

"What's my part?" I asked.

Strangely enough, a lightning flash of intuition told me what he was going to say, but the foreknowledge made the actual hearing of the words all the harder.

"Bobbie's in a romantic mood," he went on. "You've struck her imagination. She's looking on you as the persecuted hero. I suppose that you can guess all of those things, because in my experience, a man generally knows what impression he's made on women—young women, particularly. Now, then, the moment you are free, I want your word of honor, which I will trust, that you will step out of this part of the country and never come into it again until you have my permission, and that you'll make no endeavor to get in touch with Bobbie."

It was, somehow, what I expected— not that my forethought had been as exact as that, or as bald, but that I had had the vague premonition. And a sort of agony came up into my throat and choked me, and stung my eyes.

"Mr. Meade," I said, "I suppose you're being as generous as possible. I'm thanking you for that. You're a fine man or you couldn't be Bobbie's father. But I want to tell you that I'd rather sign a promise to go to hell than to agree to what you want from me. I'm innocent, and if—"

Now comes the shameful part, and what's hard to write down. For when I thought of my innocence and the prejudice that was working against me to cut my throat, my eyes filled up, and the infernal tears started trickling right down my cheeks, where those cool eyes of Robert Meade could plainly see them!

The shame tortured me. It made me outrageous.

I jumped closer to the bars of the cell, and I called out to him: "I'll see you damned first. Go tell Bobbie that she saved me from hanging once, and that if I keep my life, I'm going to come to her, if it has to be on my hands and knees, and tell her that the rest of the world is a dead leaf to me, and she's the only thing between heaven and hell that matters to me!"

Well, as I poured out this silly, stilted, melodramatic speech, I saw through the dimness of the tears an expression of incredulity and disgust on his face.

I did not blame him for that expression. I despised myself. I knew that if he were in my boots, he would play the part of a man, no matter what happened.

I turned on my heel and groaned. If I had not groaned, I would have sobbed, I think. That's a moment that fills me with ice, even to remember.

Then I heard a cold, steady voice saying behind me: "I'll come back when you're more master of yourself!"

I heard his step start away, and the hysteria mastered me still more, so that I cried out: "I never want to see you again, you cold-blooded sharper!"

There was a pause in his departing step. Then it went on again, and he said never a word more to me.

When I was sure that he was gone, I dropped on my knees and grabbed my face in my hands and wondered how such a hysterical, unmanly, nervous, ridiculous fool as I could walk the face of the globe and call himself a human being.

I've been through many bad times, and moments of danger, and all that, but the moment that I least want to recall is that interview with Robert Meade, in the jail at Cat Hill.

16

THE RISING STORM

After that interview with Meade, I think I preferred dying to living; certainly I never wanted another man to see my shameful face!

And that day went along, and when George brought me lunch, his eyes were on the floor, and he would not lift them to look at me, which I was glad of. He knew—everybody in the world knew—that I had broken down. I told myself that I was no good at all, I never would be any good again. I had taken water. I would run, after that, from a Chinaman!

That cold poison was seeping into me and distilling and redistilling in my brain. And always my mind turned back toward the Porsons, and I would remember that on account of them I had come to this day, which I hoped would be the last in my life.

There were no more visitors. Not a soul. No word from the Porson or the Meade family. Only one man came, stood silently for a moment, and turned away with a shake of the head. That was the sheriff.

I bowed my head, after he went. He was the right sort of a man, the stuff that heroes are made of, and when he found me not worthy of a single word of greeting, it meant that I was lost in the outermost darkness.

With my supper, George brought me a copy of the evening paper. Again he said nothing to me. I looked at his face, and the black of the skin was dusted over with gray. He was afraid, but afraid of just what?

I opened the *Bugle* at once and found a strange display on the front page.

At the very top it carried lines in small print, which said:

The advertisement below we do not pretend to understand. It was handed in by an unknown party or parties, together with a sufficient sum to give us a profit in printing it.

And below that, in great capitals, was printed the following weird statement or appeal:

MEN OF CAT HILL. AT TEN O'CLOCK TO-NIGHT, WHEN THE BELL STRIKES.

IN THE MAIN STREET, OR IN THE PLAZA,

EVERY MAN WHO CALLS HIMSELF A MAN, BE THERE.

COME AS THOUGH PREPARED TO DEFEND YOUR HOMES AND YOUR HONOR.

THE FAIR FAME OF CAT HILL HAS BEEN DARKENED.

JUSTICE MUST BE DONE.

IN THE NAME OF JUSTICE, YOU ARE CALLED UPON, MEN OF CAT HILL.

WILL YOU BE FAILING WHEN THE HOUR STRIKES?

AT TEN O'CLOCK, BE THERE!

Well, when I had finished reading that, I understood why George was frightened. It was enough to scare every soul in the jail, every man who was hired by the law, because it said, as clear as daylight, that at ten o'clock there would be a mass meeting in the plaza, and from that point the mob would roll on toward the jail to break it open and to take out that miserable sinner, Nelson Grey. Who would then and there receive "justice" from the hands of the men of the town. And the "fair fame" of Cat Hill would be redeemed and washed clean in my blood!

That was all as clear as could be, and my heart dropped into my boots.

Somehow, there was nothing that I feared about death so

much as the means by which I was to come to it. The masked faces, the brutal voices, the commands that would be shouted they seemed to me worse than the prospect of the harsh rope that would bite into my throat and the force that would wrench me from the earth and leave me dangling in the air. How would I be able to meet that hour, I who had lost my name and place as a man that very day by shamefully disgracing myself right before Robert Meade?

I fell into a stupor. George would come, before long, to get my supper tray, and then I would ask him some questions about what the sheriff and his assistants were doing in preparation for the defense of the jail when the mob attacked it. But no matter what the sheriff did, I knew that I was lost. What officers of the law can induce themselves to open fire on otherwise reputable citizens who have come to take quick vengeance upon a murderer?

George came.

"Where's the sheriff?" I asked.

"He's gone away, Mr. Grey," said George, in a faltering voice, his eyes on the floor. "He was called away, sir, right after he came to see you. He had to ride out and try to catch that devil of a Don Pedro, that greaser that's been robbing and murdering on the Tracy Trail!"

And George went hurriedly away before I could get another word past my numb lips.

The stupor came over me again. I thought that it was only a moment that I sat here, brooding, when I heard a bell strike, and numbered off the beats—nine of them.

It was nine o'clock, and I had one hour of life left to me!

Now, suddenly, a new idea came home to me. No matter how much Josh Acker had been to blame, according to the old law of an eye for an eye and a tooth for a tooth, was it not right that I should die for killing him?

I looked at my watch. It was stopped at half past five. I set it again for nine ten. Fifty minutes, about, were before me. Perhaps a little longer if it took the crowd some time to get under way.

Then I began to hear the beating of hoofs that swept down the street toward the little plaza. Never a rider came from that direction, but all of them were pouring toward it. And I understood that, also.

A wind had risen, and it was beating the boughs of the big trees that stood beside the jail against its upper walls and roof. I thought it was another sound of the rising storm that seemed to come down the aisle, toward me, and then in the dimness of the lantern light that made everything unreal, I saw Bobbie Meade, gripping the bars of my cell.

"Nelson Grey!" she called out in excitement.

I started up and strode to the bars. Our faces were only inches apart, and I saw that her face was white, and her eyes wonderfully large, so that I could hardly recognize her.

"Do you know what they've planned?" she asked.

I nodded my head.

"The cowardly scoundrels!" she breathed. "I'm going to try to speak to that masked mob of brutes in the plaza. I don't know—I might be able to stop them. If I can't, it's good-by, Nels!"

I stood against the bars, my face as cold as the iron. And I heard her saying:

"I've seen brave men before, but I've never known anything as brave as you are. I think I'd die if that would help you. I know that you're as steady as iron. I can see that you're not afraid. And I've only one hope—that God won't let such a man as you be murdered!"

I felt the grip of her hands on mine, and then she was gone, and I stood there blankly, looking into nothingness.

What a man that father of hers was!

He could have blasted me in her eyes forever, turned me into a figure of brittle straw, struck me out of existence, as far as Bobbie was concerned, by merely mentioning how the tears had poured down my face, and how I had grown hysterical, that day. But I could see that he had spared me. And he had even allowed her to come into Cat Hill and do her best to stop the rush of the crowd. No doubt he was waiting for her outside the jail at this moment. No doubt that he would also do his best to use his authority and check the rising.

Well, that was generosity on a scale that staggered me, and was almost too large for my mind to conceive!

So she had gone away, not realizing that as I stood there against the bars of the cell, I was in such a cold funk that if I had tried to speak, I could only have mumbled. She would hear of my death, after this, and if only I could manage to bear myself like a man, at that time, then she would remember me as a hero!

What false nonsense! And yet it gave a thrill to me, and made me lift my head. It gave me a last purpose in life.

I was still standing there, while ideas rushed through my mind like water through a mill race. And then, as though right over my head, I heard the terribly steady and regular beating of a bell. It seemed to me that it must be in the jail. Only gradually could I realize that it came from well outside the building.

One by one I counted the beats, like the last breaths of life in my body—ten heavy strokes, and at the end, like the wide-swinging roar of an echo washing back from hills, I heard a sound of voices. Unlike echoes, they did not fade, but grew and grew, as when the wind ceases, and lets the sound of a great river come ominously in upon the mind.

That was the crowd.

I did a very foolish thing, then, and a thing that I have never been able to understand, it was so puerile, so vain, so ridiculous—I stood back from the bars and shrugged my shoulders to get my coat straight, and dusted off my trousers, and then straightened the bandana at my throat. I picked up the sombrero which had lain unregarded in a corner of the cell.

Then I tried my voice, and made it reasonably clear and loud, as I said: "Well, boys, here I am!"

You see, I was rehearsing, instinctively, for the moment that was to come, and I saw that the only possible way for me would be to assume a cheerful air, and so try to carry it through to the end!

Would I turn brittle when I saw the rope? Would I dissolve like sand before water when the crisis came?

God alone could tell that!

I made a prayer, then, not for the salvation of my worthless soul, not for mercy in the hereafter, but a prayer that He would send me strength enough to let me die well before the eyes of men!

Oh, I'm enough ashamed when I remember that frightful day, but there is a curious, bitter pleasure in writing down the facts. They are enough to take away a man's most secret vanity for as long as he lives!

I tried my voice again, saying, quite loudly: "Well, here I am!"

This time another voice answered me: "I know where you are. Speak soft, partner! Speak soft, old boy!"

And there was Lanky, crouching at the door of my cell!

17

ANOTHER TALE

Instantly, everything in me changed. I had been ready to pray for nothing but a chance to die well before other men—men whom I hated and despised—but when I saw that lanky form, those wide, capable shoulders, when I glimpsed that ugly, long, crooked face, I forgot all the thoughts of despair instantly, and hope rushed in a burning flood through me. I wanted to yell and dance. I wanted to scream with joy. There was such a happiness in ten seconds of mere hope that it was worth a lifetime of facts.

But I neither yelled nor danced, for as I saw the fingers of that strange fellow working at the lock, my next emotion was a tremendous flood of wonder.

It would be the second time that he had saved me.

Back there in the anteroom, there was no doubt that Tom Acker would have made a shambles in which both Dan Porson and I would fall. Lanky had prevented that, coming mysteriously in darkness that was, no doubt, of his own making.

Now he was laboring to save me again. Why?

I was nothing to him. I had shown him a few courtesies at the ranch, but so had all the other punchers—we were so glad to sit around and listen to his yarns. Well, no matter what the reason, here he was, though he must have known perfectly well that if I were caught with a man trying to get me free, the second fellow would be in most prodigious danger of dying with me at the hands of the crowd.

Awe overcame me. I went to the bars and said:

"Lanky, old man, what brought you in here?"

He was crouching with his eyes blinked shut, and his head turned so that the ear was close to the lock, and his fingers were probing at the inside of the lock with a tool so small that I could not make it out, only the twistings, some times rapid and sometimes slow, of the long, bony hand.

And yet even at that moment speaking in pauses, and in a whisper he could not resist telling a yarn!

"Why, it's like this, Nelly," he murmured. "It's like a time when I was down in Yucatan, and I was riding 'longside of a gent that was going to look over the land down there where the slaves work at the tobacco. They rake 'em in there to the Valle Nacional, and a man, a good strong man, will last a year, maybe, but mostly they die quicker. Between six and seven months is enough for most of 'em. Contract labor, it's called, but slavery is the right name. That gent I was with, he was thinking of spending some money and buying land in the Valle Nacional, so we had a right good time of it, and we lived on the fat and drank of the best, I can tell you!

"We seen a good many sights, when we were down there. We seen the slaves dropping in the field. We heard 'em moaning and howling in the dens where they were penned up at night. Yaquis, a lot of 'em. The Yaquis are iron, and they last longer. But the queerest thing was a gent that we passed sitting by the road, one day. He'd been turned loose to die. They used to do that a good deal. When one of the workers got too skinny and poor and down, so's he couldn't work and wasn't even worth the handful of food that they doled out every day sometimes they'd turn the poor beggar loose, and let him die struggling toward liberty. And here was one of 'em sitting by the road, and laughing to himself. He wasn't no man, Nelly. He was just a bundle of bones. You could see the skull through his face. Right through!"

He paused, here. I found myself listening to this strange and horrible story with a fascination with half my mind, and with the other half, I was listening far more intently to that sound of the mob like a rising storm at sea—for now the sound was growing louder in volume, and pouring nearer. It was coming like a great head of water when a dam is burst.

After an instant of silent working at the lock, I heard Lanky continue, in the same muffled, interested voice, as though *he* had not heard the approach of the sound that meant death for us both: "Well, we stopped, and I said to that gent, I said: 'What's the great joke, brother?'

"And he says back to me, he says: 'Well, señor, I sit here and laugh, because of a very funny thing.'

"'What's the funny thing?' says I.

"'I'm the funny thing,' says he. 'Here I float like a chip on the vast wave of life, señor, and think how I was a strong man, free and happy and safe, a year ago, with land of my own, and a wife, until I heard that my brother, who had disappeared, had come to this valley of death. And then I shook myself, and felt all my muscles at once, and said to myself that I was so strong that I could come here to find him, and take him away to safety once more! And so I came down here, and as soon as I put my nose into the valley, they caught me, and made me labor in the field. Every day for a month, they gave me a beating. That made me much less strong. And every day for a year, I have been wondering a little that I should have been such a fool. Do you see? I had seen the shark eat one man, but I did not think that the shark could eat two. But it could. And now it is digesting the last of me. That is why I laugh, señor. And in all of this time, I never have seen my brother. No doubt he is dead, and is also laughing, in hell!'

"That's the story that the Mex told me, sitting there by the road in the Valle Nacional, waiting for death, too weak to get up on his hind legs and walk one step to meet it!"

No doubt Lanky would have talked on in the same way, but now the roar of the crowd reached the jail, and broke around it, and I felt a sense of physical shock, as though an electric bath were pouring about me.

"Lanky! Lanky!" I cried.

He did not raise his head, but merely muttered: "Well, brother?"

"It's too late to help me, Lanky," I said. "And if they catch you here, they'll murder you along with me. There's the devil in them. Listen to it howl!"

And there *was* a devil in the throat of every man that swept up to the jail, a ravening, hungry devil that was demanding food.

"I tell you what, Nelly," said Lanky, "that reminds me of a yarn of a gent that was going to make a choice between mince pie and pumpkin pie, and when he seen the two pies before him, he says to himself, the mince pie is good, but the pumpkin pie might be better than the one that Aunt Maggie used to make in the old days, and I dunno whether I oughta try—"

Suddenly there was a decisive clicking sound, and the door

yawned open before me. I fairly fell forward into the aisle of the jail.

A gun butt was thrust into my hand. It was a big Colt which was still warm with the warmth of the body of Lanky.

"Now, Nelly — we prance along!" he said.

We ran down the aisle of the jail, and as we ran, we saw other prisoners standing at the bars of their cells, and when they saw us running, they raised a shout and a howl that matched the yell of the crowd outside.

We passed the front door, still running, and heard a stentorian voice that thundered: "George! George! You lazy, worthless hound, open up this here door, or we'll wring your neck for you!"

Like the dying man in the Valle Nacional that Lanky had been speaking about, I felt laughter in me. For certainly George must be away from the jail long before this. He would not have stayed to hear the music begin. No, not if the gray dust of fear that I had seen on his face meant anything.

The jail was being protected against the entrance of the crowd by no more than the strength of its locks. I gave up a prayer of gratitude to the firm that had made them of such good steel.

Then a thundering of heavy blows began against that front door. I looked back, as we turned down an empty corridor, and I saw the strong door shaking and sagging under the immense pressure of the blows it was receiving.

There was wonder in me. Lanky seemed to be running with a definite goal and purpose in his mind, but I could not imagine what it was. For the noise of the savages surrounded the entire jail. They had not come to the front door, only, but they had spilled all around it, and as the hammering continued at the front of the building, in the same way I heard it commence now in the rear.

Everywhere the sea of threatening sound surrounded us.

We came to a door. Lanky laid hand on it and jerked it open. He caught me by the shoulder and fairly flung me up the stairs inside the door, and then paused behind me, and I heard the sound of the bolt being shot home again.

At the same time, as I staggered to the top of the stairs, I put my head with a bang against a rafter.

Lanky was instantly beside me, and the ray from a dark lantern slashed here and there in sword strokes through the dark, revealing the limits of a long, narrow attic, in which the rafters went this way and that in a crazy pattern.

Lanky, stooping over low, ran forward and showed me the way, and as he moved, I heard a great, explosive crash that shook the whole building.

The front door of the jail had gone down, and now the ocean of noisy fury was roaring and thundering inside the walls of the place.

We came to a place where Lanky paused, and pointed to an open trapdoor in the ceiling of the attic.

"There's where I come to leave my calling card on you, Nelly," he said. "You think that you can jump that high?"

I tried, and failed, falling inches short of the mark.

"Let me go first," said Lanky, and instantly, with a tiger's bound, he was up to it, and had drawn himself through the gap.

I saw his monstrous bony hands thrusting down into the dimness above me.

"Jump!" he commanded.

I jumped. My wrists were caught in two vises. I was snatched upward, and hauled onto the top of the roof. Then Lanky lowered the trap behind me.

I felt that we were hardly better off than when we were in the jail, but nevertheless, there was the wild wind of the night beating in my face, and the electric hope of freedom was building inside me until I began to feel the strength of a giant.

Yet beneath us, half buried in the darkness, I heard, and I saw, the dim stirrings of a human sea.

18

TREE RIDING

Besides the feeling of the free wind against my face, there was the vast difference of having a gun in my hand and of having big Lanky beside me. I shall never forget his calm, swift movements. He was at home in the dark of the night and the wind as any hunting cat.

We went rapidly forward, walking—not crawling—on all fours. I followed as well as I could until I came to a place where the great branches of two trees, two lords of a forest that had otherwise been cut down around the town, thrashed against the roof of the jail, tossing their shadowy heights wildly up into the air, rebounding, and lunging again toward us.

"That's the only bridge that we've got to safety," Lanky said in a whisper. "That's the way that I came to call on you, partner, and that's the way that we've got to go back again."

Imagine trying to hurl yourself onto the back of a horse at full gallop—in the dark of the night! Even that would be comparatively secure, I thought, compared with catching one of those whipping, weaving, lurching branches, fumbling through the foliage to get to the timber of the branch, and then being snatched wildly away with the recoil of the bough.

Lanky, beside me, was saying at my ear: "They'll be up here on the roof, in a coupla jiffies. Watch me, kid. It ain't so hard to ride a tree, if you can ride a bronco."

A wild howl of rage came upward from the jail. It seemed to me that I could feel the vibrations of passion through the roof. It seemed as though this were the force that suddenly thrust big Lanky upward from his crouching position.

The dark shadowy form of the nearest bough flung toward him. He bounded upward and forward, sank into the leaves, and was then swept away.

Well, he had done everything that one man can do to save another. He had taken for me everything except the final leap to safety, and that I would have to take for myself.

Besides, to spur me on, I had the pretty safe deduction that that general outcry from the jail signaled that the crowd had found my cell with the door of it open! That meant that they would presently spread out in search in all directions, for at their present temper they would not give up the hunt very readily!

But when the great bough swayed back toward me, shuddering under the blow of the wind, I merely stretched out my arms toward it like a dummy, and failed to take my chance.

Yet the news seemed to be spreading from the jail to the crowd on the ground. For now a howl went through them.

Again the branch swayed toward me; again I stood up, shuddering, and strove to spur myself to take the chance, and again the nearness of the fall stopped my breath and my heart at the wrong moment. I could not leap!

There was a nearer sound.

It was the slamming back of the trapdoor leading to the roof. In another instant, they would be leading me back to the cell from which Lanky had taken me. It was not courage that made me take the leap, at last. It was simply that I dare not have such a shame heaped upon my head. As the dark and irregular mass of the branch swung toward me, more slowly, this time, and with less promise of coming in right over the roof, I actually nerved myself to take two running steps forward. Then I leaped high, closed my eyes, and clutched widely, with arms and legs.

I got to the limb, well enough, for my embrace practically surrounded it, and in a moment I was swinging down along the length of the bough, wondering why I had hesitated so long to do such a simple thing.

In an upper fork of the tree, a dark protuberance, like that of a climbing mountain lion, was clinging.

"Lanky!" I gasped.

"All right, brother," said Lanky. "I was just waiting here to get my breath for a minute. Now we can go on down, I guess. The boys seem considerable stirred up, don't they?"

Down beneath me, I could see the sweeping of many forms back and forth, like the racing of waves in a cross current. And the yelling rose and rose in volume and in pitch.

"We might as well go down," said Lanky. "Follow me, partner!"

So he went ahead of me, always showing the way, to the last acting as guide.

He crawled rapidly down the tree, came to the lowest fork, and then slid down to the ground. I followed his example. When I reached the earth, which I did with a jolt and a jar, and in a sitting-down position, instantly a hand fell heavily on my shoulder.

"Who are you? Where'd *you* drop from?" demanded a loud voice.

Was I wrong? Or was it the voice of Tom Acker?

No, as I scrambled to my feet, I saw that it was a far larger man, and now he shifted his grip and locked an arm around my throat.

I never could tell what devil enabled a perfect stranger to recognize me in the dark of the night!

But there I was, in a strangle hold, and there was he, yelling at the top of his lungs:

"Hey, I've got him! I've got him!"

He was behind me, mind you, and I saw the dim gleam of his gun as he jerked it out—I saw the flash of it as the crook of his arm shut off my wind, and as I realized that I had come again to an impasse.

There was no Lanky before me. He had disappeared. No, there I saw him—or a tall shape like him, working back through the crowd toward me, but he would not come in time.

I stamped fiercely down and back, and by the grace of good luck, my heel crunched on the instep of my captor. He howled. His arm released my throat.

And as I darted forward, a gun exploded, though the bullet must have been fired in the air, for certainly no man would have been insane enough to fire a gun in the midst of such a jammed crowd as that!

"There he goes! Catch him!" screeched a dozen voices.

Hands tore at me. I dived under a mass of striding legs and came up in a tangle of struggling bodies. More hands reached for me, and caught me.

"There he goes!" I yelled.

"Where? Where?" said the men around me.

"That gent with the bare head!" I howled in answer.

Oh, what a little thing to turn a stampede!

A fresh impetus was given the crowd in a wrong direction and little by little I worked into a slack of the throng, and then to the outer edge of it, where I found a tall man leaning against a fence, and looking on with folded arms at the jamboree, and listening to the uproar as though it were all upon a stage, and done for his benefit.

"That was a good dodge, brother," said the voice of Lanky. "They'll remember you for that longer than they'll remember you for the way you busted out of the jail."

It was true. Of all the queer tales that ever developed out of the jail break at Cat Hill—and I've told how small a part I had in the whole affair, from beginning to end—there was nothing that was magnified so much as that. I'll have occasion to mention several instances of the wrong conceptions that people got of me, owing to that hurly-burly. They seemed to think that I had fought my way, single-handed, straight through a hundred men, all trying vainly to bring me down. And that was the reason that nearly every one believes, to this day, in spite of all that I've said, that I actually got out of the jail single-handed, without the help of a single man!

But to get back to that moment in the dark of the night, when the lounger by the fence hailed me, and turned out to be Lanky. I grabbed him by the arm and said:

"Now which way, Lanky?"

"Why, out to where I've got the horses," said Lanky. "It's about five miles out, and that's pretty far for me to walk, considering how dog-gone bad my feet are. We'll just borrow a coupla the best horses over there at the rack in front of the courthouse, and jog out to where I've left our pair."

"How'll we get to the rack in front of the courthouse without being seen?" I stammered.

"Nobody'll know us if we walk," said Lanky. "Whoever Nelly Gray is, he's a gent that's running and running fast to get away. He ain't anybody that's walking along with a friend."

And straightway he stepped out and walked with me right down the middle of the street.

There was a tremendous outcry and a firing of guns on the farther side of the courthouse, at about this moment; and the whole crowd began to stream toward that point of excitement.

Lanky walked up, and carefully looked over the horses. He seemed to be able to see in the night as well as in the dark.

"This one'll do, and this one," he said finally.

He pointed the way to one of the horses, and I took another. By the time I had mounted, he was already jogging down the street, and I hurried after.

19

UNDER THE STARS

When we got out of town, at a dogtrot, I was fairly foaming with questions that had to be asked. But Lanky simply galloped those questions down my throat, because he cut loose as fast as the ponies would drive, and he never let up for five blessed miles, until the mustangs were staggering, and winded, and stumbling as though they were ready to give up and come down with a crash.

He had been cutting right across open country, most of the time, not sticking to roads or trails more than two miles out of the five, and now he turned the horses down a dry-bottomed draw, with a growth of trees on either bank of it.

A hundred yards of this brought us to a shack that stood on one bank among the trees, and here Lanky dismounted, tied the reins to the horns of the saddles, and following his example blindly, I flogged my mustang and made it gallop off through the darkness.

No mustang is ever really lost. Before long that pair would fall into human hands and drift back to their masters.

Well, I hardly cared about small points like that. Whoever their masters were, they owed me something for having gone into Cat Hill, that night, to join a lynching party!

Now Lanky strode ahead of me, rapid and purposeful, to the door of the shack, which he kicked open.

As he went forward toward the shack, he had exclaimed to me, over his shoulder: "Stay back among the trees!" So I stepped into the deeper shadow and waited. I was prepared for almost anything but what followed.

Voices muttered inside the shack, and then out came two men, one of them obviously having the elongated outlines of Lanky. It was his voice that said:

"You hear me?"

"Yeah, why not?" said the other.

"What I said was true," said Lanky. "If they'd hanged up the kid, you'd 'a' paid for it, Acker!"

Was it the great Tom Acker, then?

Yes, it was Tom Acker, for I recognized his voice perfectly, as he said in answer:

"I'll tell you this, Lanky. You're a fool for turning me loose like this. Because one of these days, I'm going to get you, and get you bad!"

"Maybe you will," said Lanky. "But there you are. You're free."

"Except my hands," said Acker.

"You don't need your hands to walk until you get to help," said Lanky.

"Tell me one thing," said Acker. "How did the kid manage to bust out? Did you help him?"

"Why should I help him, and what's he to me?" asked Lanky with justifiable indifference.

"Oh, I just wondered," remarked Acker. "You got a queer habit of shoving your long nose into business where it don't belong, haven't you?" Then he added: "What do people say about the way I disappeared?"

"They don't say anything. They don't know. They wonder if you'll be on hand for the funeral—is all they wonder about you."

"I oughta stay away," said Tom Acker savagely. "He was never nothing but a trouble to me, the big half-wit. He never had no real sense. He was always mixed up in some fool play. Then he gets into a mess with that Porson kid. I didn't give a damn if Porson's bullet put him down and out, or not. But being the brother of Josh, I had to stand up for him, that was all. Otherwise, what would people have thought of me?"

That was a staggerer for me—that gunman, and thug, that man of many killings, who existed on the very outer fringes of the law—he was compelled to do great things for the sake of public opinion!

"I sure understand," said Lanky dryly. "Well, so long, Acker."

"How did the kid bust loose out of jail?" asked Acker.

"I dunno," said Lanky. "With his two hands and feet, I reckon. Maybe he didn't get clear away, either. I just heard the yelling and the news that was in the wind, was all I heard. He didn't step up and *tell* me that he'd got loose."

"I wouldn't 'a' thought that the brat had it in him," said Tom Acker. "I never forget the sick face of him, when I seen him there at the dance. I dunno how he ever dropped Josh, neither. Josh was no holy smoke with a gun, but he could shoot."

"So can the kid," said Lanky. "It ain't the boys that love a fight that make the best fighters, Tom. You hitch yourself to that idea, and you'll find that it works out right along. So long."

I saw Tom Acker fade out into the darkness. His voice came back:

"The next time is going to be a fair fight, and in any kind of a fair fight, I'm going to cut you in two with bullets, Lanky!"

"Any way of getting you is fair to me," said Lanky. "Why I don't cut your throat to-night, I dunno. But there's so few coyotes left that can give a gent a run, that I thought I'd leave you free again. When I want you, it won't be much trouble to catch you up and put you in a bag, ag'in!"

This taunt and I must say that it was a mean one drew a stream of curses from Tom Acker. Then I could hear him crashing away through the underbrush.

I can't say exactly how I felt about that man Lanky he seemed to always have a whole extra pack of cards up his sleeve.

While I was still wondering about the way he had cached Tom Acker away, out here, he went on to a shed behind the house, and introduced me to a couple of horses standing there.

"One hoss is mine, and one hoss belongs to Tom Acker," said Lanky. "You take my hoss, and I'll take Acker's, and away we go."

"Where do we go to?" I asked.

"Anywhere you say, brother. Some place far, I reckon?"

I was silent, considering. Of course, the range would soon be buzzing with parties sent out in pursuit of me.

"You name the things that you'd like to do or have?" said Lanky in query.

"I want that pinto gelding from the Porson place," I said. "And I want to tell the Porsons, the pair of 'em, in front of their men, what I think of 'em. After that, I've got to see Bobbie Meade."

"Bobbie Meade made a right good talk for you this evening, in the plaza," said Lanky judicially. "She and the old man, they both spoke up, but nobody's got as long a tongue as that gent Carter. That Reginald Channing Carter, he could talk down anybody. He reminds me of a gent that I knew in Missouri by the name of—"

I hastily dodged this story.

"Lanky," said I, "I've taken enough from you, and I'm not going to take any more. You keep your horse. If you ride Tom Acker's horse, you're a horse thief. You know that!"

"Well, brother," said he, "I'd almost as soon be a horse thief as ride any more, just now, on that bear horse of mine. There's parts of me and my brain that get plumb tired of him! Anyway, we'll ramble along over the trail and get to the Porson place. I reckon that you *do* wanta have a little chat with old man and young man Porson. We'll be there about sunup and breakfast time."

I tried to argue against his going with me. I said that I had some money coming to me from the Porsons, and that I'd walk to the ranch to get it. But finally Lanky shut me up, by saying:

"You come along with me, partner, because wherever you walk, for a few days, you're going to be drawing more of a crowd than you want to have. Me? Why, it's fun for me, and something to do."

At any rate, I saddled the "bear horse" of Lanky, and he saddled the beautiful gray of Tom Acker.

We rode out side by side under the stars, and I heard Lanky saying:

"Never sat on nothing better than this in all my born days, brother. He's all springs, and they're all set the right way. He don't step nowhere, except on cushions. How does the bear horse go under you, Nelly?"

I had climbed so far up in the world that I could feel the sting of that nickname again. But I could not afford to show bad temper to Lanky, after what he had done. I said:

"It's this way, Lanky—the bear horse, as you call it, is all made of springs, too, but they all work the wrong way. When he's walking in front, he's getting ready to gallop behind. He's got a wabble in his middle section that would make a man seasick, in a long ride. And he seems to want to sniff the ground all the time. I'll tell you what, Lanky, there's a strain of bloodhound in this mustang, and he wants to smell out the trail."

"That's what comes of a good education," said Lanky

mournfully. "All this time, I been casting around to try to find the right words to describe that broncho, but they never come to me, and here you hit the picture off the first time you put your hand to it. Yeah, education is a mighty powerful thing, I'd say."

I managed to laugh a little, at this, and I can tell you what, it seemed to me a year since I had laughed before—and that had been at Lanky, also, it seemed to me!

"Lanky," I said. "You mind telling me what it's all about?"

"What?" he said.

"All this mystery business," said I, "about you and Dan Porson, and why you oared in to save him, and how it was that you got all clawed up—by thorns and brambles and such. And what sort of a thorn tree was it, really, that clawed you—wasn't it a Mexican tree that grew knives? And why did you take the trouble and risk your neck to come into Cat Hill and save my bacon when it was already just about in the fire?"

"When I hear a lot of questions like that," said Lanky, "it gets me all confused. I got a single-track mind, brother. It ain't quick, and it runs slow and careful in one direction at a time. I dunno how it is, but that's the truth."

"Well, pick out any one of those questions, and tell me the answer," I pleaded with him, burning up with curiosity.

"Why, Nelly," said he, "that would be like the boy that stands in front of the mince pie and the pumpkin pie, that I started telling you about back there in the jail, and when—"

I made a last effort to nail him down to the point.

"Lanky," said I, "just tell me how you got into the dance hall, there, in the nick of time, and how you handled Tom Acker, will you?"

"There you go crowding me," said Lanky. "You oughta give an old hoss a lot of rope, Nelly. When you start crowding an old hoss, it gets all bothered in the mind, and don't know where to go. And that's the way that I feel. Now, where was it that you wanted me to start talking? And that reminds me of a time that I came to a crossroads and—"

"Oh, all right, Lanky," said I, throwing up my hands literally and figuratively. "You beat me. It's the last time that I'll ever try to pry an answer out of you."

"Speaking of prying," said Lanky easily, "there was a dentist once who was working away on a tooth of mine, and I says to him: 'What you prying at, brother? The roots of that tooth, or the jawbone?'

"And the dentist, he says to me: 'It's this way, partner—you're over thirty, ain't you?'

"'Yeah,' says I, 'I'm over thirty.'

"'You take a hoss over thirty,' says the dentist, 'and the teeth they're apt to grow into the jawbone, and if I took a good pull on this tooth of yours, I dunno but I would pry away half of your face.'

"'Well,' says I, 'I dunno but that would be a good idea, maybe. It ain't much of a face to look at, though there's a lot of it. But I'm used to it. Just you leave that tooth tied in the same old stall.'

"And there that tooth still is, son, and doing me good service ever since, like it was grateful, and recognized that I was a kind master. Only, I don't bite agin' no bones on that side of my face, and maybe that's why my face has growed kind of crooked, lately."

"Has it changed a lot—your face, Lanky, I mean?" I asked, chuckling.

"Why, Nelly, when I was young," said Lanky, "I was as fine-looking as any dummy that a tailor ever hung clothes on, but I got older, my face it sort of went out of fashion. Speaking of fashion, I can tell you a yarn about a girl that got a job slinging hash in Tucson, one time—"

He rambled on; I listened rather vaguely, with my face upturned, wondering if this were really I that was riding under the stars, or my disembodied soul, in a dream.

20

AT PORSON'S

We reached the Porson place at about the time we had expected to get there. To me, it was like going back into a dream and seeing a familiar face in an atmosphere of unreality; for everything, of course, was as usual, but I was not a part of it and I probably never *would* be a part of it.

When we came up, the fellows were busy, here and there, washing up for breakfast. We rounded the side of the house suddenly, and so we came on them before they had had any warning. Lefty was just pumping water into a graniteware basin, and yawning the sleep out of his eyes. Dan Porson leaned close to the kitchen door, his feet crossed, rolling his early morning smoke, because he was one of those hardy fellows who have to begin the day with a smoke. And his father was walking up and down with his hands clasped behind his back and his head bent in thought.

That was a very usual custom with him, and very often I had watched him going up and down and back and forth and felt that he was a real type of the fine old patriarch, the type of the men who had made the great West.

Well, my attitude toward him was a good deal changed now. It was true that he might be a maker of empire, but he was also a confounded old skinflint, and something worse. Yet I never felt

104

about him as I did toward Dan. No doubt it had been the Old Man who shrugged his shoulders at my bad plight in the town of Cat Hill and made light of it, but Dan should have broken through his father's ideas and sneers and really done something for me, anyway.

It was Dan who saw us first, and the cigarette makings fluttered down toward the ground from his hands. He gaped like a child at a nightmare. Then Lefty saw us, and let out a yowl. And last of all, Old Man Porson turned sharply around and scowled at us both.

It was pretty plain that he would have been more pleased if I had been hanged, than to see me on the loose, like this.

"Hello, boys!" Lanky sang out. "Look what I met up with, wandering along the road! There's two pieces of luck that I've had. I found that Tom Acker's hoss straying with a saddle and bridle on, dog-gone me, and the next thing I know, I come onto the kid, walking along with his hands in his pockets, and whistling a tune, like there wasn't no sheriff in the world!"

He laughed loudly, as he ended this speech.

The fellows came swarming in around me as I slipped out of the saddle, and they shook hands with me, and slapped me on the back, and wished me luck, and were mighty glad that I had managed to get out of the jail, after all. They wanted to know how it all happened that I had been turned loose.

I brushed their questions aside, and simply said that I had been lucky. Of course I couldn't talk, because every word that I said would make Lanky a criminal in working at a jail break.

Then Dan Porson came to life and pushed his way through the rest of the punchers. His face was a bright red. He held out his hand.

"I'm glad to see you, partner," he said.

I disregarded that hand. For, looking at Dan, and seeing the red in his face, I realized that he must have known he was playing the part of a low-down hound all the while.

I went by Dan and walked up to his father. He stood there and looked me up and down, as sour a picture as you could imagine, his hands still clasped in the small of his back, and his jaw sticking out, and the muscles working in and out at the base.

"Well?" he snapped.

"What's the matter, Mr. Porson?" I asked. "Aren't you glad to see me back?"

He blinked two or three times, as fast as a bird blinks at a light while it's sitting on a perch.

"Why, I'm glad enough to see you, boy, but you been and got yourself into a pile of trouble," he said.

"*I* didn't get myself into trouble," said I. "I was dragged into trouble by your son, over yonder. I rode into Cat Hill to stand by him; but when the pinch came, he cut and ran for it; and left me with the fighting to do."

"You up and murdered Josh Acker," he said.

"I've got a piece of hair gone, that a bullet from Acker's gun clipped away," said I. "And now I want to tell you why I've come back here. It's not to collect any gratitude from you."

"Ain't it?" said he, cocking his thin face a little to the side and looking at me with his bright, beady eyes.

"No," I said. "You owe me some back pay, and you've got a mustang here that I'd like to have. I'll trade you the pay for the pony. What say?"

Old Man Porson looked at me with narrowed eyes.

"That's the best dog-gone hoss on the place," he said. "That's got the makings of a cutting hoss—if you mean the pinto. I was dog-gone glad when Dan brought that hoss back to us from Cat Hill. I'm glad you didn't take *that* hoss to jail with you!"

"What sort of a price would you put on the pinto?" I asked.

"Two hundred fifty dollars," said he, as quick as a wink.

That was a mighty tall price for a horse. And when I considered that I had only about thirty or forty dollars coming, I was ready to throw up my hands. Besides, considering that the Porsons were under some obligations to me, that because of Dan Porson I was an outlawed man that *needed* a good horse, and because I couldn't do honest work again—perhaps forever—it seemed reasonable that they'd let me take the pinto at my own price.

It seemed so to most of the punchers, too, because I could hear a murmur of disgust go around the circle of them. A loud murmur it was, too.

Dan Porson came up. His face was redder than ever. "We ought to do something for Nels, father," he said. "He's got something coming to him from us."

"I'm going to learn why he ain't back there in jail, where he belongs to be by the law," said Old Man Porson.

"Wait a minute," said Lanky unexpectedly. "I've got some loose change around me, somewheres. And I've always had an eye to that pinto. Look here, Mr. Porson, I'd be kindly obliged to you if you'd gimme a chance at that hoss, for two hundred and fifty."

"Two hundred and fifty? You got two hundred and fifty dollars floating around about on you?" snapped old Porson.

I was amazed, too, when Lanky counted out the money, and not in chicken feed, either, but in five fifty-dollar bills.

Porson held them up to the light and stared.

"Well," said he, "I reckon that I called that the price of the pinto. He's out in the pasture, maybe. Yeah, there I see him now."

"Thanks," said Lanky. "Go out and fetch that hoss, Nelly Grey, because he belongs to you. You can pay me back when your ship comes in."

"You can't take that money, father," said Dan Porson.

"Can't I?" snapped the old man. "I can, though, and I do. The fool might've had the pinto for half of that money, if he'd had the brains to bargain for it. But now I got the money, and he's got the hoss, and there you are!"

He snapped his fingers under the very nose of Lanky.

Well, it was too much for me, and I boiled over.

"The world knows what a skinflint you and your boy Dan are, Porson," I said. "Everybody knows that after snagging me in this deal, you let me down. Everybody knows the shyster lawyer that you sent to fight my case. He wanted me to sign a confession and get ten or fourteen years in prison. But I'll tell you what: The price you put on that pinto that I broke for you and turned from a worthless man-eater into a fine horse   the price that you've put on that horse is going to hurt you more than ten murders. There's not a man or a woman on the range that won't sneer at the name of Porson, from this time on."

"Come back here, you loud-mouthed brat!" shouted old Porson.

Well, I was red-hot all the way through, by this time, and I turned away from old Porson and walked up to Dan, who was red and white and purple, and looked ready to fall in a fit. I said to him:

"You're the worst and lowest hound that I ever saw. You're the worst cur that I ever heard of even. You would have let me hang without spending a penny to help me out. Besides, you're a sneaking coward, and the proof of it is that you're taking water from me right now!"

And I whacked him across the face with the flat of my left hand.

I sort of knew, somehow, that he wouldn't draw a gun. It makes me sick when I look back on that moment and remember how well I knew that. But at the time, I was half crazy.

For it had all come over me in a wave that I was giving up my right to live as a good citizen inside the law and its protection, that I was doomed to be an outlaw the rest of my days, that all of my dreams of becoming a cattleman with a growing herd and with increasing acres—all of that dream was gone forever. I would have to live like a hunted wolf, and all because I had thrown in my luck with the wrong people that was what made me insane. If they had been great-hearted, if they had been the sort of men that the West *can* produce, it would have been a different matter. But they were wrong from the start to the finish, and I groaned as I thought of them.

At any rate, young Dan Porson did not make a move to slug me, or to pull the gun that I saw making a bulge inside his clothes.

I turned on my heel and walked off from him, and as I went, I heard old Porson screech out:

"Gimme that gun! Gimme that gun! You yaller-hearted quitter, you're no son of mine! Gimme that gun, and I'll show him what it means to talk to a Porson. I'll show him that old hands can shoot straight and fast, too!"

I hurried on. And the calm, deliberate voice of Lanky drifted after me, growing fainter and fainter, while he said:

"Look here, Mr. Porson, I ain't no fighting man, but I would like to say that it ain't your fight, but your boy's fight. Here's poor young Nelly Grey that's got himself outlawed, and that's had to break jail, and that's going to be hunted with a price on his head, and that won't dare to live the life he's got a right to live here he is double-crossed and abandoned, a lot of folks would say, by your boy. And it looks to me like it's Dan's fight."

I turned back, nearing the fence of the pasture, and I saw poor Dan Porson hang his head and go to the house with an uneven step.

I realized that it was a more terrible thing than the killing of Josh Acker. That had been quick death and an end of pain, but this meant a living hell every day that young Porson existed. The story would be told in all its shamefulness in every part of the range. But, for my part, I was sure that what had kept Dan Porson from lifting a hand was not fear for me, but the sickening weight of his own bad conscience.

21

LANKY'S LUCK

We rode over the hills away from the Porson ranch, I on the dancing pinto, and Lanky astride the "bear horse" once more, with the long-legged thoroughbred gray mare of Tom Acker on a long lead, following.

Lanky said that he had the mare in reserve; if a pinch came when speed was needed, then he could cast the "bear horse" adrift and take to the speedster. I agreed that the mare looked capable of running away from a hurricane.

"But look here, Lanky," said I, "what happens if you're accused of stealing that mare?"

"Stealing her?" he echoed. "Why, brother, nobody but Tom Acker would accuse me of stealing his hoss!"

"And why wouldn't Tom accuse you?" I asked.

"Well," said Lanky, "it's like this. When a gent gets into a room where they's a lot of flies, he sort of expects them to be lighting on him and biting him, and he just waves his hand casual, and tries to keep them batted away. But if he's in a room where they's only one fly, and that fly keeps landing on the tip of his nose, or the tickling places around his ears, then he's likely to grow peeved, ain't he? And pretty soon he puts down his newspaper and he gets up, and he starts out to corner that fly and murder it, don't he?"

"Yes, he does," said I. "At least, that's what I do."

"Well," said he. "Tom Acker used to be like a man in a room with a lot of flies. Understand? He was bothered a good deal, and he had to keep busy. But pretty soon he worked up a great big name for himself, as a real gunman, and a dangerous feller, didn't he?"

"Yes," I said. "He did."

"And now," went on Lanky, "he's like a man in a room where there's nothing that bothers him, and then along comes one fly, and leaks in under the door or through a crack in the window, and starts singing around and lighting on the head of the gent inside. And that fly is me, Nelly, understand?"

"I understand," I said. "And now there's nothing that he wants in the world except to corner you and murder you, eh?"

Lanky shook his head.

"No, sir," he said, "there really ain't nothing in the world that he wants so much as to kill me. He'd like to have my throat under his thumb and shut off the air, little by little. He'd like to roast me a slice at a time. Because he's mighty worked up, is our friend Tom Acker. And the funny part is that I ain't a fighting man, Nelly. You know that, don't you?"

I looked him fairly in the eye. Those eyes of his were perfectly open, and convincing as the eyes of a child.

"I only know one thing about you, Lanky," I said.

"Do you? Only one thing?" said Lanky, looking more innocent than ever. "If you only know one thing, then what might that one thing be?"

"The only thing I know is that I'd hate worse to have one Lanky on my trail than twenty Tom Ackers!" I declared.

He gasped and shook his head at me.

"I'm surprised at you, Nelly," said he. "And you with an educated brain, too, and yet you can't see that the only way I ever been able to do anything with Tom Acker has been through having all of the luck my way!"

He shook his head at me, and seemed very earnest, and almost sad about it.

"Me, I'm about the most peaceable man in the world, Nelly," he assured me.

"Are you?" said I, grinning.

"Are you smiling, Nelly?" he asked.

Why, his voice was actually raised a little, as though he were growing angry.

"Look here, Lanky," I said, "as long as you live, you can be anything you want, as far as I'm concerned. I'll swear that you're black, red, or white—exactly what you say you are!"

He sighed. "That ain't exactly the same thing," he muttered.

He grew silent, which was a strange state for him to be in, and from time to time I could hear him clearing his throat, as if he were hunting for something to say, but not finding the right thing in spite of all of his efforts! Finally he said:

"Going back to that idea about hoss stealing—I might say, partner, that Tom Acker wouldn't never accuse me of stealing his hoss, because that would mean that he would have to explain about how I might 'a' got it, and he wouldn't wanta lose no reputation, any way you look at it. No, sir, he'll set out on my trail by himself, and not talking. Tom Acker never called in the law to help him to fight his fights. That reminds me—"

I forget what it reminded him of. My own troubles were so heavily on my mind that I could not follow the story he told. I know that we rode on through the hills, I blindly going where he led, until we found a good thicket of trees, and on the edge of that thicket, two jack rabbits jumped up and scampered away. Instantly the long Winchester which was in the saddle holster under the right leg of Lanky came flashing out like a sword blade, and he fired twice in rapid succession, and those two rabbits lay still.

It was as beautiful a bit of marksmanship as I had ever seen. And after the second rabbit had fallen, Lanky looked at me whimsically and quizzically.

"It's my lucky day with a rifle," he said.

"Sure," said I. "I could see that that was nothing but luck from the minute that you first moved a hand for that gun."

I gathered up the rabbits, and we cut them up and roasted them for breakfast and lunch. The horses were staked out to feed in a clearing among the trees, where the grass grew long, and we wrapped ourselves up as well as we could and went to sleep. It was the middle of the afternoon before I wakened.

I yawned and stretched and sat up with a dizzy head that throbbed like a malarial fever. I saw that Lanky was already up, sitting cross-legged and whittling at a twig, which was one of his favorite diversions.

As my brain cleared, I said: "Lanky, I suppose that here's where the trails branch, for us."

"How come?" he asked.

And he squinted carefully down the length of the white bit of wood, as though it were a very important matter for him to trim it off straight and true from end to end.

"Well," said I, "nobody knows, as far as I can see, that you helped me to get out of jail. But everybody knows that I'm an outlaw, and people who help outlaws are apt to get themselves into jail. You've given me my life and a horse to ride. That's about enough. I hope I can pay you back for the horse, one of these days. The other thing I never *can* pay back. We'd better say good-by for a while."

"Sure we'll say good-by," said he, "but you got something ahead of you for this evening that maybe you'll want my help for—any kind of help that I can give you."

"What have I got ahead for this evening?" I asked.

"Well, you wanted to call on the Meade girl, didn't you?" he asked.

"Yes, I want to see her," said I. "If I can manage it."

"I thought you might want to," he said. "So I went down to the Meade place and made the date for you, while you was sleeping."

I jumped to my feet.

"The devil you did!" I exclaimed.

"Why," said he, "it's right down there in the hills, not more'n three miles away. We was aiming at the Meade place ever since we left the Porson ranch this morning, wasn't we?"

"I was too thick in the head to know where we were aiming, this morning," I confessed. "I was letting you do all the thinking. You mean to say that you've been down there to see Bobbie Meade?"

"Not exactly her," said he. "It was old man Meade that I seen and talked to. Kind of a bright and upstanding sort of a man, I take him to be, Nelly."

"He is," said I. "But what did you see him about?"

"Why, about you coming down to pay a call on his girl," said Lanky, opening his eyes at me. "Wasn't that right?"

"But he doesn't *want* me to call on her," said I.

"Well, sir, I found that out right away." Lanky nodded. "Fact is, when I allowed that you was coming down, he said that you couldn't see her, which he had the will and the means of stopping you, too. And I said that I was sorry to hear him talk like that, because you was mighty set on your ways, and that whether he wanted you to or not, you was likely to walk right in, and see the girl, and walk out again, because you had a lot of respects and things to pay to her."

I gasped. I could not say a word.

"It was an amazing thing to see how bad Mr. Meade took that," Lanky continued. "He fair exploded right before me. He says that he'll see you damned first, or something harsh like that, and that the only safe thing for you was to keep away from his girl. And of course I told him that I didn't know nothing about it, but that safety was the only thing in the world that you wasn't interested in, so far as I could find out."

"Confound you, Lanky," said I, "why do you make me out a desperado? I'm not a dare-devil."

"Why," said Lanky, "I was just talking the way I thought that you'd want me to talk for you. Matter of fact, he damned a bit, here and there, and said that he'd handle you and the whole situation in a way that you'd never forget. And I says that you, being always punctual, would arrive sharp around nine-thirty at the ranch house, and call on Bobbie Meade."

"Oh, Great Scott," I said faintly. "And just what did he say to that?"

"Why," drawled Lanky, "I'm mighty sorry to say that he allowed he'd be setting with his wife and his girl in the front room of the house, and that there would be a man watching it on every side, and if you could get by them, guns or no guns, he'd be very pleased to see you, but that if his gents seen you, they'd shoot you down like any outlawed dog!"

I put my back against the tree, fairly staggered.

"And what did you say to that?" I demanded.

"Why," said Lanky, "I nacherally said that when you went to call on your girl, you didn't aim to do any shooting, and that you wouldn't fire a bullet to-night, but that at nine-thirty sharp, you'd walk right into that there front room and have a cup of coffee with 'em, if the coffee was handy. And he up and says that the *coffee* would be waiting for you, and him and the girl, too, mighty willing to oblige!"

22

LANKY ON LOVE

It came over me with a rush that perhaps this friend of mine, Lanky, was a little touched in the brain. He would almost have to be wrong in the head to have taken the immense risks he already had gone through in order to help Dan Porson and me—two strangers to him who meant no more than the man in the moon.

And as I stared at Lanky, finally I broke out: "Lanky, Meade and Bobbie Meade are going to think that I'm crazy!"

"Well, partner," said Lanky, "tell me something."

"Sure I will," said I.

"You're kind of in love with her, ain't you?" he asked me.

"I suppose I am," said I.

"Then it's all right," he said.

"What's all right?" I asked.

"Acting sort of crazy," said Lanky.

"Well, how do you make that out?" I asked.

"It's this way," said Lanky. "There never ain't much sense about a gent when he's in love. You can figger it out like arithmetic."

"That there's no sense in love?"

"Yeah. Just like adding one and one."

"Go on and show me how," I said.

"It's like this, partner," said Lanky, stretching out his vast, bony hands and sticking the long forefinger of the other hand into the palm of the first.

That was a favorite gesture of his when he was talking, explaining anything. But he was full of gestures with his hands and shoulders. To look at the back of Lanky, you'd think that a Mexican or a Frenchman was talking, he moved around so much. And his feet moved, too, and his long legs were always twisting around each other, and he sort of pointed with his feet as well as with his hands.

"It's like this, partner," he was saying. "How many men are there in the world?"

"I don't know. Six or seven hundred million, say."

"And mostly all of those men will get married?"

"Yes," said I, "I suppose so."

"And mostly because they fall in love?"

"Yes," said I.

"And every man will think that his girl is beautiful and smart and mighty talented all kinds of ways, even if she ain't much in the kitchen?"

"Yes, that's true," said I, wondering where he was leading.

"But looka here, Nelly," said Lanky; "look at all the women that there are in the world, mostly made sort of lopsided, and their feet queer, and their knees all crooked, and their shoulders stooped, and they're just sort of hitched together mostly, like the way that a tenderfoot hitches together a pack the first time that he builds one!"

I nodded. I began to see his drift.

"And you take their faces," went on Lanky. "While they're on the near side of twenty-five they ain't so bad. Smiling, and grinning, and squinting, and arguing, and bargaining, and such things ain't wrinkled 'em up, or laying awake at night, or having babies, and all of that. Those things ain't bulged them out of shape in the face, or gaunted them up, or taken a tuck in their mugs in the wrong places, has it?"

"No, perhaps not," said I.

"To say nothing," went on Lanky, "of them girls that was born out of luck, them with their cross-eyes, and their fade-away chins, or their lantern jaws, and mostly of all, them with the buckteeth that smile even when they don't want to. Them are the kind that are poison to my soup. But mostly all of 'em will get married to some gent that gets dizzy about 'em. And why do they get dizzy? You answer me that?"

I stared up at the blue sky through the trunks of the trees that surrounded us and shook my head. Lanky picked up two brace of mountain grouse and threw me a pair of them to prepare for the fire, while he started to work on the other pair, but lost interest pretty soon and laid himself back against the trunk of a tree and put his hands behind his head, and went on talking while I worked.

"I don't know that I have an answer ready," said I.

"I have the answer, though," said Lanky. "It's because love is a kind of craziness. When a gent's in love, he's a little batty, that's all. My buck-toothed sweetheart, you can't see nothing in her, and I can't see nothing in your girl who has the overdose of teeth. You see, we each like our own separate kind of poison, and when she looks at us, our hearts is on the waves, just plain dancing! It's a kind of insanity, is what it is. And that's why it don't matter if you act sort of crazy about the Meade girl. The crazier you act about her, the more she'll think that you're in love with her. And the more common sense you are, the more her pa and herself will think to themselves that you ain't really interested. Do you foller me, Nelly?"

"I follow you," said I. "But to say that I'm going to walk in on them at nine-thirty, through men carrying guns with orders to shoot me on sight—"

"You see how it is, partner," said Lanky, lighting his pipe and then extending one hand in a broad, liberal gesture, "you see how it is? If old man Meade hadn't sort of got interested in the idea himself, he wouldn't of suggested making it that hard for you."

"What do you make of it?" I asked, starting to kindle the fire.

"Why, I make it that he's been kind of romantic himself, and when he boils up and gets mad about you seeing his girl, he don't just nacherally say that he won't let you, and that you can't have a look at her, but he says he's going to make it *impossible* for you to see her. And impossible is a mighty long word, brother. It's a word that can be said, and it's a word that can be wrote, but it ain't a word that can be made true very easy. He says that he's going to make it impossible for you to see her, and he's a rich man, and he's a smart man, and he's got a lot of gents with guns that'll do what he tells 'em to do. But just the same, maybe he'll build a wall with a rotten brick in it, and we'll crawl through the hole after we've punched out that one brick!"

He twisted one long leg around the other as he said this, and I never saw a look of more contentment than that which came over his face.

"But how'll we find the one bad brick in the whole wall?" I asked.

"I dunno," he said. "I gotta think about it. The best way to think is not to worry, and take deep breaths, like you was asleep, and pretty soon, when you're all relaxed, you begin to get an idea; just like the beginning of a dream, vague and thin at the start, and fleshing out and taking on features and a whole face before long."

I looked askance at him while I went on with the preparations for the supper, and I was so hungry myself that, judging Lanky by my appetite, I prepared those four birds by skinning 'em, and I set the portions on twigs set at a slant in front of the fire, and that way I aimed to get them all roasted to a brown turn.

After that I watched and tended them. Lanky had a coffeepot and coffee, and salt and hard-tack in his outfit that was strapped behind the saddle on the "bear horse." I broke out that outfit, and found water at a little stream that was burbling among the trees, and started the coffee heating up.

I looked at Lanky, and his hands were still behind his head, and his eyes were on the trees above him, and the only thing about him that moved was his pipe, which he shifted with a waggle of his long jaw from one side of his face to the other, and sometimes just bobbed it slowly up and down, and his look was as blank as that of a sleepwalker.

After a time I could stand it no more. I asked:

"Ever fall in love yourself, Lanky?"

"Yeah, couple or three times," he answered.

"Then tell me about it, will you?"

"Aw, I had all the symptoms that I reckon you have right now, brother," said Lanky. "Awake when you're asleep, and asleep when you're awake, and all of that; and empty in the stomach, and all of those things!"

"Who'd you fall in love with, Lanky?" I asked.

"There was a lady that lived down near El Paso, up the river a ways," said Lanky. "She was about as bad as ever I was hit. She had a little house, and she raised goats."

"Was she Mexican, Lanky?" I asked.

"She was kind of Spanish," admitted Lanky with a thoughtful frown. "The dog-gonedest eyes ever I seen."

"No mustache?" I asked.

He cocked one eye at the upper branches.

"There was a kind of a shadow, you might say, on her upper lip," said Lanky. "I took to playing the banjo to her, and all of that, and I used to go out there and see her mostly every evening."

"Well," said I, "what happened?"

"What happened was a sad thing," said Lanky, "and I don't like to talk about it, except me being older than you, I'd oughta give you the advantage of my more experience. But one night in the full of the moon I rode out her way, and I seen the big yaller moon go floating through the branches of the trees beside me, so close down that I could've climbed up and bit a hunk out of it.

"Well, I get out there, and I see that the door of her shack is closed, and there is a light inside, which gives me kind of the wigwams. And I taps on the door.

"'Who's there?' says Chiquita.

"'Me, sister,' says I.

"And a man's voice cuts in and says in Mexican: 'Who's me?'

"Says that Chiquita, that deceiving bit of calico: 'Why, it's just a worthless Yankee out there that's been trying to bother me some time past.'

"'I'll go and throw him on his ear,' says the Mexican.

"And out he come, as big as a house, with the ends of his mustache sticking out past his cheeks."

Lanky paused.

"I guess he didn't throw you very far, Lanky," said I, grinning with anticipation.

Lanky shrugged those wide shoulders of his.

"It was a long time ago, brother," said he, "and besides, I ain't a fighting man, and I never remember fights very good."

23

THE MEADE HOUSE

I'll never forget how we polished off those birds. There was hardly enough left for a hungry dog to be interested in. I asked Lanky how many bullets he fired to get the four, and he told me six shots had been needed. I was surprised by this, because I'd seen him knock over two running rabbits in a row, and that was shooting as perfect as I ever have seen. But he explained in his serious and modest way that he never liked to shoot at game when it was sitting—as mountain grouse will do until you're near enough to knock them over with a club, almost. He always scared the game and tried for it on the run.

I digested this information quietly. A man who, with six bullets, and out of a rifle, can kill four grouse on the wing, is a man to be counted on in a pinch.

"How many men have you dropped, Lanky?" I asked him suddenly.

He shook his head at me.

"You always get to talking about fights, Nelly," he said. "And that's the kind of talk that starts the chills up my spine. How many times I gotta tell you that I ain't a fighting man?"

After we'd eaten we smoked a cigarette, and I washed up the coffeepot and put up the pack. I always noticed that around camp Lanky was no good at all. He seemed ready to starve rather than do any cooking. And as for cutting wood, or starting a fire, or staking the horses out, or saddling, or packing, or doing even as much as fetch the water for the coffee, he would groan and heave and make false starts until it gave a man a pain to watch him. So I did all the chores around camp. And I was glad enough to do them. A man needed never go hungry when that rifle was in the company with Lanky behind it! If so much as a ground squirrel showed its head an inch above the ground, he'd clip off its head as far as he could see the black speck. He was one of those fellows who can't miss, and while I've known some who were about as accurate as Lanky, I've never seen a man who had his sureness together with his speed.

After things were cleared up we started.

It was nearing sunset, and the sun was down when we came to a big thicket, where Lanky dismounted and told me to do the same. We tied the horses there, and then I walked forward with him, and the thicket thinned out and turned into an open grove. Presently, at the edge of some trees, I saw a big garden opened out before me, and beyond the garden there was a fine big house, painted white and with huge sun awnings stretched out around it here and there. And the wing nearest to us had a wide veranda going around it. It was as comfortable a place as I ever had seen, but it looked more like a house at a fashionable resort than the houses I was accustomed to see on big ranches.

Instantly it showed me the distance that I stood from Bobbie Meade. It's all very well to talk about everybody being born free and equal, but the people that have the money and the advantages are bound to have a great advantage over the people who are born poor and have to rub through the crowd.

No wonder that Robert Meade wanted to keep me away from his daughter, so long as she happened to be interested in a plain cow-puncher with nothing in the world but the clothes he stood up in.

I took it pretty hard, sitting there among the trees and watching the darkness swallow up the house and the lights commence to shine.

There were more than lights and house to see, moreover. For on that veranda that I've mentioned men began to appear. I could see them sauntering up and down. More even than the men was the fact that they were carrying double-barreled, sawed-off shotguns, Sawed-off shotguns are not guns at all; they're just murder!

I remembered the strong jaw and the steady eye of Robert

Meade. Well, it was plain that he could more than live up to his face!

"There's the place, brother," said Lanky. "There's the front room. And at nine-thirty sharp—that's a mite more'n an hour from now—you've gotta step into that room, because that's where I reckon that they'll be setting with the after-dinner coffee, and the drinks, and what nots!"

He chuckled as he said it. I remember how he sat on the ground, hugging his knees against his chest, and grinning, and still chuckling so loudly that I wondered why the men on the veranda did not hear him.

"Is it a good joke, Lanky?" said I rather bitterly. "Maybe I'll enter that room at nine-thirty, all right, but I'll be considerably overweight with buckshot when I get there."

"Yeah, it looks pretty near impossible, don't it?" agreed Lanky. "But it's a hard thing to find what's impossible. Because men, they've got hands and feet, like animals, but they've got brains, too."

He let go of his knees, rubbed his bony hands together, and I heard the skin rasping in the darkness.

"What's the answer?" I asked after a moment of silence.

He said nothing. The long minutes went by. And at about nine o'clock I could see the shadowy images of people enter the room behind the veranda. I could see them, because there were French windows all the way around the room, and they had only very filmy curtains over the glass. It was about nine o'clock, because just before they came in we heard clearly the chimes of a big clock.

Before that clock struck the next half hour I was due to walk into that same room and accept a cup of coffee!

Well, I can tell you that the sweat started on my face when I thought of that prospect. But still, when I murmured a question to Lanky, he had no reply for me.

After a time he got up and silently disappeared among the trees, while I vaguely wondered how his big feet could cover the ground with so little noise. There was only one comfort to me/ that perhaps Bobbie Meade would think that my messenger had overstepped and said a lot of things that I never had intended him to say.

But Lanky could put on such a simple look that one would never guess how strongly his imagination was likely to be working! No, they were apt to write me down a silly fool and a braggart!

That would finish me with Bobbie. I felt finished already after one look at that garden and the huge size of the house, and the sense of luxury that leaked out of it.

Presently Lanky came back to me with something snaky in his hand.

"What's the rope for, Lanky?" I asked him.

I whispered, but he said, out loud so that I jumped:

"Just a little idea of mine. We got ten minutes left for you to get ready for the grand entrance, brother. Are you ready to start?"

I swallowed.

"But what's the idea, Lanky?" I asked.

"I'll show you," he said. "You'll find out just what it is as we go along."

I groaned.

"Ain't you willing to go it blind?" asked Lanky curiously. "Because I really got a smallish idea, partner!"

I made a wild gesture into the darkness.

"All right," said I. "I'll take the chance. You've pulled me out of as bad a rat hole as this, Lanky—only, it sort of seems like putting my head into the noose for nothing."

"Ain't the girl something to you?" snapped Lanky.

"All right," said I, and stood up.

"Get down on your hands and knees again," said Lanky, "because this here is mostly crawling, the way I see it."

"I only want to point out something, Lanky," said I. "Those are sawed-off shotguns, and sawed-off shotguns don't miss. They don't know how to miss, as far as they can carry!"

"Yeah," said Lanky cheerfully. "They don't miss. And they're what's been keeping me here thinking so long. You angle in behind me, Nelly, will you?"

And out he came from the trees, crawling along on his hands and knees, and sort of flattening himself out, so that he was close to the ground.

By thunder, he went straight out from the trees, and I crawling behind him with my heart thumping in the hollow of my throat. For there was a big, powerful light shining from each side of that veranda, and out of the hallway, too, and whole fountains of illuminations were pouring across the lawn in front of the place! It was like noonday; it was worse than noonday, considering those sawed-off shotguns!

We came to a small hedge that ran around a part of the lawn, and behind that hedge I flattened out for a minute to get my breath and half of my nerves back, but I saw that Lanky was going steadily on, and I could see the light from the lamps striking on his shoulder—the one that was farthest out from the shadow of the hedge!

If the light was falling on that patch of him, couldn't the guard walking up and down that side of the veranda see him? Of course he could! And big Lanky was simply taking a chance that the moving little spot might not be noticed!

I can tell you that I made myself small enough to pass through the eye of a needle as I went along behind him up the length of the hedge.

Finally we came to a break in it where the graveled path curled in through the hedge and wound across the lawn, and beyond that path rose up the side of the veranda about two feet.

"Now," whispered Lanky as I lay flat beside him, colder than the ground beneath me, "all we've gotta do is cross that path without making a noise when the boy on sentry-go turns and starts back up the veranda. I'll go first. Then you come right behind me. We lay down there under the edge of the veranda, and when he comes by on his next turn, I snake him right off the porch with this here rope, and you bounce onto the veranda and finish his beat, and give the word at the corners, the same as him, and when I've got him tied I take your place and keep on with the beat, and you just step through one of them French windows and walk in to get your coffee. Ever hear of anything simpler than that?"

24

ON THE VERANDA

An idiotic, hysterical laughter came bubbling up in me; I had to grit my teeth hard to keep from fairly shouting at Lanky's idea of a simple thing to do!

Then, looking through the upper twigs of that little hedge, I watched the man on guard come striding down the porch with a long, slouching step. He was a fellow to count on in a pinch; a whale of a man, not so much in his size as in the build of him and the look of him. He had one of those fighting faces where the jaw and the cheek bones and the eyebrows are massively made, and the nose is only a button—a face made for receiving shocks. And you can take it for granted that a man who is made for receiving shocks is also just the one to deal them out.

One of the French windows pushed open, and there was Bobbie Meade in the gap, dressed in white that made her sunburned skin look as dark as that of a Mexican, but her smile lighted her up as she looked at the man on guard.

"Hello, Bill," she said. "How's everything?"

"Everything's all right," said Bill, "but if I lay an eye on that fellow Grey, there's going to be a change in the landscape. That's all! Is that going to be all right with you, Bobbie?"

"Nelson Grey isn't an idiot," she said. "He wouldn't try to

break through a wall of gunfire like the one father has built around this room; he wouldn't be such a halfwit."

"I hope he wouldn't," said Bill. "Would he be likely to come swarming at us with his guns popping?"

Robert Meade came up behind his daughter and stood looming, with a very handsome woman with silvery hair and a young face at his shoulder. That was Bobbie's mother, I could guess. And a fine thing she was to look at.

"He won't fire a shot," said Meade. "That's what his messenger told us. He's not to fire a shot, and yet he's to walk in on us in this room at nine-thirty."

He laughed a little as he said this.

"You're betting on a sure thing. That's not fair, father," said Bobbie.

She looked over her shoulder at him with real anger. I was glad of that. And I saw a wriggle go through Lanky as he lay there on the ground in front of me. I guessed, somehow, what that wriggle meant—it was total and immense joy, almost more than he could endure, because of the situation that we found ourselves in. And for the first time an inkling, a vague hint of understanding of the true character of Lanky came into my mind; but the answer was so wild and strange that I dismissed the conclusion at once. No human being could really be like that.

"As for betting on a sure thing," Robert Meade was saying, "I'm only meeting your friend Grey on his own ground—the ground he's chosen, Bobbie. I wouldn't have done that much, even, if I hadn't known that you like him and believe in the rascal."

"Why do you call him a rascal?" she demanded quickly.

I liked her better and better. I worshiped her from the outer darkness I was lying in.

"Bill, what would you say of this Nelson Grey?" asked the gentle voice of Mrs. Meade.

"Why, ma'am," said Bill, scratching his head so that his hat was shoved far back on his head, "I'm here to pack a riot gun, not to do no thinking. But a gent that needs riot guns to talk to him is a pretty hard-boiled hombre, I'd say. You can't tie him and keep him with a diamond hitch, and that's sure. I dunno but I would like to see that wild cat, but I'd rather see him in a cage, because anybody that can fight his way through a mob of about five hundred punchers, all heeled for trouble, is sure all-fired hot to handle!"

I shook my head in the darkness, remembering how I actually

had ducked and slithered and talked my way through the crowd around the jail; that was the first time that I heard the legend that was to grow up around my escape from the Cat Hill jail. And, of course, not a word of credit was given to old Lanky.

I saw another wriggle go through Lanky, and again I guessed what it was—laughter this time.

"There's nothing against him," said Bobbie, "except that he stood by a friend in a pinch and—"

"Never mind, Bobbie," said her mother, putting her arm around the girl. "We won't get your father started in that argument any more. You're too much alike, you two. Come back in here."

"We'll leave the door open," said Robert Meade, chuckling, "to show young Grey that we're ready to welcome him. We can't do more than that for him, can we, Bobbie?"

As they turned from the door their voices became obscure, and Bill continued on his beat.

As he got to the next corner, the fellow who was pacing the adjoining side of the veranda sang out quietly:

"Well?"

"O.K.," said Bill, and turned on his heel and marched back toward the door that opened into the lighted hallway.

The moment he was past the gap of the hedge, Lanky was on his feet—rather, he seemed to be on all fours, and like a great daddy longlegs, he ran noiselessly across the gravel of the path with his shadow trailing out behind him. The shadow disappeared, and Lanky was crouched under the side of the balcony as the sentinel turned at the end of his beat and started back, having given the word again to the man who was marching up and down in the hall.

It was a formula that varied—just any interchange of words: "Here we are again," or "Once more," or "Say when," or anything that came to mind, so long as it kept them from having to finish out to the very verge of the corner.

Perhaps Bill felt a little silly marching up and down on this beat, but he failed to show it; he was as keen and alert as could be.

He reached the next corner down the veranda, singing out quietly:

"Yeah?"

"Yeah," responded the other man, and Bill turned back up the veranda.

As he went by I tried to follow Lanky's example and run out

through the flare of the electric light, but I simply couldn't make myself budge. I kept remembering what a signboard looked like after a charge of buckshot from a scattergun had been thrown through it one day in my own home town. The lettering was mostly knocked out, and the whole center of the sign was one big hole with ragged edges.

Well, the riot gun that Bill carried was quite capable of doing the same thing to me, and something told me that I couldn't manage to cross the gravel of that path as noiselessly as old Lanky had done.

So there I crouched, sweating, behind the hedge, and heard Bill march up to the hall entrance and give a mutter and turn about. He completed his round, and as he passed the gap in the hedge again, it seemed to me that I heard the click of the clock chime in the hall of the house for half past nine. I hadn't heard anything, as a matter of fact. It was simply a snapping of my own nerves that rang a bell in my foolish brain. But it was like the dig of a spur into me. Suddenly it seemed easier to face a charge of buckshot and old scrap iron than to hear the chime of that clock for half past nine before I got into the room where the Meade family was waiting—with coffee hot and ready.

So I got up, and, stooping far over, I went spraddling across the gravel of the path.

But not silently! No, it seemed to me that I was shod with iron plates, and that I made a noise like a charge of cavalry.

As I sank down into the shadow of the edge of the veranda I could see Bill twitch suddenly around before he came to the hall entrance.

He ran straight back, and I felt him leaning out above us. I felt him as clearly as one would feel a knife point pressing at the base of the skull!

I waited for the roar of the double barreled gun that would blow us out of existence, Lanky and me.

I might have taken off my boots before crossing that path—I remember that that regret and afterthought came sneaking into my mind.

Then the guard at the farther side of the veranda sang out: "Hello?"

"Come here," said Bill. "I seen something on the path—I heard something, I mean, and—"

A heavy, leisurely step approached us.

"You heard something—you seen something—maybe you drunk something, brother!" said the other, coming up.

"Yeah, I heard something, and as I turned around up there by the hall door, I sort of seen a shadow switch across the tail of my eye," said Bill.

"You're getting nervy, because it's right close to half past nine," said the second man.

"Me, Tucker? I ain't nervy—I tell you I heard something scuff through the gravel."

"A skunk, maybe," said Tucker, chuckling.

"What's the matter?" asked the guard from the entrance to the hall, having missed the watchword at the end of his beat.

"Aw, nothing," said Tucker. "Bill's got a case of nerves, is all it means."

"I ain't got nerves. You're a liar!" said Bill, getting hot at once.

"He's got nerves, Les," Tucker continued. "He's seeing things with his ears, is what he's doing, and pretty soon he'll be hearing 'em with his eyes!"

"Go on and get moving ag'in," commanded Les, who seemed to be in charge of the guards. "You boys get your eyes peeled now, because they's only a couple or three minutes left before half past nine."

"Nothing is going to happen," said Tucker, the optimist.

I remember that a boiling of cold excitement—if you can understand such a thing—poured up in my brain. For, suppose that we *were* able to do something, after all—in spite of all of these handicaps that had been placed against us?

They went back to their beats, Bill still grumbling, and as he turned and went up the veranda again, I saw Lanky pull off his boots and rise, not with the lariat, but with a naked Colt in his hand. One step brought him onto the veranda. The next was a catlike bound that carried him to Bill. The revolver fell with a very soft thud across the back of Bill's neck, and he dropped, a loose weight, into Lanky's arms!

25

NINE-THIRTY

I found myself on the veranda—I still can't remember how I got there!—and stepping right out, letting my heels come down with rather a thud, as though I needed to walk heavy in order to assure every one that I was Bill walking in Bill's own shoes!

And I gave my sombrero a jerk, so that the brim flared down in a lop over my eyes and kept the upper part of my face in shadow.

It would serve as a mask if either of the two adjoining guards gave me no more than a casual glance. As for the rest, Bill was a heavier man than I, with wider shoulders, and he was perhaps a couple of inches taller. But his outfit was mine almost to a *t*, and that was not strange. Most cow-punchers dress pretty much alike, especially when they come off the same range—likely they've bought their togs all at the same store!

There were differences, of course. His coat was newer and better than mine. It was a checkered gray, and mine was a striped gray. But that might pass. And his flannel shirt was blue, and mine was a dark-gray. But the shirts showed hardly at all, except around the throat.

In fact, anybody who was suspicious would have been able to tell at a glance I was not Bill; but a fellow convinced that I was Bill might not register the differences. But what I hoped was that neither Les nor Tucker would step out around the corner and take a full squint at me.

I talk about myself and my own problem, but what about that panther of a Lanky?

Well, as he caught up the weight of that bulky prize fighter of a Bill in his arms and carried him with wonderful lightness and rapid, gliding steps to the side of the veranda, it seemed to me that he was like a great hawk that's dropped out of the sky and struck a commoner bird to death with one whang of its talons. Or he was like a huge, long-legged wasp that's stung a bloated spider to senselessness with one touch, and then carries and drags the bulk away to its hole in the ground.

There was something terrible in the sight of that long form and the lean, ugly, twisted face and the eyes of Lanky I had just a glimpse of, and which were like bright bits of metal.

It came home to me with a frightful rush that that fellow was not afraid at all—no more afraid than a boy is when he's playing an exciting game. This was the way I would have felt as a child playing blind man's buff, or some kind of tag.

In this case we were due to be tagged with a couple of handfuls of lead. That was the only slight difference! But Lanky didn't seem to care. It was just a game, and a good game, at that!

I saw him disappear over the edge of the veranda. There was only a two-foot drop, but he was able to collapse all of himself and the weight he was carrying into that space which was so much too narrow and crowded for his height. It was like the way a jack-in-the-box can be crowded back into place!

The next instant I heard the voice of Les in the hallway saying:

"Yeah, Bill?"

I had been forming the voice of Bill in the back of my throat all this while. Now I brought it out, but I brought it out too hard, and fairly shouted:

"O.K."

"Say, what the devil?" said the voice of Les.

I turned on my heel instantly and started back, moving my shoulders a little as Bill had done in his walk, and holding under my arm, in exactly his way, the riot gun which Lanky had lowered softly to the floor of the veranda, and which I had taken in turn.

And behind me I felt the keen eyes of Les drilling into my back. I heard him mutter:

"I pretty near thought for a minute—"

Then his step began again as he walked back on his beat, and a nervous wave of joy leaped through me.

It seemed now that we could not fail to win; that the game was already ours.

Twice I walked up and down the length of that veranda, speaking to Les at one end, and to Tucker at the other, and then arose the form of Lanky, and he stepped onto the veranda with the boots once more on his feet.

I paused near the open door of the room. His own great, slouching stride was shortened, and as he came up past me, he gave me such a glance as few men have seen in this world—a look of utter and absolute joy, a flaming look that burned into me! What a man he was!

And now, as he walked, his case was very different from mine. To be sure, he had pulled down his hat so that his face was pretty well shadowed most of the time, but of course the instant that Les or Tucker stepped around a corner and glanced at him, his great height would make it clear that he was not Bill, and betray him—to what? To the blast of a riot gun fired at point-blank range!

I didn't dare to think of his peril.

It half unnerved me simply to visualize it for the split part of a second before the clock in the hallway clanged out a single stroke.

That banished everything else from my mind. I was there at nine-thirty, and, thanks to Lanky, I was stepping through the half-open door into the front room of the Meade house.

The impossible had been accomplished!

As the bell chimed and I stepped in, I saw the three of them sitting in very interesting positions.

Mrs. Meade had her head bowed a little, and one hand was pressed over her eyes; her husband leaned back in his chair, his arms folded across his great chest; and Bobbie Meade sat on the very edge of her chair with blazing eyes.

She saw me instantly and jumped up, but she kept her voice down.

"I knew—in spite of *everything*, I knew you'd come!" she said to me.

Mrs. Meade opened her eyes and snatched down her hand from her face. I saw her pale lips part for a cry. I lifted a hand and said rapidly, softly:

"Please don't shout—that would mean a killing outside on the veranda!"

Robert Meade had not turned his head as yet. Now, gradually, as though he were forcing it about with a separate and strong act of the will, he moved that head, and his eyes rested on me, not with amazement, but with a keen, cold, critical regard.

"You're here, boy," he said. "I didn't think you had it in you."

"I didn't," said I. "I was helped. It's nothing to my credit that I'm here."

"Stuff!" exclaimed Bobbie Meade. "He always backs away from a compliment like a horse at a broken bridge."

"You bribed Bill!" said Robert Meade, pointing his finger suddenly at me.

"No," said I.

I remembered what had actually happened to Bill, and could not help smiling. A whang at the base of the skull is not exactly to be called a bribe.

When Meade saw me smile, his own face darkened.

"This is the strangest thing I've ever been messed up in," he declared.

Mrs. Meade picked up a silver coffeepot and poured some coffee into a cup.

"We're forgetting," said she, "that Mr. Grey came in for coffee."

I blessed her inwardly for saying that.

Meade began to make deductions. "You've just stepped through that doorway; a man is still walking up and down on that veranda; therefore the man who's walking there is not Bill."

He started for the door.

"That's not in the bargain," I said, my voice a little sharp because of my haste to stop him. "Suppose you stay where you are?"

He swung about on me angrily.

"Is that a threat?" he asked.

"It's not a threat. I'm reminding you of the bargain—I was to step in here at nine-thirty without firing a shot. And here I am."

I turned directly toward the door that opened on the veranda, and raised my voice so that I thought big Lanky would hear me.

"Do you mind stepping to the hall door there, Mr. Meade, and telling Les to call off the boys? I got in here, according to the agreement; it may take shooting to get out again."

"And why not?" asked Meade, more and more angry.

"Oh, father!" cried out Bobbie Meade, her voice half stifled with anger.

Meade gave way suddenly.

"It's true," said he. "I've been beaten fairly and squarely. And I'll take the beating."

He went to the hall door, opened it, and said:

"All right, Les. You can call in the boys now. It's after nine-thirty."

"Better keep 'em on the beat a while longer," said Les. "He might show up and say he was a mite delayed as soon as we go off the beat."

"The game's finished," snapped Meade. "Call in the boys."

What would Lanky do? Disappear, of course, under the veranda—at least, that was what I hoped for.

Presently I heard the voice of Les calling at the back veranda:

"It's all right, Jim, Tucker, Bill. Come on, fellows!"

They trooped toward the back veranda, and then went down the steps. No doubt the bunk house lay in that direction from the house. Bill would not be with them, but perhaps Bill would not be missed. If he cared to loiter at the house, that would be his business.

At any rate, I began to breathe freely and easily for the first time since that moment in the afternoon when Lanky had announced to me the challenge that he had given to Meade on my behalf!

I stood there, in the meantime, looking incredulously down at the cup which I held in my hand. That hand was shaking so that the cup chattered softly against the saucer. Meade, turning back from the door, regarded me rather sourly.

"Nerves shaken a little, Grey?" he asked me.

"Shaken so badly that they're almost gone," I admitted.

26

COFFEE AND CONVERSATION

I could feel the glance of Robert Meade going over me, and I knew that he was comparing me and my shaking hands with the fellow he had seen unmanned in the jail, with tears pouring down his cheeks. It sickened me to realize that he was making that comparison, and I felt that in all honesty I ought to make a full confession of just how I had come there. But a fellow as sure of himself and as reliant on hard facts as Robert Meade deserves to take a little beating and mystifying on occasion. And, after all, I couldn't help remembering that he had posted men with riot guns to keep me and my foolishness away from the house!

"Who was that man who was walking up and down the veranda in the place of Bill? And where was Bill disposed of?" he asked.

I managed to smile straight into the keen, aggressive eyes of Meade, and said to him: "I'll tell you what, Mr. Meade—you ought to answer a few questions yourself first of all—and one of 'em is: How much have you got against me? Why did you put those fellows out there with riot guns? Wouldn't rifles have been bad enough?"

"I put 'em there with riot guns," said Meade, "because I hate a bluff. I hate it worse than poison. You sent down that long-legged fellow to throw a bluff with me; and, by thunder, I still feel that it was a bluff and a trick."

He walked right up to me and stood with his face mere inches from mine as he said this.

"Robert," said his wife quickly, "aren't you letting yourself go a little? Mr. Grey, come here and sit by me, will you? Bobbie, you take that chair. Robert, you'll want to walk up and down like a lion, I suppose, and I can't stop you."

"I'm walking up and down like a fool," said Robert Meade. "This is the most infernal mystifying affair that I've ever heard of. Certainly the worst that I've ever been mixed in! Bill is the best fighting man on the place. How could he be made to vanish in thin air, or blinded while another man walks right past him across the veranda?"

I said, as I sat down beside Mrs. Meade: "You know, Mr. Meade, there really is such a thing as hypnotism."

"Ha?" said Meade with a start. He came closer, glowering down at me. "What's that you say?"

"You agree that there's a hypnotic power in the eye?" said I.

"Hypnotic? Utter rot!" roared Meade. "I don't agree to anything of the sort."

"You mustn't be so positive, Robert," said his wife.

"D'you claim that you hypnotized Bill?" asked Meade, as aggressive and matter of fact as ever.

"I'm merely offering an explanation of how the thing could have happened," said I.

"It's all stage stuff—some simple trick," said Meade. "Confound it, it's just some simple trick. And now that you're here, young man, what about it? What have you to say for yourself, and what do you mean by—"

"Robert," said Mrs. Meade, "Mr. Grey is having coffee with us!"

Her husband snapped his fingers and flung himself down in a chair that crunched and groaned under his weight. He stared straight before him, gloomily, and it was an amazing thing to me to see a fellow who had seemed a tower of strength and perfect self-possession so utterly upset and beside himself.

Bobbie watched him with amusement and surprise. Then she turned back to me. You'll have noted that she hardly had said a word.

I started explaining to Mrs. Meade that the fellow who had come to the house that day had said a great deal more than I had wished him to say, and that I was sorry for it, and that of my own free will I never would have made such a ridiculous proposal about stepping into the house at a certain hour, regardless of the wishes of the people of the house.

And as I talked I felt the eyes of the mother on me anxiously, probing, weighing, deciphering me.

"You want to talk to Bobbie," said she. "I can't monopolize you like this."

"No, you talk away   you two," said Bobbie Meade.

I felt that she was watching me, also, and with far keener eyes than those of her mother.

"I wanted to talk to Bobbie," I admitted. "I should have swung to a rafter in the dance hall except for her. Then she came to see me in the jail. She persuaded her father to try to help me."

"Why didn't you accept that offer of help?" broke in Mrs. Meade.

I saw Meade himself lean a little forward in his chair. He kept an expression of indifference, but suddenly I understood what he had done. He had struck a balance in his report of that conversation. He had not told the family of the shameful way I had broken down; neither had he told them of the suggestion he had made that I should move away from the range and never see his daughter again. In that way, I dare say, he had made it even between us.

So I simply answered Mrs. Meade: "You know how it is— one doesn't like to take important help from strangers. And then, it was clear that the money would be coming out of his pocket when he really thought that I'd taken advantage of Acker—and murdered him."

Mrs. Meade opened her eyes a little; I saw her husband turn his head quickly and look at me in a new way.

"I agree with Bobbie," she said. "I don't think that you took that advantage."

Now I thought of poor Lanky out there in the dark with his prisoner to guard. How he had fixed Bill I could not guess, but within the few seconds he must have tied and gagged him securely. I would have to get back to him as soon as possible.

And as I finished the last drop in that midget of a cup, I stood up and put the cup on the table and said that I must go.

"You've only just come!" said Mrs. Meade. "Bobbie's talked a lot about you, and we want to know you better, Mr. Grey."

I had to find some excuse, and I said: "You know that they're following me, and if they run me down, I don't want it to be here."

"Run you down?" exclaimed Mrs. Meade. "Something has to be done about that. Robert, we must do something about it!"

"Why?" said Meade. "Looks to me as though he has enough

tricks up his sleeve to handle the law very comfortably, no matter what happens."

I turned fairly to Bobbie Meade for the first time.

"They haven't found my trail yet," I told her. "When they do, they'll keep me hopping. I had to see you before they started chasing me. This all seems very melodramatic, the way I've come in on you, but I hope that you'll see it wasn't my fault."

"I know," said she, and smiled at me.

Well, there are a lot of people in the world who have to talk words by the thousands before they can make their point, and there are others who can say a volume with a nod of the head, and Bobbie Meade told me sufficient volumes with those two words and the look of her as she said them. For there was a sympathy, and kindness, and something more than kindness, too, in her face. It made me happy, but it frightened me, too.

You know how it is when you appear in a false light. If the light is too bad, it doesn't matter so much, because time will put that right if you've been wronged. But if the light is too favorable, it's a miserable feeling because it means that other people will sooner or later feel that they've made fools of themselves about you, and nothing is worse than that. People who deceive themselves are always angrier than people who have been deliberately deceived by others.

I had to say: "The few times you've seen me, Bobbie, I've been on the center of the stage one way or another. That's not my talent. What I hope some day is that I can have a chance really to talk to you. You've seen the wrong side of the coat. I'm not a dare-devil or a gunman, or even a specially good shot. I'm as easily scared as the next fellow, and the only way I broke out of jail was because I had help. The only reason that I wasn't moved out of the picture at the dance was because another fellow got Tom Acker away in the first place, and then you and the sheriff took a hand. The only reason that I managed to get through to you to-night was because that long, lean fellow who came down here to-day engineered it for me."

That was about all I could say. It made me feel like a fool, too—as though I knew that she had too high an opinion of me, or put me in too important a place, and had to have her eyes opened to the truth.

But she took that in the best possible way, too, and smiled at me again.

"You have to go, Nelson?" she asked.

"Yes, I have to go."

She came up and gave me her hand.

"I want you to come again," said she. "And if you can't get near enough, send me word and I'll come to you. We ought to talk. We *have* to. And all the time in between I'm believing nothing but the best of you, and every trick that goes against you will hurt me, too."

I like to think back to what she said and the way she said it. Try to figure in your mind how a girl could come cleaner than that or be more out in the open—I mean, when you think of the simpering, silly false pride of most women, and the way they hold themselves back on a pedestal and have a man make a fool of himself.

I was in a golden haze as I said good-by to Mrs. Meade and watched her glance go from me to Bobbie—and even while she was speaking to me, her look of concern and trouble was settling on her daughter again.

Robert Meade went with me to the veranda. I closed the door behind us and said:

"I think there's something here that you need to see, Mr. Meade."

"What is it?" he asked.

"It ought to be here," said I.

I stepped down from the veranda, and Meade with me, and there lay the form of a man.

I sat the figure up with difficulty, and that was because Bill was bound stiff and fast with a running twist of rope. It didn't seem that he could have been wound up like that except on a machine, never by hand.

His eyes were wide open and purple, and there was a gag stuffed between his teeth. I jerked out the gag, and with the first breath he said:

"Damn!"

27

A PROMISE

I had the rope off him and got him to his feet while he was still gasping and panting. I ran my hand behind his head and found a lump the size of a hen's egg, but otherwise he seemed to be all right. I could have known that Lanky would understand exactly how hard to hit; as for me, I would either have killed him or not even have given him a shock.

"Are you all right—is your head all right?" I asked him.

"You're Grey!" he exclaimed. "You're Grey, and by thunder you got here, after all! Yeah, my head's all right. Kind of singing, is all."

"What happened to you, Bill?" asked Robert Meade.

He stood there big and doubtful, with a scowl on his face.

"I dunno," said Bill. "I was just walking up the veranda, and it seemed to me that a shadow sort of slid up behind me and breathed on my shoulder, and just as I was about to turn my head—wham! I got it, and the lights went out. That's all I know, till I woke up laying down here on the cool ground, wrapped up like a mummy. And I could hardly move even my fingers of one hand!"

He turned and stared at me.

"Is this all a gag?" he asked. "Is this fixed up between you and Mr. Meade?"

"It was a bet," said I. "That's all. It was a bet. Can you walk all right, Bill?"

"I can walk all right," said Bill sourly, "and I'm going to use my legs to walk outta this here job. There's too damn much funny stuff going on around here to suit me!"

He turned about and stalked off from us with a little hitch in his step, for he seemed to be constantly leaning to the left, and inclined to steer in that direction. I suppose that that was an after effect of the blow.

A hard grip came on my arm, and I turned with a start. It was Meade who had grabbed me.

"Boy," said his terse, harsh voice close to my ear, "either you're the pure quill and the straightest that can be made, or else you're a damn scoundrel. And on my soul, I don't know which you are!"

I looked up at him and smiled in spite of myself.

"You'll have to trust time for the proving of that one way or another," said I. "You'd never believe me."

He went on, unmoved by the smiling.

"Either you're a man of steel with a quick soft streak in you, or else you're the silly coddled egg that I saw in the jail the other day, with a streak of steel appearing now and again."

"I'll tell you this," said I. "I'm nearer to the coddled egg than I am to the man of steel, if you want to know it. But the other day you caught me when my guard was down."

"What d'you mean by that?" he asked.

"I mean," said I, "that my nerves sneaked up behind me and got the upper hand. That's all. I've got to go, Mr. Meade. I'm waited for."

"By how many men?" he asked.

"One," said I.

"You did this job with one man to help you?" he asked me sharply.

"The other fellow did the job, with me to help him," I corrected Meade.

He snorted at that.

"I hope this modesty's not a fake," he said.

"Look here, Mr. Meade," I put in. "I'm not so modest. I'm a pretty fair cowhand. I've had a decent education. I could lead an honest, average life and get by with it. But I'm not a dashing, crashing hero; on the other hand, I'm not a sneaking cur, and neither am I a murderer. You think that you've got to underline me in black and red, and that's not fair."

He studied me for a moment, with his big jaw muscles working.

"You talk well enough," he said. "I wish that talking were the man, though!"

I shrugged my shoulders. He was against me, and that was plain, but I liked him. That is, I knew that I *could* like him, and I *wanted* to like him. He was so absolutely straightforward.

"What d'you think is going to come out of this?" he asked me.

That made me angry. After all, I had been through a good deal that evening—even though I had been hanging onto the coat tails of Lanky most of the time. Just to follow Lanky was a man-sized job, as you may agree.

"Look here, Mr. Meade," I said. "You want to be logical and businesslike and add everything up at the end of every day and find out where the profit and the loss may be."

"What way would you suggest for a man to conduct his life and his thinking, young man?" he asked.

"I'd suggest crossing bridges when you come to them," said I.

He stared at me for a long moment.

"What do you mean by that?" he asked.

"You know well enough what I mean," I told him, staring straight back. It's wonderful how a little anger stiffens one's backbone.

"Perhaps I can guess," he said finally. "But I'd rather have it straight from you."

"Well, then," said I, "you think that your girl has lost her head a little about me. You're afraid that she may actually do something rash."

"I think just that," he admitted. "I understand why you made that speech to her in there, too. You were talking to her, but you intended it for my ear. You wanted to make an impression on me by talking down about yourself—as though she'd believe you when you tried to pull the wool away from her eyes after pulling it over them so thoroughly."

"Tried to make an impression on you?" said I, raging. "Mr. Meade, you've made a big success in life—you've won a lot of points in the game. But don't fool yourself now. For my part, I care tons for every idea that comes into the head of Bobbie, but I don't give a damn what you think about anything, beginning with myself. Your money's nothing to me. Not if you had billions."

He looked me over keenly and nodded his head, not as one who agreed with me, but who agreed with a former thought he had had. It wasn't a favorable thought, either.

"I'm not standing here to wrangle with you," he said. "I'm trying to talk straight. But you can't stand straight talk."

"You're the one who can't stand it," said I. "But go on with your straight talk. You think I'm a fortune hunter or a cradle robber, or something like that. What are some of the rest of your precious thoughts, eh?"

I must say that he kept himself well in hand, and all the time he kept probing me with those straight-looking eyes of his. I had nothing on my conscience about him, but still it was hard to stand that examination.

"I have money," he said at last, "but Bobbie is more to me—her little finger—than all my possessions. She's lost her head about you, and you're clever enough to have seen it. You could bleed me to the heart through her."

"Wait till I let you spend a penny on me!" I snapped.

He made a pause. I felt that my outbreak had been simply silly, and lost practically all of my heat.

Then he went on: "I want to think that you're straight. There's one way that you can prove it."

I shrugged my shoulders.

"If you want to see Bobbie in the future," said he, "will you let it always be as to-day, through me?"

"Through your riot guns?" I asked.

Again he made a pause, and again I felt like a fool. I saw that he was talking simply and straight from the heart.

Then I remarked: "You know, Mr. Meade, that I'm not trying to wring any tears out of you when I tell you that the law is likely to corner me long before I see Bobbie again, and if the law gets me, it'll hang me sure, since I confessed guilt, so to speak, when I broke out of the Cat Hill jail."

"That doesn't ease my mind a great deal," he answered. "You don't know Bobbie, my lad. She's impulsive, but when a thing gets under her skin, she never forgets. You've gotten under her skin."

It gave me a chilly feeling of awe. I said nothing.

He went on: "This may be the last time that I see you for a long time. Frankly, I hope that I never lay eyes on you again, because in the marrow of my bones I think you're a trickster, and I don't trust you. It isn't that you're poor. That doesn't matter to me. I have enough coin to put money in its place. You want to be a cattleman, you say, and I think that's the finest career in the world. But I smell the charlatan in you somehow, and I hate a trickster. But I want to say this: For Bobbie's sake, if you're ever in a pinch, let me know and I'll help out."

I could not help blurting out: "I'd rather cut my throat than ask you for help."

At that his patience left him.

"You talk like a young fool!" he said. Then he added: "Not that I care a straw about you, but I don't want Bobbie to grieve the rest of her life because of her poor, unbefriended cow-puncher who was done to death by a process of law. I'm thinking of her. I hope that you're thinking a little about her, too."

I could only say that I wanted to do what was right and fair, but that his charity would choke me.

"We can't agree," he said. "As her father, I hope that you break your neck before you've gone a mile. As a mere man, I would like to know you better. If you're not a charlatan, you may be an extraordinary fellow. Good-by."

He was about to turn away. I stopped him.

"I'd like to say a few things to raise your hair," I said. "I won't. There's only one thing that I'll shake hands with you on. And that is that I'll never go sneaking when I try to see Bobbie. I'll see you first."

He got hold of my hand and gave it a good grip. But as I turned and went stumbling away from him into the darkness of the night, I knew that I had not won his confidence or his trust.

Why should I, since I knew that I could hardly trust myself on that point?

28

HIDING OUT

When I got to the edge of the woods, there was no sign of Lanky, but when I went on to the place where we had left the horses, there I found him waiting, stretched out on the ground.

"Hello," he sang out in his usual way, a good deal louder than he needed to. "Back again?"

"I'm back, Lanky," said I. "You heard me talking in the room about calling off the guards? I thought that would warn you to make your get-away."

He yawned as loudly as he had spoken.

"That's all right," he said. "Mind peeling those saddles off the ponies? We'll have a snooze here."

"Sleep here?" I exclaimed, my hair standing on end. "Why, man, the news will be in Cat Hill before long, and the sheriff and his gangs will be piling out here to find us. And we've left tracks all over that they can follow."

"Aw, I dunno," said Lanky. "So many tracks all around the place that they ain't likely to run us down, I guess."

He yawned once more.

I kneeled down beside him and touched his shoulder.

"What's the matter with you, Lanky?" I exclaimed. "You haven't been drinking, have you?"

"I'm just kind of tired," said Lanky. "If you don't like it, you troop back into the hills, and I'll join up with you there to-morrow."

I was amazed. It seemed to me insanity, but by this time I had come to feel that Lanky could hardly be wrong in any of his decisions. I had seen him do so many extraordinary things that I was even prepared to follow him blindly, as I did on this occasion. I simply shook my head and decided that I would have to stop thinking on the question. Perhaps his game was to lie close in, while the hunters were apt to range far out in the search for us!

At any rate, I unsaddled the horses and found them a pretty good place to graze among the trees, and then I lay down in turn near Lanky.

He was snoring like a slide trombone, and that noise and the excitement that I had gone through kept me awake so long that I was sure that I would not close an eye all night long. But that decision was no sooner made than I was asleep.

When I wakened, the sun was clear up above the horizon and the full brightness and the warmth of it was sifting through the trees. Near by one of our horses neighed, and I leaped to my feet in a tremble, remembering where we were.

But when I looked down, there was Lanky with only one eye open.

"What's the matter?" he drawled.

"The sun's up now," said I, "and if we try to get away we run a good chance of being seen."

"And why get away?" muttered Lanky. "This—pretty good place to—"

And he was asleep again and snoring in a sweet content.

I looked down at him in a gathering amazement. It was true that he had remained awake the day before while I slept, but that was not a reasonable excuse for this drugged and heavy weariness that seemed to fill him. I shook my head, completely baffled.

I went to the horses, took them off their long tethers, and got them to a trickle of water that came down through the trees. I brought them back to the clearing—it was hardly big enough to call that and saddled them and put on the two packs. Then I went back to Lanky. He was still asleep.

And there he remained asleep until the middle of the afternoon, more like a drugged man than one in full health.

In the meantime, I had sneaked to the edge of the trees a dozen times, and twice I saw parties of riders swinging out from the direction of the big ranch house of Robert Meade. I did not spot the sheriff, but I gathered that they must be his men, and they had a businesslike air about them. From the way they rode and looked about them, I knew that their hearts were in their business, and that was depressing.

We could not move by daylight, when the air was so full of hornets. And again I admired the cunning of Lanky in remaining so close to the last place we had been seen that nobody thought of looking for us there!

In the middle of the afternoon he woke up, yawned, took a drink of water out of his canteen, and ate a few bites of hard-tack. Then he smoked a cigarette, in spite of my protest that the smoke or the scent of it might get us into trouble, and lying down once more, he was soon asleep again.

I don't think that he uttered more than a grunt during this time he was awake, and now I was greatly alarmed, because I was certain that he was badly hurt in some way, or else that a fever had hold of him.

The night fell on one of the longest days of my life, and still Lanky was flat on his back, softly snoring. Finally I went to him and put my hand on his forehead. Whatever was wrong with him, he had no fever. My hand on his forehead was not sufficient to more than half rouse him. So now I gave him a shake by the shoulder.

"Well, well?" he said irritably. "What's the matter now?"

"It's all right for you to stay here, Lanky," said I. "There's nothing against you so far as I know. But I've got to ride on. If I don't get into the clear this night, I may never get away."

He said nothing, just looked up at me through the dimness.

"All right, Lanky," said I. "I've got the horses saddled, and I'm going on ahead. Good-by, and God bless you."

He held onto my hand and pulled himself to a sitting posture by the aid of it.

"Wait a minute," he said. "Dog-gone me if you ain't as restless as a traveling salesman. You'd make a first-rate drummer, Nelly. It ain't pain to you to have to keep on the move. You like it. Every time that you sleep two nights in the same bed you feel that you're getting old and useless. But what's the matter with this place? Ain't the ground as soft here as it'll be over the hill?"

"It's all right for you, Lanky," said I. "But I've got to go on. It was a mighty slick move to spend a day here, where they wouldn't look because they wouldn't dream that we'd have the nerve to stay here. That was a bright idea; but if we stay on, luck is going to go against us."

"It wasn't any brightness on my part that made me wanta stay here, but I was sleepy," said Lanky. "And I'm still sleepy. I need a coupla more days of sleep, I do. But if you're dead set on moving, I'll travel on a piece with you, but no long stretch, mind you!"

Well, I was glad enough to get him out of those woods and over the rim of the hill, out of sight of the roof of Meade's big house. But as we sank behind the hill, I rode close to him and said:

"Lanky, you've been the best partner in the world; but you can see for yourself that if you stay on with me you'll be getting into hot water. I'm an outlawed man by this time, and everybody who helps an outlaw is liable to arrest, the way I understand it."

"Yeah?" he drawled. "Where do we camp for the rest of the night is what I wanta know!"

I watched the way he sat in the saddle, with his head down and his feet dangling loosely in the stirrups, his knees sagging outward, and his back was so bowed that it looked like a permanent deformity.

"What's the matter with you, Lanky?" I asked.

"I'm sleepy, is all. Ain't a man got a right to be sleepy? You remind me of the story of the gent that got tired of sleeping so much valuable time away, and so he took and made himself a barbed-wire collar, so's every time that his chin dropped he would—"

Here Lanky yawned prodigiously and muttered: "I forget the rest of it."

We went on for about two hours, I think, and then, as we came to a patch of big, scrubby brush, Lanky slid off his horse and swore that he could ride no farther, and he said if I went off and left him, and didn't give him a chance to see some more of this game, I was a quitter and a piker!

He gave himself a roll in a blanket, lay down on the bare ground, and was instantly asleep again.

I could make nothing of it. I had heard about sleeping sickness, and, not knowing what the symptoms of it were, I wondered if he might not have something of the kind. At any rate, there I camped with Lanky in a very bad place, because there was no water, and the brush was not thick enough to make really good shelter. But there I had to stay, because I give you my word that Lanky was not awake for more than two hours out of the two days—at least, not while I was around him. He slept most of the time flat on his back, and flies that settled on his nose or leaves that blew against his face, or even a sizable dust storm, made no difference to him.

The morning after we got there a young deer walked out of

the brush twenty yards from me, and I shot it before I had a chance to remember that I didn't want to make a noise. So we had plenty of venison to eat, and Lanky would wake up to swallow a couple of meals a day, and then fall asleep again like a log.

I began to think that he would never get on his feet again, and I was badly worried, because certainly it was a bad place to remain. I had to take the horses out of the thicket to water twice a day, and no matter how I varied the course to the water, I was beginning to leave a whole pattern of tracks around that patch of shrubbery.

Well, on the morning of the third day I woke up, stretched, got into my boots and hat, and then by chance glanced at Lanky's bed. I fairly jumped when I found that he was not in it.

He was not back when the gray of the morning turned to pink. He was not on hand when the sun rose. And with him, the fine gray that was the pride of Tom Acker's life was gone, and Lanky's saddle and bridle.

I had a chilly feeling that he must have slipped away in the night, not wanting to stay and say good-by to me. It was the right and the logical thing for him to do, but somehow it hurt me a good deal to think that he would pull out in that way.

Well, about the middle of the morning, along in the hollow to the east of the brush, I heard a horse neigh, and I slithered through the scrub and looked out, rifle in hand, wondering what might be on the way toward me, and half expecting to see a long line of riders, with rifles balanced across the pommels of their saddles.

I'd hardly got to the edge of the brush when the horse neighed again, and was answered by the "bear horse," confound its unlucky hide! And there, jogging up the hill, came Tom Acker's gray mare, and old Lanky jouncing in the saddle.

29

AN IDEA FROM AN ENEMY

Mind you, Lanky was not the only thing that jounced, because all around him there were tied big, awkward bundles, and I could hear a tremendous clattering of tin.

He came up and saw me, and waved his hand and laughed as he went by me. There was no sleep in him now. He was all lighted up, and as he came to the little open spot where we had our things, he dropped down out of the saddle and waved his hand to the pack.

"Go on and unload her, brother," he said. "I done the loading, and you do the unloading. Because there's things there that'll do your heart a lot of good to see!"

There were, at that.

When I unlimbered that load of stuff I found a fine sugar-cured ham, and half a side of the best bacon you ever saw, and coffee, and sugar, and tinned tomatoes, and canned corn, and fine baker's bread, and a couple of big packages of cookies with dates and raisins and such things in them, and there were cans of plum jam, and strawberry jam, and black-currant jam, which has the world beat, in my opinion. There were a lot of other odds and ends.

"Great Scott, man," said I, "I never saw so many good eats."

"Lay 'em on the board, cook," said Lanky. "Don't just stand

there for to admire, but lay 'em out where we can taste 'em. That's not looking food; that's eating food!"

A meat diet was about all that I had been used to for a good many days, and at the thought of that treasure my mind stopped working. I broiled some venison steaks that were prime, and made coffee, and then we sat down and ate until we nearly busted. And even when I couldn't hold any more, I still wanted to keep on eating.

Lanky lay back against a hummock and canted his hat over his eyes and grinned at me, very pleased with himself and with me and the world. He hadn't stirred his stumps, and for that matter, he never did stir them around camp if he could possibly dodge the jobs. I admired the way he could get out of chores; but, of course, any odd jobs I could do to make Lanky comfortable I was glad of.

Now he smoked a cigarette, and fed cured sweet dates into his face all the while with one hand, and kept snapping the slippery pits out from between his long, strong, white teeth, that were so like the teeth of a horse.

"Where did you buy all of this stuff, Lanky?" I asked him as I pulled the smoke of a cigarette deep into my lungs.

"I don't know," said Lanky.

"You don't know!" I exclaimed.

"You see, brother, it was kind of dark when I called at that grocery store, and nobody was at home. I had to pick the lock of the front door."

I gasped.

"Great Scott, Lanky," said I, "you didn't commit robbery just for the sake of some groceries, did you?"

He grinned at me in the highest good nature.

"I left a couple of times what that truck is worth," he said. "I left it behind me on top of the counter. But I wouldn't 'a' wanted to wake up the proprietor at four in the morning, would I? And besides, anybody that seen me might start to asking a lot of questions that I wouldn't want to answer. Look at what they're saying already."

With that he pulled a newspaper out of his pocket and threw it across to me. One glance at the front page of that paper and the spread of the headlines made my eyes pop, I can tell you.

I won't try to put it down word for word. It would take too long. The main item concerned one Nelson Grey, a young man I knew very well, and whose fortunes I was as interested in as I was interested in myself. It said that he had appeared at the Porson and the Meade ranches under spectacular circumstances; it said that the countryside was roused and was busily looking for him; and it said, above all, and this was what put the ice in the marrow of my bones, that the town of Cat Hill, by popular subscription, had raised a reward for his capture, or information leading to that capture, and the reward was just over two thousand dollars!

I leaned back and groaned when I thought what that meant. A good, first-rate cow-puncher in those days felt that he was being rather overpaid and a pretty lucky fellow if he got forty dollars a month and found. He thought he had a regular position that was too good for him, and he wanted to keep it the rest of his days. Two thousand dollars meant a year's pay for four such fellows—men who could ride anything on four legs, and who could shoot the eye out of a hawk on the wing. That was what a cow-puncher would collect by sending a bullet through my skull!

I dragged out an extra bandanna and mopped my face with it, though the day was cool.

Suddenly my memory flew back to the table that night at the Porson ranch, and the whole scene at that moment when young Dan Porson had invited me to go with him to the dance at Cat Hill. I was bitter.

Yes, I had killed one man because I had to. Now I wanted to kill another, and I wanted it bad.

I sat there with my jaws locked hard together for a time, looking straight before me, tasting the thing that I wanted to do.

And all at once I was hard, and cold, and calm, and collected, as I had never been in my life before.

You see, I felt that I was a dead man. With such a price on me, with so many men looking for me, it hardly mattered what I did. I would die, and probably before very long. So nothing mattered that had mattered before. The good opinion of other men— what was that, when society was to hang me as soon as it got its hands on me? And self-respect? Why, that was nonsense, and so were all the other ideas that I had been raised with. Men had cornered me like a wild beast, and like a wild beast, not like a man, I felt that I was privileged to fight back.

I made a cigarette, lighted it, and went on smoking and reading. Suddenly I had been able to push the whole picture to arm's length, and look at it as though the news had little or nothing to do with me personally.

There were long articles about me. There was a rehash of the jail break, on which the reporter spilled all kinds of adjectives. There was a report that I was known at the Porson ranch to be a dead shot. And poor Josh Acker had to be killed again to excite the reader against his "murderer." It appeared that I was the worst and most determined character in the West in years. I was a "desperado," I was a "criminal by nature," and all the way through the reporter was referring to "this scoundrel," "this desperate and dangerous man." It was a wonder that such a villain could be such a youth.

Then Lanky was dragged in. He had appeared with me at the Porson ranch; he had preceded my coming at the ranch of Robert Meade. It was probable that the poor, simple fellow was an attendant upon me, and that he was the first member I had taken as a unit in my gang!

Yes, that was the way the thing went.

Then I looked at other articles.

Tom Acker, said a whimsical notice, had lost his matchless gray in a poker game, and Tom was so glum on the subject that no one cared to ask him who had won the famous horse.

I chuckled a little when I saw the way that Tom had chosen for dodging the really humiliating manner in which that pony had been lost to him! Lanky had been right again; Lanky was always right!

But fully one half of the front page was given to the celebration of a great exploit on the part of Sheriff Loren Mays. He had cornered the gang of the great Don Pedro, that Mexican savage who was better known, even south of the Rio Grande, as "Don Pedro the Cruel," and Loren Mays and his posse had shot down five of the bandits before they could break away.

All their captives were dead, because the survivors, as they fled, first made sure of the silence of their former companions by shooting each of them through the head. It was an old tradition of the gang of Don Pedro the Cruel that none of the band should fall into the hands of the law alive, for fear that he might confess secrets that would involve the safety of the entire organization!

Like wolves, those who fell in the hunt were dispatched by their own friends!

I had heard of that horrible practice by the bandits before this, but it was a shocking thing to see it down in black and white, and so newly done.

Among the dead, however, Don Pedro himself did not appear.

"But," said the newspaper account, "who would know Don Pedro even if he actually were killed? A thousand conflicting descriptions of him are abroad, but hardly two people in the West will agree as to his actual appearance!"

There was another pleasant suggestion later on in the column. I took it up with Lanky.

"You see something here, Lanky?" I asked.

"I seen quite a pile in that paper," he said. "What's the point you mean, brother?"

"The newspaper says that perhaps I'll throw my hand in with Don Pedro. It says that Don Pedro would probably be glad to have a star as dark as mine to tack onto his long list of murderers."

Lanky nodded his head. He was still eating dates. There was no limit to his capacity. Like a snake, he seemed able to expand his entire frame in order to accommodate more food supplies.

"You know what I think?" asked Lanky.

"Go ahead and start thinking," said I.

I looked through cigarette smoke comfortably at Lanky. It seemed to me at that instant that the hope of ever seeing Bobbie Meade again had disappeared; a far sterner reality was before me.

"I think," said Lanky, "that a gent that has got any brains about him oughta always be willing to take good advice."

"What good advice is in here?" I asked.

"Why, don't they advise you to join up with the gang of the greaser?" said Lanky.

I stared at him, half smiling, half disgusted even by the suggestion.

"Take any good idea, even when it comes from an enemy," repeated Lanky. "Now, this here ain't a bad idea at all. You wanta get back inside the law. You wanta get back bad. You gotta pay to be let in. That's all right. Here's the price set out before you. You bring the law Don Pedro's head on a silver platter, and the law is certainly going to slap you on the back and call you a bright boy and wipe away all the bad-conduct marks, ain't it?"

30

AMBUSHED

They say that if you name the devil, he's likely to appear. Now let me tell you a queer thing. It didn't happen at once, but about half an hour after we had started this subject, and while Lanky was easing his way into it step by step, sort of feeling his way along and getting more and more interested all of the time, we heard a drumming of the hoofs of horses, and then the clanging of rifles—plenty of shots fired irregularly.

We ran out to the edge of the thicket, and, looking through the outer fringe of the bushes, we saw three men riding on three dead-beaten horses.

The strange thing about them was that although each of those horses, dying on its feet, was having the last of its strength whipped and spurred out of it, not one of them could get a length ahead of its companions. The fellows who rode were working harder than even jockeys do to win a great race, and the reason was that they were playing for greater stakes—because life rates a little higher than money, no matter how you figure it.

Behind them came with a fine sweep fourteen riders on fourteen tired horses. Yes, you could see that those mustangs were worn out, but you could also see by the strength of their bodies and their necks that they were not so tired as the three they were chasing.

It's often that way when a bunch are chasing one or two. Because the fellows who are being chased have to keep ahead of the others every lick of the way, whereas the gang can let their sprinters go out ahead and run the enemy hard. And as the sprinters fall away, run out, then the main body comes plugging along, and the sprinters jog along in the rear till they get their wind back and can work up to give the poor devils another run for life.

It seemed that something like this must have been going on in the chase we were watching the end of, and the end it certainly would prove to be, because the three were heading down the valley toward the creek, where there was ordinarily a ford, as I had been able to tell by the deeply worn trail that went down either bank. But that ford was unusable now, as I very well knew from having taken our three horses to water there every day lately. There had been rains in the hills, or an extra melting of the winter snows in the highlands, and the stream was running like a thousand yellow and white devils.

I sang out with a groan: "The three of 'em are goners, Lanky."

"Yeah, they're gone, all right," said Lanky, squinting a judicious eye at the scene. "But they'll last it over to the creek there, maybe, and beyond the creek there's woods."

"They'll never be able to cross the creek," said I. "It's raging and roaring, bank full. If you half open your ears at night in a calm you'll hear the water devils talking things over clear over here."

"Then they're gone," said Lanky, "and by the looks of those boys behind 'em, they're going to eat the three when they catch 'em. Him in the center of the three, he sure rides powerful well!"

It was a man so tall and gangling that he made his mustang look like a midget; he must have been a man of considerable weight, owing to his great height, but yet by his riding he kept his horse up with his companions.

Now he turned in the saddle, a rifle gleamed at his shoulder, and he fired.

"Beauty!" murmured Lanky.

One of the pursuers went down, horse and man.

I blinked with horror. When I looked again, the horse lay still, but the man was up and shooting wildly with a revolver as he ran forward.

"That tall gent, he can shoot," said Lanky with a nod of approval. "But he can't shoot good enough to put down fourteen of 'em. Yeah, and even a good shot like him can't hit the mark all the time, shooting backward off a running hoss!"

As he spoke, the tall man turned in the saddle and tried twice more in rapid succession, but the pursuers came on uninjured. They replied with a rattling gunfire, and I heard the echoes of their yelling come with a ring through the air.

It was horrible. It was like the baying of dogs on the traces of three tired and gallant stags.

"Can't we do something to stop that?" I asked.

"You know how it is, son," said Lanky. "They're chased because they most likely need catching!"

"God help them!" said I.

I had brought a rifle along with me, and instinctively I raised it toward my shoulder, and then realized that I was being a fool, and that I certainly would not shoot at one group of men to save others until I knew what the cause of the trouble might be. But as I lowered the gun, Lanky said:

"That ain't such a bad idea, neither. Lemme have it, son, will you?"

He picked it out of my hand and sank on one knee, and leveled the rifle.

"Look out, Lanky! Don't shoot, man!" I exclaimed.

"Leave me be, Nelly," said Lanky. "First you wanta help those three gents in the lead and then you wanta keep them behind from being hurt. There ain't any point in that, Nelly. You remind me of a gent I knew in Kansas," he continued, settling his aim while I watched the muzzle of the rifle travel very slowly, creeping bit by bit to the left as it followed the running of the horse, "and across the street from his butcher shop there was another gent that had another butcher shop as good as his."

As he spoke he fired. The gun recoiled slightly, the shell was ejected, and as the bolt clicked home, I saw that one of the pursuers had ducked flat in the saddle, and now, as he sat up, he was looking wildly about him!

"Don't do it!" I shouted. "Don't do it, Lanky!"

He went on with his story: "And this here friend of mine, he was a biggish-sized gent, and when he seen that the people was going more to the other fellow's store than to his, he got madder and madder, and finally he says that he'll lick any gent that's damn fool enough to go to the butcher shop across the way."

He fired again—and the hat flew off the head of the leader of the bunch!

Straightway he reined in his horse. I could scarcely believe my eyes; horror choked me.

But Lanky went on: "And when the trade stopped coming to

him, the little butcher across the way, he come over with a cleaver and he run my friend out of his shop and clean down through the main street of the town, and finally he run him up a telegraph pole and kept him there till night, and my friend, he hung on till he nearly died, and he says: 'Hey, Mike, will ya listen? I didn't mean no real harm to you nor your customers, but I was only sort of wearying because of the fine beeves that would have to hang up in my shop and nobody whatever to admire them none.'"

Again Lanky fired, and now the whole gang left off their pursuit and scattered here and there, while the three rushed on to a long lead.

"You better get the hosses, brother," said Lanky, "because that whole fourteen, they got the look of folks that mean business. I'll stay here and keep 'em sort of amused as long as I can, d'you see?"

I saw, well enough. The fourteen were stretching out their line from side to side and taking what cover they could. It was plain that they could not continue their original hunt when there was such a murderous skillful marksman playing upon them from the flank, but now it seemed apparently that they were going to try to find out who that marksman was!

Bitterly I regretted that I ever had expressed compassion for the fugitives!

"The rascals," I said to myself while I sprinted for the horses, "they probably do deserve their hanging! Otherwise why would fourteen people be riding after 'em?"

That was my mind on the thing as I got to the horses, and while I flung on the saddles and jerked up the cinches, groaning with fear and snatching in my haste and missing two handholds out of three, I heard the rifle open up again from the side of the shrubbery and maintain a steady fire. Other guns answered Lanky from a distance. Bullets began to crackle like fire through the brush.

I could imagine that Lanky was shooting to keep the gang from spreading out too far on the two sides, and so being able to surround us. Once that happened we were done for, because all the fourteen would need to do would be to touch a match to the grass, let the fire scorch us out, and then they could shoot us to bits as we rode out of the smoke.

I was desperately in haste and making bad time of it, but finally I got the saddles on, and even threw on most of the packs, when Lanky came through the thicket like a bounding deer.

"They're coming on the charge," he said as he leaped into the saddle on the gray horse of Tom Acker's. "They mean business, and we gotta mean the same."

"The bear horse?" I asked.

"Let him go. If he's going to give me any more luck, he'll have to do it at a distance," said Lanky.

And as he talked he was getting the gray under way. We shot crashing out of that thicket and down the farther pitch of the hills, while the two wings of the riders swept around on our flanks, screeching like Indians.

However, we were going like the wind, and it seemed to me that we were fairly riding away from the bullets that they began to fire at us.

Their tired horses were no match for our fresh ones. The gray led by an increasing distance down the first slope and over the flat, but when we hit the up-pitch beyond, the pinto held its own and then began to gain. Which warmed my heart a lot, particularly considering where we were.

Well, I don't think that that pursuit took more than three minutes altogether, because by the end of that time the posse had pulled up its horses—at least, we took it to be a posse—and we were flying away ahead of them down the same valley where the three had ridden.

I looked across at Lanky and saw a great grin fairly splitting his face in two as he pulled the gray back to an easy jog.

"Lanky," said I, "were you shooting to kill?"

"What you think, son?" he asked.

"You knocked a hat off," said I.

He squinted, as though aiming again.

"I was just shaving things a leetle bit too fine," said he.

We turned down the side of the brimming creek, came to a narrow passage along it—and from behind a rock heard a voice say:

"Hands up, gents!"

31

A GUN OUT OF THE AIR

It was too good for even Lanky. There was a sharp cleft in the middle of the rock, and a rifle barrel stuck out clean and clear.

Lanky stopped his horse with a jerk. I made the pinto stand on his heels.

"Get 'em up!" said the rough voice behind the rock.

I hoisted my hands. So did Lanky. When he got his almost shoulder-high, they seemed to be struggling against rising any higher.

"I know them kind of hands," said the voice behind the rock. "They got proud fits. But hoist them hands up, will you?"

And Lanky's hands went up, finally, as high as his shoulders.

At that point they seemed to stick in the air, as though it were thick, and now the man with the rifle stepped out from behind the rock.

He was a middle-sized fellow with a face blackened with unshaven beard, and with the flesh around the eyes sunburned red. A bad pair of eyes were those, though they were now wrinkled with a smile.

"Run right into hot water, brothers, didn't you?"

He dropped the rifle into the hollow of his left arm as he said that, and the next instant something twinkled in the air under the chin of Lanky.

It was a little two-barreled revolver, one of those pocket

beauties that throw a slug as big as a .45. They won't shoot true, and they won't carry any distance, but at point-blank range they'll kill a man as well as a cannon could.

"Freeze!" said Lanky out of one corner of his crooked mouth. "Don't budge."

The black-bearded fellow froze, all right. His jaw swung open on a well-oiled pair of hinges. He only needed to move the muzzle of his rifle a foot to bring it to bear, but the look of Lanky with a gun ready in his hand was not a thing to inspire any confidence, I can tell you. He just looked hungry, and as though the other fellow were meat.

"Just slack that rifle to the ground," said Lanky, "and when you straighten up, friend, lemme see your back, with your hands over your head. Reach for the sky. Get right up on your toes while you're reaching, too."

The other very slowly put down the rifle. I could see a flash in the corner of his eye, and for a full second after the rifle was on the ground he kept his grip on it, but then he seemed to think better of the dodge, and gradually straightened, with his hands high in the air.

"I never seen nothing like it," he complained. "Where'd you pick that gat out of the air?"

Lanky produced his man-sized everyday Colt from his clothes and dropped the little pocket pistol inside the vast, loose collar of his shirt.

He was still flushed. I think he was terribly angered because he had been held up in this way, even though he had turned the tables so quickly.

"Go fan him," he said to me. "Get all his hardware."

I dismounted to do the favor.

"You boys are all wrong," said the black-bearded one. "I was just playing a trick on you."

"A mighty good trick, too," said Lanky. "That trick was all aces, stranger, except that I got a gun out of the air. What's your dodge? Getting yourself a couple hosses?"

"We could use 'em," said the other. "But we ain't that low. We know that you and the gent on the pinto saved our bacons a minute or two back. When we seen you ride out of the brush, it looked like they'd get *you* instead of us, too. But while the boss and my partner cooled off the hosses, I was sent back up the trail to see if you'd come this way—or trouble in place of you. That holdup was just a game, brothers."

He spoke as if he meant it. I had his weapons by this time— they consisted of a pair of big revolvers and *three* knives. One was a little stiletto affair. The sight of its needle point made my heart wince under my ribs. One was a plain clasp knife, but with a blade nearly five inches long. The other was a plain, old-fashioned bowie—a real murder tool!

I had the itches as I looked at that assortment.

"You been used to tough meat at the table, brother, ain't you?" said Lanky.

"Yeah, and all kinds of colors," said the stranger.

He chuckled a little as he spoke, and I admired his nerve.

"Who's your chief?" asked Lanky.

"You don't know, eh?" said the fellow, chuckling again. "You just opened up and fired from the brush for fun, maybe? You just wanted them fourteen to climb your frames for fun—was that it?" He added: "The chief's down the line a little ways. Come along. I guess you wanta be thanked, and I'm damn certain that he wants to thank you. How we were beginning to fry when you boys opened up on that gang of swine!"

He groaned at the memory, so great was his relief from that near danger, and I could sympathize with him.

Lanky stood aside, regarding the other. Then he said:

"It's all right. Give him back his stuff, Nelly. We wouldn't wanta make him show like a fool in front of his boss, would we?"

I was not very willing to do it, and as I hesitated, Lanky surprised me by saying:

"Not that I got any right to give you advice, boss."

"Hey," said the black-bearded one with a snort and a start. "You mean to say that the kid is your boss?"

I was about to protest, also, but I saw Lanky shake his head meaningly at me, and I held my tongue, though I was badly embarrassed.

"Why, brother," said Lanky in return, "you dunno who my side kicker here is, do you?"

"No, I dunno" said the man as I returned his weapons and he began to put them away. Facing me squarely, he looked me over from head to foot with eyes that made me uneasy.

"That's Nelson Grey," informed Lanky.

The man fairly jumped.

"You!" he said.

His eyes rolled.

"What kind of a joke is this here?" he demanded. "Nels Grey is about three times as big as this!"

"Oh, he's big enough, brother, he's big enough," said Lanky, smiling. "When he gets in action he's big enough. He'd fill *your* eye for you."

"Would he?" muttered the fellow doubtfully eying me more darkly than ever.

"Quit it, Lanky!" I said to him, shaking my head.

"There; that's him," said Lanky sadly. "Always shutting me up—never letting me speak a word. I tell you what, Nelly—you give me the chills, the way you're always shutting me up."

"Quit it, Lanky," I said again, embarrassed and half angry as I saw through his game of drawing back behind me and making poor me the important member of our pair.

"All right, I'll shut up," said Lanky. "But you act all the time like nobody knew you, Nelly. You can't possibly get by that way all the time!"

The man shook his head and shrugged his shoulder.

"He left the play to you," he said to Lanky.

"Sure," said Lanky. "With him there to take your attention—I could squeeze by on the side."

"*Him* take my attention?" said the fellow. "Oh, well—"

He let his voice trail off and left his thought unexpressed. Then he said: "Come on along, boys, and meet the chief, because he ain't far from here. He's going to be dog-gone glad to see you." And, turning on his heel, he added over his shoulder: "That was slick. I still don't see how you got that gun out of the air."

"The air is where I grow my guns," said Lanky cheerfully. "Ever since Nelly Grey told me how to do it, and showed me, too."

I half groaned, but Lanky winked broadly at me and grinned with a great inner satisfaction.

The black-bearded man went scuffing down the narrow trail before us, and Lanky had a chance to pull the gray close beside me.

"Watch, kid!" he murmured, with that skill of his in pitching his voice so that it reached only the ears for which it was intended, and no others. "Watch sharp. We're about to see the great Don Pedro, or I'm a goat."

"Here we are," said our guide as we rounded a great boulder that half obscured the trail.

There in the water at the edge of the creek, sloshing down their spent horses to cool them off, I saw a young blond-headed fellow, and close beside him a great, awkward crane of a man—none other than the central one of the trio, whose face was known to me as that of Reginald Channing Carter!

32

DON PEDRO'S GANG

The minute he saw me, that long crane of a man stepped up the bank and came toward me with a grin on his face and his hand held out. I took a back step and said:

"You long-drawn-out drink of poison, what d'you mean by trying to shake hands with me. This is the bird," I added to Lanky, "who tried to have me lynched in the dance hall!"

"Is he?" said Lanky, giving the stranger a hard look.

"Of course I am," said Reginald Channing Carter. "And why? Because I wanted to get him out here, away from people. I wanted to get him for myself. D'you think, my boy, that I would have let them go through with the hanging? Why, I had a dozen men there, waiting for a signal from me. They would have knifed through the gang of fools and got you loose in a minute and carried you off. That was my game, partner. I was going to have you with me or bust, because the first slant that I took at you, I says to myself: 'That's the kind of a gent that Don Pedro would pay his weight in diamonds for!' And look how it's worked out? Here you're with me, and the Don is going to be one happy man when he sees you! That's why I'm reaching my mitt to you, boy!"

He stood there smiling, and his eyes shining at me, and I, all the while hesitating about whether to back away from the contagious nearness of that long claw, or to step right in and flatten his long nose for him and then kick him into the creek.

But Lanky said: "Oh, you're one of Don Pedro's boys, are you, brother?"

"I am," said that long, lean hypocrite instantly. "I'm his friend and his companion, and he's a gent worth having for a friend, you can take it from me! There's a *man!*"

"Why," said Lanky, "everybody's heard about him, but I didn't know that even any of his men knew him very well, and mostly all of 'em never seen anything but his signet ring!"

"Because he can't trust most of the gents that he meets up with," said Reginald Channing Carter. "Fact is, partners, that there ain't very many people in this here world that you can throw in with and know that you're going to come out right. A mighty sad and sour gent is Don Pedro, from some of the experiences that he's had in the world. But you two—you're the kind of meat that he'd want to have with him!"

"Would he?" said Lanky very innocently.

Just then a rattle of hoofs came up the trail beside the creek, and half a dozen riders hove in view around the next bend, going like sixty.

"Let's get out of this, Lanky!" said I.

"It's all right," said Carter with a wide gesture with both hands. "It's all right, boys. Those are friends that are coming. And if they'd come sooner, we wouldn't 'a' had to run so far from Loren Mays and his hired gang. We'd 'a' turned around and ate them up!"

His face changed as he spoke, and I tell you what, he looked hungry, that fellow, and ready to consume some raw meat.

I was turning Pinto, which was as neat-footed as a cat and already pricking his ears, and ready to start like a coiled watch spring because he could sense what I felt by the electric current that runs between a man and the horse he loves, but Lanky amazed me by saying:

"Why, what's the hurry, Nelly—when your friend here says that everything's all right?"

That nearly knocked me out of the saddle—for Lanky to refer to Carter as my "friend." Because, of course, he knew all about what that rascal had tried to do, and how he had raised the crowd against me in Cat Hill when I was in jail.

And yet there was something that stopped me a little— because his ill will had seemed so entirely devilish that I always wondered what malice there could be behind it, and now he had offered a reason for his behavior that was a strange and far-fetched reason, to be sure, but nevertheless a reason.

At any rate, what Lanky proposed to do was good enough for

me. Where he stayed, I had to stay—there were still a good many things about the character of Lanky that I would have to learn!

These fellows from around the bend came whooping down on us while those thoughts went swish through my mind, and as they came, Carter stepped out and held them up with a raised hand.

At that sign they pulled up their horses and stopped them in a length or two, the way cattlemen and range riders knew how to do. It takes a lot out of horseflesh, and human flesh, too, to halt like that, but the fellows prefer to make their halts in just that way.

As they stopped, Carter lighted into them.

"Where in hell were you? Why weren't you five miles up the trail an hour ago, where you were supposed to be?"

"We got the order late," said one of them.

"Why was it late? What was the matter with Bench?" asked Carter.

"His hoss stepped into a hole in the ground and busted his leg and throwed Bench, and he landed hard and busted his collar bone. That's why he ain't along. He had to travel the rest of the way on foot, and though he run all the way till he was near dead, he got there pretty late."

"Busted the collar bone on the right side, and he can't use his gun hand," added another man.

The mouth of Carter writhed a moment before he said: "Harry Wayland is lying back there on the trail, dead, because you boys was late."

"Well," said one, "that's too bad, but Wayland never was much of a hand. There's plenty more where he come from."

"There's plenty more where you're going to, too," said Carter fast and mean, "and maybe you'll start there more pronto than you expect!"

The fellow he told this to was a big, mean-looking chap, but he shut up like a clam when Carter addressed him in this manner. It was fairly plain that Carter held a strong whip hand over the gang. Among the lieutenants of Don Pedro, he must rank very high indeed.

Carter went on in a different tone: "If it hadn't been for these two gents, all the rest of the four of us would have been rode down by Loren Mays and his sneaking hired men, but these here, they stepped out and drew Mays off—the prettiest thing that I ever saw in my life. You should've seen what Lanky and Nelson Grey done to-day when they took fourteen fighting men on their hands for the sake of the three of us."

He turned back to us and said to Lanky: "And Don Pedro is going to hear about it, mind you! You come on with us, now, and whether you want to join up or not, you can stay with us the night and make up your minds in the morning. There's a comfortable camp for all of us not five miles from here!"

I looked at Lanky and tried to get his eye and give him a sign to say no, but I failed completely. Ordinarily, he was as sensitive as could be, and always would feel the weight of an eye; so that I guessed he did not look at me because he *knew* what I would be feeling, and did not wish to have to disregard my sign.

At any rate, I couldn't go counter to him, of course, and the first thing that I knew, we were riding down the trail with that gang of nine outlaws. For every one of them was a man belonging to Don Pedro. You hardly needed to be told that. They looked the part. A meaner, more savage lot I never will see in my life.

There were three Mexicans—or half-breeds—in the lot, and there was one full-blooded Negro with a face made to take the part of a devil in the darkest part of hell. But even he was not so bad to look at as some of the white men. Carter stood all by himself in detestable qualities to me, of course, but some of his companions of the same color ran him a close second. You could see that these men had left behind them everything that is decent in human nature—or, at least, so it seemed to me. I've known outlaws and man-killers, in my time, who were as good a lot as you would care to see. They simply had too much temper for their judgment to balance against. But this crew was different. Any one of them, except perhaps the blond fellow that I referred to a moment ago, looked ready and willing to cut a throat or pick a pocket, or do both things one after another.

We headed down the stream with this gang, and at a place where the creek flattened out to shallows, we crossed over and made an easy fording. All of this way Lanky had been chatting first with one man and then with another, and it seemed plain that he liked the outfit and everything that they suggested to the mind!

After we went up the farther bank of the creek, I found a chance to ride beside him with no one else in easy earshot, and then I laid into him as fast and hard as I could, though in a low voice.

"Lanky, are you crazy?" I demanded.

"Why, what's the matter, Nelly?" he asked.

But by the look in his eyes it seemed to me that I could read that he felt rather guilty and some shame.

"You know what's the matter," I told him. "You've thrown in

here with the hardest lot of cutthroats in the world. It's as bad as murder to be with them at all. For Heaven's sake, Lanky, let's get away from 'em! Let's do it soon, and stay away!"

"I don't understand that, partner," said Lanky. "All of these people are grateful and friendly. We've done them a good turn, and they'll do *us* a good turn now."

I stared at him.

"Lanky," said I, "do you think that there's any kindness or decency or gratitude in the whole of that gang of murderers?"

He turned his head to me with a very odd look in his eyes.

"You know, partner," said he, "that I don't pick up many friends in the world?"

I was silent. I hardly saw what that had to do with the case, unless he were going to add that he felt these bandits would make the proper sort of friends for him.

"Once I had a friend by the name of Ray Joyce," he went on. "He was about as good a friend as I ever had. He was about as good a friend as any man *could* have. And one day he disappeared, and nobody ever heard a word of him since that time. Well, I've always had an idea that the gang of Don Pedro—which was playing up a good deal about that time—might have accounted for him. I've always had that feeling down in my bones. And now's my chance to find out."

"What'll you be able to do if you manage to find out?" I asked, both horrified and curious.

"I might be able to kill a good few," said Lanky cheerfully. He added: "There's another thing."

"What's that?" I asked.

"You remember what we were talking about back there in the brush?"

"Not exactly," said I. "There have been a good many bullets between me and my ideas in that camp!"

"We were talking about Don Pedro," he said. "And what could be as pat as this, I'm asking you? We talk about the chance of catching Don Pedro, and a minute later we're in the midst of his gang. Ain't that a sign?"

"A sign of what? A sign of trouble," said I.

"A sign that the luck is going to be with us, and we'll be able to pay Don Pedro against everything that you owe the world—or the world thinks that you owe it!"

He snapped his fingers as he spoke.

"And even suppose that we don't win either of the points that I been speaking about," went on Lanky, "look at the game that we got before us—look at the beautiful time we're going to have, partner, will you?"

33

OUTLAW STRONGHOLD

Altogether it was a pretty picture that Lanky's conversation gave me. He was to attempt to locate the men who had killed his friend, Ray Joyce, and if successful, he was to try to pay off that old debt. Furthermore, he and I were to endeavor to spot the great and famous Don Pedro, and when we located him, the idea was that we were to fold him up, put him in a vest pocket, and, riding to the governor of the State, say to him: "What about a free pardon for young Nelson Grey even before he's tried, in exchange for the possession of the famous Don Pedro?"

Yes, that was the scheme which Lanky had broached to me, and whether it failed or no, we would be repaid by the wonderful time that we would have while playing around with this gang of cutthroats!

Yes, I was beginning to step farther and farther into the intricacies of Lanky's nature, and I must say that I was finding myself lost in a jungle!

What was play to him was walking a tight wire a thousand feet above nothing. It was not play to most other people, beginning with myself!

In the meantime, I took closer and closer stock of the gang we were riding with. I had to dismount to tighten the cinch of the pinto, and while I was doing that—and I took my time—I noticed that two of the toughest of the lot remained to the rear of me, apparently finding enough to wonder at in the shape of a twisted pine tree to cause them to draw rein.

But there was no doubt in my mind that Carter had given them word not to let me drift out of the party. And if I had prolonged my stay, I felt certain that they would have prolonged theirs under one pretext or another. Perhaps they would actually join me.

At any rate, after I mounted and went on, it was not ten seconds before they were under way and trailing after me, and I noticed all through the ride that the two resolutely remained together. In the nature of things, a five-mile ride through rough country, and a great deal of it over no trail at all, shuffles a party about like a pack of cards in play. But the two of them remained all the while as a sort of rear guard, and I knew perfectly well that they were there by appointment. One of them was the Negro with the nightmare face.

We covered the five miles without any sign of the sheriff's men coming up behind us—which was one way I hoped that our cozy little party might be broken up, so that I could have a legitimate excuse to slip away from them—and finally we came on the wreckage of an adobe village. There were trees sweeping up to it on all sides in a regular sea, so that there was no good excuse for using dobe brick, except that the first inhabitants were so used to that material that they couldn't think of houses in the terms of any other building stuff.

That was all long ago. Now there was hardly a roof intact. The houses were spilled down to the street, and the rains of several generations had been melting them away, so that some were no more than just smooth-backed mounds, though others had stood the gaff in better style, and trees and small shrubs grew everywhere about the ruins. Only the walls of one place were reasonably intact, and that was the "fort." At least, it seemed to be that, as well as the residence of the chief man of the place in the old days. It was pretty broken-shouldered and weak-kneed, at that, but it kept together enough to have a certain amount of dignity, and, compared with the one-room huts of the rest of the village, it certainly looked like a giant.

There was an arched entrance, and as our leaders came out, a pair of ragged boys ran out from the shadows, waved their hands, and darted back inside. We rode through that same archway, and I saw that it was sagging to one side, as though it were ready to fall to pieces. Inside was a big patio, with a wrecked arcade running around it. The pillars of that arcade were not built of the dobe bricks, but were composed of rough stones, cemented together, so that while the roof had fallen in here and there, the pillars were only minus some of the top stones.

A Mexican came hurrying out to greet us, and he salaamed like a Turk to Carter. That gawk had stepped out of his saddle to the ground, and he began to fire some snappy orders and directions that soon had everybody busy.

Some of them stabled the horses, and others looked after the feeding and watering of them, and others broke up some firewood, while the whole Mexican family that lived in this caricature of a castle was chattering and scampering and singing in the kitchen, getting food ready.

But as for Lanky and me, Carter got us under his wing and conducted us into the main room of the place.

There was a good deal of dignity about that hall—for it was big enough to deserve the name. It must have been twenty feet high to the ceiling, and more than halfway up the side of it a balcony was bracketed out from the walls, and ran around the bedroom doors. The raining was intact, and it was a fine bit of hammered iron that would have been worth a price in any city. There were other fine bits, such as patches of colored tiles let into the walls here and there, and a pattern of big copper nailheads on the doors. There were more tiles in the recessed window places, and the windows themselves were guarded on the outside with grilles. Best of all, because the place was damp and a cold mountain wind was beginning to hum and whistle in the corners of it, there was a great fireplace that a dozen men could have stood up in—yes, and lifted their hands above their heads.

That fireplace was soon working. For the men brought in a monster of a log for a back piece, and then built up a fire that volleyed and thundered up the chimney all evening long.

All this while that scoundrel of a Carter was sitting talking to Lanky and me, and I was nodding, and Lanky was talking back.

Most of the time Lanky talked about Don Pedro, and wanted to know what sort of a fellow he was, because he said that he was not fool enough to believe all the newspaper reports and the gossip that one hears about an important man.

Carter struck in on that word.

"Important, that's what he is," said Carter. "And looka here—if he wasn't a man, and a decent man, at bottom, would so many men foller him till they dropped?"

"Why, no," said Lanky, "though I been hearing all along that once in the gang, a man ain't *allowed* to leave it."

"Nobody wants to," said Carter. "The fact is that the boys have too good a time, and make too much money, and are let out on their own so much that not a one of 'em ever wants to break away."

"Is that so?" said Lanky, nodding his head like a fool who would believe anything.

"Yeah," said Carter, "that's the truth. Them that ride with Don Pedro ride free and fair and far, lemme tell you!"

I listened with a good deal of concern to the talk, and the way that Lanky was appearing to take it in, but it seemed clear to me that he was really interested in this talk about freedom.

Carter went on: "Little jobs, little fool ten-cent jobs, they ain't the kind that Don Pedro goes after. No, sir; you never hear any cheap job blamed on to the shoulders of him and his men. Sometimes there'll be three months, four months, and not a hand to lift. The boys can just lay around. If they run out of money on a few sprees and spend all the cash that they made on the last job, what difference does that make? Don Pedro, he's got an open pair of hands. He don't let the left hand know what the right hand gives away. No, sir; to a gent with a nature as big and wide and deep as Don Pedro's, the thing that counts is to have his men satisfied, and after that he lays in and gives the boys something to do that's worth doing. When he makes a plan, it's a plan. It means hundreds of thousands, likely. It's a job to fill a man's imagination first, and his hands afterward. The size of the job will never hold him back. And when he starts to take the cream, he takes a ton of it, enough to last a while."

"What sort of a looking man is he?" asked Lanky.

"Him?" said Carter. "He ain't so much to look at. He ain't pretty. But he's got the brains, and the brains are what counts, I'd say."

"Yeah, I'd say that they're what count," agreed Lanky, nodding his head.

I looked at the pair of them as they talked about brains, and wondered that two such ugly men could be gathered together at one time and place.

"I've heard that there's a way of spotting Don Pedro," said Lanky.

"Have you?" asked the tall man with a start. "What way?"

"Why, by the scars on his back."

"Humph!" said Carter. "I dunno that I never heard about that, and yet I've heard a good deal about Don Pedro. What kind of scars, then, would they be?"

"The scars made by a wet rope end," said Lanky. "Down

there in the Valle Nacional, in Mexico, they tell a story about him. They say that they had Don Pedro there and that he didn't want to work, and that they give him what they give the rest of the slaves that hang back."

"What's that?" asked Carter.

He humped himself over and hugged his bony knees with his long arms, and his eyes winked fast, like the eyes of a bird.

"Why," said Lanky, "they line the poor devils up in the morning—I've seen it myself—and after they're in line, if one of 'em needs disciplining, another gent takes him astride his back, and his clothes are peeled off, and then the whipping expert, he steps up with a rope that's been soaked till it's heavy with water, and he begins to slam that whip into the naked man. The time I seen it, the gent that owned the plantation was standing by, and he puffs at his cigar slow and leisurely, and every time that he lets out a puff, *wham!* goes the whip. The first coupla lashes they raised their welts, and the third brought out little pin points of blood. After that the blood started to run. Along about the ninth or tenth stroke, the poor devil I seen, he begun to moan a little, and about the twelfth he begun to howl like a wolf. He was a Yaqui, and they're iron, but even iron can't stand that kind of pounding very long. He howled like a poor dog. And the plantation owner seemed to like that. He begun to smile and smoke his cigar a little faster, and part of the time he looked at the gent that was being flogged, and part of the time he looked at the rest of the slaves, because those slaves were all shuddering as though a cold wind was blowing on 'em. Most of 'em had had that medicine before their ownselves, and most of them would catch it ag'in."

Carter had half closed his eyes, and he was nodding his long, hideously white face.

"Did they say that Don Pedro got that kind of medicine?" he asked.

"Yeah," said Lanky. "They say that he got it day after day, till he went and crawled on his hands and knees, not being able to walk, and licked the hand of the fellow that had been beating him. Anyway, if he got even one flogging of that kind, the scars would stay with him for life—big, broad, white scars. I seen plenty of 'em while I was there."

Carter was silent for a moment, still nodding his head.

"In the Valle Nacional," he said, "every one dies. No one ever escapes."

"Yeah," said Lanky. "One in a thousand gets away. And Don Pedro happens to be one in a thousand, I guess."

Carter lifted his head suddenly, as though from a dream.

"That's a fair thing to say," he agreed. "Yeah, I'd say that Don Pedro is one in a thousand. But about them scars—why, I wouldn't have the nerve to ask him to peel off his shirt and show 'em to me. Don Pedro, you gotta know, is a man with a whole lot of dignity about him. He ain't any ordinary kind of a man at all!"

"Sure," said Lanky. "But I'm thinking that if he's ever caught, that's one way he could be spotted as the real Don Pedro—by the scars."

"Aye, but who knows if the story is true?" said Carter suddenly.

"I dunno," said Lanky, "but I heard it myself. I guess that a lot of people have heard it besides me. How about you, partner?"

I searched my mind, and then remembered. "Yes," I said. "I've heard something about scars on his back, but never about the Valle Nacional."

34

THE MAN-EATERS

The fire was now roaring up in the chimney, and the flare of the light was brighter than the radiance that came in through the windows from the sunset. The shadows from the fire went dancing in waves along the walls and over the ceiling. Carter got up and put his back close to the blaze and spread out his hands to it, though even where I was sitting, back from it, the heat was searing my skin. But Carter, like a white snake, seemed to need continual thawing.

"About Don Pedro crawling and kissing the hand of him that flogged him—" he muttered.

"Not kissing it—but licking it," said Lanky, "same as the overseer told him to do. That was to break his spirit, but he got away before they killed him."

"It's hard for me to see Don Pedro doing a thing like that," said Carter. "But nobody can tell—nobody can tell. When we going to eat around here!"

He roared out in a high, ringing, nasal voice: "Hurry it up! Hurry it up!"

They hurried it up, well enough, and pretty soon all of the men were in the room, and the food began to come in, and the crowd gathered around the table. It was a rough sort of a meal. There was a kid roasted in two halves, and each half laid on a big wooden board.

A fellow would come up to one of the roasted portions and slice off half a dozen ribs with his bowie knife, and then he'd lay that on top of a stack of wet tortillas and go on to a big caldron that was filled with soup. In that soup there was chicken that had been torn up and thrown in in chunks, a quarter of a chicken at a time, and there were vegetables, like cabbage. A man would take the big, black, iron ladle that stuck out of the pot, and into huge earthenware bowls, of which there were numbers scattered about on the table, he would ladle as much as he wanted. Into another bowl he might put a lot of hot Mexican beans, cooked with peppers and pork.

Then he would sit where he chose. He might pull a stool up to the table, but most of them had lived out so much that they seemed to prefer sitting cross-legged on the floor, at the distance from the fire that pleased them. They dumped the water out of their canteens and filled them from a bucket of red wine, and drank this with their meal.

Lanky and I followed the example of the others, and I don't think that I ever tasted anything better in the line of food, because for a long time—up to the canned-goods feast—Lanky and I had been eating chiefly hard-tack and roasted meat, which is a diet that one tires of.

We had other company, in the shape of a number of big mongrel dogs that wandered in and looked a cross between mastiff and greyhound. Man-eaters they appeared to me, and they skulked around, and their eyes watered and their mouths slavered at the scent of the food. They got the bones. When a man had stripped a joint, he would throw the bone in the air, and everybody yelled and whooped as the dogs made a rush for it, and there was a grand fight until one of the dogs won and went over to a corner to let its wounds stop bleeding while it chewed up the bone. Then one of the men would get tired of his soup and push out his bowl toward a dog that he favored, and that lucky dog would lap up the soup with its big red tongue, wagging its tail, and splashing the soup around a good deal.

Altogether, it was a wild sort of a scene, particularly with the roaring fire and the shadows that flung out from it. And as the sunset light died out, the fire red came on the faces of the men. I've said before that they were a villainous lot, but daylight flattered them; firelight brought out the true devilishness of the crew.

They made me feel young—younger than a baby. It seemed as though I knew nothing, and had been nowhere. There was not a man there, I'm sure, who had not killed one or two fellows.

And if there was, he was ashamed of it, I know. All, perhaps, except the blond-headed young fellow who was tending to the fire and being useful as a roustabout here and there. He did no regular eating, but now and then snatched a bit and munched it as he stood, slim and graceful, black against the yellow uprush of the flames from the hearth. He was a good-looking youth, with a fine head placed well and carried well. But there was something cynical about his fine features, and there was a keen, bold stare in his eyes as he looked the men over. He might turn out the worst of the lot; he might be the worst already, for that matter.

These scoundrels paid a good deal of attention to me, at first. A couple of the worst-looking picked out places near the corner that I had chosen, and tried to draw me out into talk. One of them got up and brought me a specially fine section of roast ribs, saying that what I had was not fit for a dog. Another filled a tin cup with wine for me. They wanted me to talk about my exploits. They referred to the killing of Josh Acker, and the escape from the jail made their eyes shine when they mentioned it. But I would not talk, so they left me, and got closer to noise and good-fellowship. I was left quite alone, and back in the shadows.

After the main eating had been done, the drinking and the talking started in. And presently there was the voice of Lanky, and the rest were silent, listening to the new companion.

The very first words that he said caught my breath and my attention.

"Speaking of low-down hounds, the worst that I ever knew was a fellow by name of Ray Joyce," he began.

I wondered at the words, because I could remember that Lanky had told me Ray Joyce had been his best friend. Now he was calling him a hound!

"Who was he? Who was Ray Joyce?" asked one of the men.

"He was one of them open-faced gents with yaller hair and blue eyes, like a girl. But man-sized, with a pair of shoulders that looked fine when he was swinging at a double jack. He had a hearty way about him, and he looked you in the eye when he talked. But inside he was a sneak and a skunk. I was raised close to him. I know him twenty years, pretty near, before I found out the truth about him. And that was when he double-crossed me. We were crossing Owen's Desert—"

"That's a sweet part of hell," broke in some one.

"It is," said Lanky solemnly. "And it was August, at that, and we'd made a dry camp, like everybody has to, halfway across. We camped on two canteens of water—one for coffee, and one to drink straight. And immediately after we camped, the hoss that Ray Joyce was riding got scared of something and started to run, and tied up his legs in his hobbles and came down with a crash. He never got up again. He'd smashed a foreleg below the knee, and we had to shoot him.

"That left one hoss for the two of us, and eighty-five miles of hell between us and the hills. And the question was, would we try to sleep a couple of hours, being dead beat, or strike right on through the cool of the night? We decided to rest and sleep a while, mostly because I had a sore leg from a boil, and was wore out from the pain of riding the day before. Well, sir, I went to sleep, and when I woke up, with the moon on one side of my face and the pink of the morning on the other side, Ray Joyce was gone. Yes, sir, I was alone in the desert, with eighty-five miles of hell before me and no hoss, and no water and a game leg!" He snarled as he finished.

"You came through, eh?" said Carter sympathetically, and a general murmur of disgust came from even those man-eaters all around the big room.

"I came through—just," said Lanky. "I nearly went crazy—but I come through, all right. And ever since then I been looking around to find the trail of Ray Joyce, but I never come onto it. And that's a funny thing, because he was the sort of a gent that people could remember dead easy, no matter where he went. But I never come onto any trace of him."

"Hold on," said Carter. "How long ago d'you say that was?"

"Why, about three years."

"And how was you crossing the desert?"

"I was drifting east across it."

"Then he likely went on to the hills east of it, eh?"

"Yeah, that's about it."

"Well," said Carter with a strange smile, "I could tell you what happened to him, all right."

"I'd like to know that!" said Lanky.

A door at the end of the room slammed. A light, rapid step crossed the floor, and then there was an exclamation.

I looked up, vaguely remembering that voice, and on the edge of the firelight, seeming to sway up and down in the waves of it, I saw Tom Acker standing!

35

DEVIL'S JOKE

Of course, the sight of him explained a good many things to me. It explained how it was that he never had any regular employment, but always had plenty of money to spend as he pleased. It explained, too, why he disappeared at odd intervals, and generally was very well heeled when he came back. He was simply one of Don Pedro's men!

He seemed to be one of the most prized of them, too, because there was a general and hearty chorus of greeting for him. But what had stopped him was the sight of Lanky at the table, near long-geared Reginald Channing Carter, whose black hat was pushed back from his lean, white face, but never removed from his head.

A sudden, dark thought jumped through my mind—suppose that Tom Acker were Don Pedro?

That thought was banished by what immediately followed.

"Who let that into the house?"

"What's the matter?" asked Carter. "What's biting you, Tom?"

"You let that hound in here, did you?" demanded Tom Acker. "Well, I'm glad he's here. Because I've got a long score to settle up with him, I can tell you!"

"Settle with who?" asked Carter. "With Lanky?"

"You can settle it right now by coming around the table and shaking hands with him," said Carter.

I was astonished that he dared to use that tone of authority to a man of Tom Acker's reputation.

"Shake hands with him? I'll see him and the rest of you damned, first," said Tom Acker. "That hound—"

Carter jumped to his feet. He was so tall that it seemed he never would stop rising.

He stretched out his gaunt arm.

"Keep your hands away from your guns, Acker," he shouted, "and come around here! You'll see us all damned, will you? I tell you, as long as Don Pedro gives me his ring, I'll run this crowd, and I'll run you, because you're in it."

"Carter," said Tom Acker, "you're pushing this game pretty far."

"I'll push it farther," said Carter. "There ain't a man in the world that Don Pedro puts a bigger value on than he does on you, Acker, and you got reason to know it. But if you start raising hell agin' my orders, I'll hang you to the first tree, and I'm here to tell you so!"

Acker stood stiff with anger and with indecision.

Carter went on, to let him down more easily: "You come around here and shake hands. Lanky is going to be one of the best we ever had. He and Grey saved my hide to-day, and the hides of two more of us."

"The kid's here, too, eh?" said Acker, jerking his head to this side and that until he spotted me.

I wanted to fade through the wall behind me when that panther's glance fixed on me at last.

"You'll shake with him, too," said Carter, "if I tell you to. Don't be a fool, Tom. You know it's all for one and one for all. That's the old rule of the game. Come around here and act up like what you are—a man!"

Acker finally rounded the table and stood close to Lanky, but Lanky shook his head.

"I'm not shaking hands with him, Carter," he said. "Not till I'm in the crowd. If I'm in, I'm in. But I ain't in till my chief gives me the word. And until he gives me the word, I'd rather cut the throat of Acker than to shake hands with him."

"Hold on," said Carter. "You fellows mean to say that you ain't made up your minds? What about it, Grey?"

I thought that my voice would never come. To refuse definitely was probably to put our necks in the noose. We had seen too many of these fellows close up. We had penetrated too far into their organization, and now, if we decided to stay out from the gang, our shrift would probably be a very short one.

On the other hand, how could we join them, pledge our hands to them, call them companions, admit the laws of their murderous gang?

Finally I said: "Why, Carter, you fellows seem to be a hand-picked lot. That's true, but on the other hand, there's something to be made by playing a lone hand in the world. We'll need the night for thinking it over."

"Oh, will you?" exclaimed Carter. "The night?"

"And in the morning," said Tom Acker, "they won't be here!"

"Oh, won't they?" said Carter. "You aim to read a gent better than I can, do you, Acker?"

"Figure it out for yourself," said Acker insolently.

I saw the head of Carter go down between his shoulders like that of a mud crane after it has swallowed a frog. And never did I see more wickedness than that which contorted his face for an instant. Then he seemed to master himself.

"You can claim to be as good a man as I am, and maybe you're a lot better," said Carter. "Only, I carry the ring from Don Pedro. And while I'm the boss of this lot, they hop when I tell 'em to hop, and sit still when I tell 'em to sit still. We'll have no brawling inside the gang. If these two ain't inside now, they'll be inside in the morning—"

"Or?" said Tom Acker.

"Oh, they'll come in with us, all right," declared Carter, looking first at Lanky and then into the shadows toward me. "They'll think it over and see what fools they'd be if they didn't grab a chance like this."

"But suppose that they don't join?" asked Acker insistently.

"What's the use being disagreeable?" returned Carter. "If Lanky won't shake hands, let it go and set down and fill your face. There's something you can say that'll make a lot of difference to the way that Lanky feels about you. I can tell you that."

Acker went gloomily toward the food and began to pick up some cold remnants here and there.

"What can I tell him that he'll be glad to know?" he asked.

"Why, man," said Carter, "you remember in the hills near to Owen's Desert, when we met up that evening with the gent on the gray hoss?"

"Oh, him?" said Acker.

"Yeah, him," said Carter, grinning. "He was the worst enemy that Lanky ever had, and had just double-crossed him in the desert. Took the only hoss between the pair of 'em."

"Did he?" said Acker. "Well, that kind of changes things, I'd say."

"Yeah, sure it changes things—and how much!" said Carter. "Go on and tell him. That was pretty slick, anyway!"

Tom Acker sat on the edge of the table, swinging one leg and laughing a little as he remembered.

"Carter and me were on a scouting trip," he said. "And we'd scouted close enough to trouble to lose a horse. We were coming along with one of us in the saddle an hour and then the other, and when we saw that fellow coming, all we could see was the gray broncho he was riding, which was a mighty prime gelding."

"Yeah, and it was," said Lanky.

"It was," said Tom Acker, "because I tried it plenty, afterward. We seen the horse, as I said, and we aimed to get it. So we hailed the rider and fell into talk with him. He seemed to be in a mighty hurry, and when we stopped to swap the time of day with him, he said something about a partner in trouble—and that he had to get to help. He'd left a partner in trouble, all right, if what you say is true, Lanky. Well, sir, here comes the funny part. He starts off away from us, and Carter, he says: 'How far you traveling, partner?'

"'I'm traveling down to Owensville,' said this man Joyce— because we'd got his name out of him while he was talking. He was one of those fools that can't keep anything to himself.

"'You're likely to go farther than Owensville, I'd say,' said Carter, here.

"'Farther?' said Joyce, turning around in the saddle. 'How far do you mean?'

"'As far as hell!' says Carter, here, and shoots him right between the eyes. He didn't say a word. He just did a flop, and we rolled him over the lip of the cliff into the creek beyond, and took the gray and moved along!"

As he remembered this witticism he laughed, and Carter laughed loudly, also, and his little, eager eyes darted this way and that, searching for appreciation.

He got it, too. It wasn't just the muffled laughter because of the fact that the chief of the gang had played the leading part; it was a wide, deep roar of mirth that came from the bottom of the heart. That was just the sort of a joke that these devils could understand.

Carter, when he saw that the jest went home, could hardly contain himself; he gripped the edge of the table with both hands and reeled from side to side.

"Yeah," he went on, "that's what I said to him: 'As far as hell!' says I, and lets him have it, *blam*, right between the eyes. That was so close to the middle of his forehead, I couldn't have picked out the spot better if I'd had a compass, could I, Tommy?"

"No," said Acker, wiping the tears of pleasure out of his eyes, "you couldn't 'a' come closer to the middle. But it wasn't the shooting that tickled me. It was the lingo that you had on tap."

"Well," said Carter to Lanky, "whacha think of that?"

Lanky was looking up from one face to the other with a grin.

"Why, I think it was slick," he said. "You told him where he was going, and then you sent him."

He put back his head and laughed. I thought that his twisted face was the ugliest thing that I had even seen.

"Hypocrite!" I thought to myself.

"Yeah, I told him, and then I sent him," agreed Carter. "You better shake with Tommy on that, maybe? And maybe me, too?"

"Why," said Lanky, standing up and stretching himself, "I'd shake with all of you fellows, and glad to—and to-morrow morning I suppose that I will. But you see how it is? Grey's been dragging me all over the face of the landscape, and I'm tired; it's the hay for me. And if he says the word in the morning, I'll step inside the gang and never step out again!"

36

BLONDY

I got up to go with Lanky. Tom Acker saw me, and he stepped toward me, saying: "Remember—there's something between us, Grey, that's going to come out, one of these days!"

I don't know what happened to me. My head went crazy. I saw myself back on the old job, a respectable member of the community. I saw my old future stretching straight ahead of me, clear and clean—and then the confounded Ackers and the Porsons had worked together to throw me down into the dirt.

I took a stride to Tom Acker and caught his arm, his right arm, just above the wrist.

"You're a dirty rat, Acker," I said. "I always thought so. I'm glad I bumped off your brother. I'm going to have a chance to do the same for you. And—"

Long arms wound around me and jerked me back. It was Lanky, who was gasping:

"Get out of here, Acker, or he'll have one of his crazy fits in a minute, and then your life ain't worth a spoiled nickel. Get out, while I can hold him!"

He yelled this out in such a desperate way, that Acker took two or three running steps back, and the whole gang got up to watch the fun.

"I'm all right," I said to Lanky, rather bewildered by the heat that had come up in me. "I won't try to touch him—"

"Not now, eh? All right," said Lanky. "Let's turn in."

He kept hold of me in an anxious way, while he said this.

"No more of this, boys!" Carter bawled out. "Blondy, show those gents upstairs. There's a decent room on the east side. Good night, boys!"

We waved to them all, and went out of the big hall, with the blond-headed young fellow walking before and showing us the way. So we climbed up to the floor above on a stairs that had a crumbling banister. And in the hallway of the second floor, "Blondy" pushed open a door, and held up the lantern that he had brought along to light the way.

He came in behind us, and closed the door behind him.

"How is this, gentlemen?" he asked. "Anything else I can do for you?"

He hung the lantern on a nail as he spoke. And as I was looking around at the ruins of the big chamber, with the huge double bed, built like a house, at one side, backed up against the wall, but a little out of line with it, I heard Lanky say:

"There's one thing more that you could do for *me*, youngster."

"Yes, sir?" said Blondy smartly.

"What brought you into a hell like this?" asked Lanky, to my amazement.

Blondy said nothing.

"I'm asking you what pulled you in," said Lanky.

"How d'you mean?" demanded Blondy. "What sort of kidding is this?" he continued, with an attempt at a laugh.

"Why," said Lanky, "she didn't mean it, after all. Not half what she said. She was only stringing you along. She thought that she'd get a reaction, but she didn't have any idea that you'd take her so serious."

Blondy stared as though he were looking at a crazy man. I was staring the same way. I could feel my eyes popping out with the strain, in fact.

"Great guns!" said Blondy. "What d'you know?"

"Everything," said Lanky.

"Such as what?"

"Such as that she's ready to fall into your arms, brother, as soon as you'll come back."

"You saw the letter," said Blondy fiercely. "You saw the letter before it got to me. They all saw it! That's why they've been laughing at me up their sleeves, these last days. Oh, damn the lot of you!"

Lanky smiled at him as he raved.

"I didn't see any letter, kid," said Lanky.

"You did," said the young fellow, "or you wouldn't know."

"I don't know anything," said Lanky. "I'm only guessing."

"You lie," cried Blondy. "You're trying to make a fool out of me! But I'll have the heart out of you, if you speak about her again."

"Why shouldn't I speak about her?" Lanky asked. "She's what you think about, all the time."

"I've never mentioned her! Who the devil are you?" asked Blondy, who seemed between a towering rage and the shakes.

"Why," said Lanky, "in spite of my face, I'm a gent that's been young myself, and that's been in love. Why don't you go back to her, brother? Why don't you go back and pull out of this mess?"

"I can't go back," said Blondy, his voice shaking, and his eyes wild. "I can't go back, because—well, you'll see—once you're in, you never can get out. You're stuck for good. Other fellows have tried to get away from Don Pedro. They never make it. They're blotted out. That's all."

"Come with us," said Lanky.

"*You* think that you can get away?" said the young fellow, half sneering. "You think that there ain't a watch over you? Aye, and every minute! Nobody comes in this far and is let loose!"

"We're going back to-night," said Lanky, with a wonderful calmness.

He smiled on Blondy in a way that made me forget the ugliness of his face. "You come with us, Blondy," he said.

"It's a frame," muttered Blondy. "You and Carter have worked it out to try me and test me. That's all it is."

"It might be that, too," said Lanky. "You'll have to use your own brains to see what it really is."

Blondy was plainly staggered. His eyes went this way and that.

I couldn't help saying: "Don't make any mistake, Blondy. Old Lanky is all gold. The straightest that ever was made!"

Blondy broke out, after a glance at me: "How d'you know so much, Lanky—about *her*, and everything?"

While I wondered, Lanky said:

"Why, Blondy, a look at you shows that you've had fathering and mothering. And when you talk, you talk school language, like Nelly here. What would turn a kid like you wrong? A little stealing that you were caught in? No, not likely. *Little* steals ain't what you're made for. Big stealing you weren't ready for. A killing? Yes, maybe that, or because there was a girl mixed up with you. She gave you the rough side of her tongue. You decided that your life was a bust, and you went out to go wild. Isn't that about right?"

Blondy ran a hand through his hair, and it stood up on end.

"Whatever's the truth," he said, "it's too late for me."

Lanky answered with a gentleness that still comes in at my ear and lives somewhere about my heart:

"Life is never too late, Blondy, as long as we're right in time."

Blondy dropped his head.

"Maybe you're right," he said. "And—she wrote just what you said—she wants me back again. It was all a mistake—I'm a fool and a hound, but I can't turn back. They'd get me, sure."

"What if they do?" Lanky asked. "Ain't it better to be tagged with a few slugs of lead than to go on living in hell? Death can't be any worse than living with devils like this bunch."

The young fellow suddenly raised his head, and I saw that he was calm, and I knew, by that, that he had made up his mind, and that he was of better metal than I, for one.

"What are you and Grey here for?" he asked.

"I'll tell you, Blondy," said Lanky, "and put every card on the table. You heard my yarn about Ray Joyce?"

"I couldn't forget what that hound did to you."

"He was the whitest man in the world," said Lanky. "He never was a hound. Lemme tell you. My yarn was straight, up to the point where I said I woke up in the morning and found Joyce gone with the hoss. Joyce was gone, all right, but the hoss was there! He knew that I wasn't fit to walk. He left the hoss for me, and hiked on foot that eighty-five miles of damnation. I rode after him. I couldn't catch up. My leg was all inflamed. I had a fever. I could hardly sit the saddle, when finally I caught up with him on the edge of the hills. He got me stretched out in some shade, and then, dead as he was from that march, he climbed into the saddle, and rode off to find help for me. He didn't find help. He found Carter's little joke, instead!"

As he paused, all the blood seemed to be frozen to a stop in me.

Blondy was silent a moment, too. Then he said:

"You *are* telling it straight. I can see that."

"You ask why we come here?" said Lanky. "We come here hoping to find Don Pedro. Anyway, we're going to kill Acker and Carter before we go back. Then would you want to ride with us?"

"Yes," said the young fellow, quick as a wink. "I'd ride to hell and back, with white men! And you're right. If I'm shot up, what difference does it make? I haven't gotten my hands dirty, as yet, living with 'em. I'll burn some gunpowder to keep my hands clean to the finish."

"I knew you had the stuff in you," said Lanky.

"Only, I want to help," said Blondy.

"You *can* help," answered Lanky.

"Tell me how."

"Go out there and saddle up some horses in the barn. Take half a dozen of the best, so that we can have a change of horses, because if we do what we wanta do, there's going to be some tall riding, around here. Go out there, and do that job, and then stay there and wait."

"I have to fill up their filthy canteens with wine," said Blondy. "And then I'll go out and do what you say. I—"

He came to a halt.

Then he went to Lanky and wrung his hand. He came to me, and looked carefully into my face, and shook me by the hand, too.

"Whatever happens, it'll be worth it," he said. And then he walked out of the room.

He had not been gone half a minute, and Lanky and I had hardly had a chance to move from our last positions, when the door was thrown open, and in stepped that long crane of a man, Reginald Channing Carter, with a furtive look in his eyes, and a cruel set to the mouth.

"What's that kid been saying to you?" he demanded, looking at Lanky and then at me.

37

A TRAITOR

The moment that he spoke, I wanted to say to Lanky: "Look out! He knows something. Maybe he knows everything." But Lanky was already talking, with a chuckle.

"Well, Carter," he started, "I thought that you was man enough to run your gang, and run it right, but this don't look like it."

"What don't look like it?" demanded Carter.

"And you're the gent that has the ring of Don Pedro, ain't you?" asked Lanky, still grinning.

He sat down on the edge of the table that was in the middle of the room and swung one leg, and made a cigarette that he lighted, still laughing.

"I've got Don Pedro's ring," said Carter, in a hard, steady voice. "And what about it?"

"Oh, nothing much," said Lanky, "except that that kid ain't going to be with you long."

"Oh, ain't he?" asked Carter, in the same voice of iron.

"No," said Lanky, "he's going to run with us."

"Oh, you're going to run, are you?" asked Carter, in the same manner.

"Yeah," Lanky said, chuckling, "the kid thinks that we're going to run to-night sometime, and that he's going to run with us."

He drew in a great breath of smoke, and inhaled it, and exhaled it with a laugh that knocked the issuing smoke cloud to rags and tatters.

I watched the face of Carter, covertly, and saw that there was a new expression in his eyes—a new expression, mingled with doubt.

In the meantime, I was staggered by what I had heard Lanky say. It appeared that he, also, shared my impression that Carter might have overheard some of our talk. But I was amazed and sickened to think that he would take advantage of that suspicion in order to betray Blondy, while the impression of Blondy's grip must still be tingling in his hand.

Lanky went on: "I just thought I'd try the weakest link in your chain, Carter, before we throwed in with you, and I'll tell you what, if you don't mind straight talk—your chain ain't worth a damn, because that kid ain't for you!"

He snapped his fingers loudly in the air, as he made the last remark.

I saw Carter grip his teeth hard.

"I heard—" he began, and then changed to: "I know enough to know that—the young cur! I'm going to make him an example, Lanky, that the boys of the gang'll remember for quite a spell. The way that I take it," he went on, "an example is needed, now and then."

"Well," agreed Lanky, "maybe you're right, at that."

"It's like in school," said Carter. "You see a word. You get it defined for you, too. But then you gotta find it used in a sentence before you know really what it is."

"You've had your schooling, too," said Lanky gravely. "By the way you handle words, a gent could see that, Carter. That's what I noticed about you before."

"Did you?" said Carter dubiously.

"Aw, you know how it is," said Lanky. "One gent can talk, and another can't. I was kind of wondering, a coupla times I heard you, why you never took up with politics."

There was the gradual dawning of a smile on the face of Carter. And then he said: "Why, I had leanings that way, when I was a kid, but I found things that paid better."

"Like Don Pedro, eh?" said Lanky.

"Well, why not?" asked Carter. "That young hound of a kid—I'm going to burn him up."

"Why not?" returned Lanky. "I've heard 'em howl, before this, when there was fire put to their feet. He'll think of a lot of words."

He put back his head, and laughed heartily. So did Carter, and as I looked at those two ugly men, with their heads tilted back, I thought that one was as like the other as a twin brother. There *must* be horrible evil in Lanky!

So I reasoned, as Carter, recovering from his laughter, remarked:

"I gotta mind to let you tackle that job, Lanky, after you're once in the gang."

Lanky gradually showed a grin like a catfish. "Have you?" he asked.

"Yeah, and I mean what I say."

"Well," said Lanky. "I could show you some tricks, in the way of torture. I've seen the Yaquis practice!"

"So have I," answered Carter, with a grin to match that of Lanky. "I'm going to be curious to see what ideas of theirs you use, son."

"Their ideas is good," said Lanky, "but I got some ideas of my own that'll make a Scotchman swear off whisky, and tell where he's hidden his coin."

Carter chuckled, delighted with this chatter.

"And how about you?" he asked suddenly, whirling about on me.

It gave me such a start that I had to pucker my face to keep the alarm from showing.

"Aw, what does it matter—a damn young fool like that!" said I, at last.

Carter grinned, when I called the other fellow "young."

"We might as well have the party now," he said.

"Yeah, and why not?" asked Lanky. "You corral him, and I'll start the fireworks."

"It's a mighty good idea," said Carter. "The boys are feeling sort of dull."

"All right," said Lanky. "Though maybe it'd be better if I had a chance to think things over a little. A real artistic job, that way, it needs careful planning, I've always thought!"

"By thunder, brother," said Carter, laughing again, "you and me could do business together."

"That's what I thought the first time I laid eyes on your ugly mug," said Lanky comfortably.

Carter passed a hand over his long, lean, pale face.

"That's all right, too," said he. "You've been around the world some, Lanky. You been around the world. And that's what counts!"

"Yeah, I've been around enough to pick up some ideas," said Lanky.

"Wait a minute," said Carter. "We oughta have a talk together. Wait a minute."

He stepped into the hall and closed the door behind him. I looked at Lanky, and he made me an almost imperceptible sign for silence. I could guess that something was in his head, that ugly, crafty, misshapen head of his.

Before I could speak, the door opened again, and Carter came back to us.

I wondered, at that, if he had not brought with him some of his men, and if he had gone into the hall to dismiss them, feeling now that he had sounded us out, and found us of the right metal. At least, I could have sworn that I heard soft footfalls departing down the hall.

When he returned, the attitude of Carter had altered completely. He took a chair, and canted it back against the wall, close to the window. Then he drew in a great breath.

"Kind of sweet, this mountain air, ain't it?" he said.

"Yeah, but kinda lonely," said Lanky.

Carter smiled with appreciation.

"Yeah," he said, "I should 'a' met you a long time ago."

"We both might 'a' saved some money," said Lanky. "We might 'a' saved some time and money, at that."

"Maybe," agreed Carter. "How about you, kid? How you feel about throwing in with us?"

"Why," said I, "I don't know. I'd hate to leave Lanky behind me."

"That's the way to talk, Nels," said Lanky. "Now you're talking like a real partner!"

Carter watched me critically.

"Back there in Cat Hill, I thought you nearly had a rope around your neck," he said.

I decided on a stroke of boldness and frankness.

"You wanted to put one there," I told him. "I knew that, all right. You wanted to see how much you could talk into the fool heads of those people of Cat Hill."

"Well?" he said.

"Why, I don't know," said I. "I wanted to cut your throat for it. But I don't know. It was a game. You didn't owe me anything. And it was a game. I don't blame you. I might try the same dodge myself, but I haven't your flow of words, Carter. You ought to be a lawyer, you snaky fox!"

I seasoned the compliment—which I had borrowed so obviously from Lanky—with an insult that might make it seem more original, and more my own.

He was as highly pleased as before by this compliment of his command over language. He cleared his throat and said:

"We'll wait till the morning, maybe, about the kid. Some of the boys have turned in already. No use waking 'em up for that kind of a party. Let 'em be fresh. They'll wanta be fresh to enjoy it. I'll show 'em how a traitor oughta be treated."

"That's it," said Lanky, "a traitor."

"The dirtiest sneak in the world," said Carter, "is a traitor. The infernal low-lives—I detest them."

"Me, too," said Lanky. "I could tell you a yarn about that."

"About a traitor?"

"Yeah, about a traitor. The worst that I ever knew."

"Let's have it," said Carter.

He pulled a long, lean cigar out of his pocket and lighted it, and the rank odor of the tobacco floated across to me.

"It'll take time," said Lanky.

"That's all right. But begin with his name. Maybe I know him."

"You do," said Lanky.

"Do I?" said Carter, his eyes shining. "Well, who is he?"

"You'd be surprised to know."

"I know him, and I don't know that he's a traitor?"

"That's it."

"Where is he?" snarled the other.

"In your own gang," said Lanky.

Carter jumped to his feet. He could move like lightning when he cared to, and now all of his clumsiness disappeared.

"What's his name?" he demanded.

Lanky pulled a gun and held it under Carter's nose.

"Reginald Channing Carter is the name he goes by," he said.

38

DON PEDRO

One whiplash glance was thrown toward the door and then toward the window by Carter. "How far you going to carry this little joke, Lanky?" he said.

"Clear to hell," said Lanky. He added: "Laugh, Carter. That's the other half of the joke you were telling last night."

"You mean that hound Joyce?" said Carter. "Him that left you stalled in the desert, man? Is that what you're talking about?"

"Joyce," said Lanky, "when he faded out that morning, left the horse behind him. I didn't put that in last night when I was telling the yarn. And when you seen him, he'd picked up the horse after I got through to water, and he was riding to get me help."

The long lower jaw of Carter dropped as he prepared to answer—but the proper words could not be found, and so the mouth hung ajar for an instant. All the while, his lithe, long fingers were working like the legs of a pair of spiders, as they hung at his side.

"Put up your hands, brother," said Lanky. "Put up your hands and try to touch the ceiling. Put 'em up slowly. Bit by bit, while I watch you."

I had a good view of the face of Carter as he worked his hands slowly upward, and I could see how his eyes darkened and lightened in turn, as desperate thoughts entered his mind and faded from it, little by little.

At length he had pushed his hands well up above his head.

"Fan him, Nelly," said Lanky.

I went through Carter carefully and brought away two big Colts, and a thin-bladed knife with a six-inch blade and a weighted handle.

"Now hold a gun under his chin," said Lanky, "and look him straight in the eye, as though you were boxing. I'll try my hand."

I was sure that I had taken every possible thing that could be found on Carter, but Lanky brought out a little .22-caliber pistol, made so small and flat that it would have been too small even for the hand of a child. Yet it could be deadly enough, of course. That little chunk of lead did not need much propelling power behind it to drive it like a ray of death through a vital spot.

Lanky considered it with a smile.

"That's a real murder gun, Nelly," he said, "and it's about what I'd expect from a Mr. Murderer Carter, I'd say."

He looked over Carter with attention.

"You can put your hands down, brother," he said.

Carter silently obeyed. There was no particular malice in his face now. It was rather a keenly attentive look that he wore, as though he were trying to work out some mental problem with which Lanky was faintly connected.

"Take off your coat, Carter," commanded Lanky.

"What's the idea of that?" asked Carter.

"I'm in a hurry, man," said Lanky.

The coat was removed.

"Now face that wall and put your hands against it," said Lanky.

I was amazed by these directions, as Carter followed them.

"Stand fast and don't move," said Lanky.

He pulled up the shirt of Carter out of his trousers and laid his back bare.

"Damn you!" said Carter in a whisper.

I thought he would have turned, for his whole body writhed. But the cold nose of Lanky's revolver was nudging his backbone, and that pressure controlled him.

"Come here, Nelly," said Lanky.

I stepped up, and stared at the back of the man. It was a sight that I hadn't expected, for the scrawny frame of Carter was overlaid with long, ropy networks of muscle. And all over the back there were long scars, half an inch wide, and looking almost like strips of silver paint against the pink of the skin.

"What in the world—" I exclaimed.

"Oh, that's the Valle Nacional," said Lanky. "I thought that we'd find Mr. Don Pedro inside the clothes of this big buzzard!"

"You mean to say that Don Pedro—that Carter is Don Pedro—" I began.

Then I remembered a lot of things with a rush—that Don Pedro himself seemed to be unknown even to most of the members of his own gang, and that his signet ring was his sign of authority. And I remembered that when Lanky told the story about the flogging of Don Pedro in the Valle Nacional, Carter's facial expression had been very queer, to say the least!

Lanky stepped back from him.

"Tuck in your shirt tail, Don Pedro," he said.

Carter turned from the wall and began to stuff the shirt inside his trousers once more. "You're talking like a fool, Lanky," he said. "I would 'a' taken you for a real brain. But now you think that I'm Spanish Don Pedro, do you?"

"Don Pedro was never Spanish," said Lanky. "I always knew that."

"What made you know that?" asked Carter keenly.

"By the kind of gents that worked for him," said Lanky. "A Mexican couldn't help using more greasers like himself. But most of the men of Don Pedro have always been Yanks. You're the explanation of it, Carter, and the explanation fits in perfectly. Everything suits me fine!"

"I got scars on my back," said Carter. "That means that me and Pedro are the only men in the world that have scars—that means that I gotta be Pedro, or nobody at all. Is that it? That's the idea of a damn fool!"

"I know," said Lanky, with an aggravating smile, "you were on a ship, brother, maybe, and the mate dressed you down with a rope end one day?"

"Why not?" asked Carter. "Ain't that possible?"

"That kind of a scar is made with a soaked rope," said Lanky. "The kind that they use in the Valle Nacional. The rope flattens out agin' the skin and takes off a wide hunk. Son, you were in the Valle Nacional, and that's where you got the floggings that left those scars. A lot of floggings, too, before you decided to crawl over and lick the hand that beat you."

The upper lip of Carter twisted in an agony of rage and shame.

"Even suppose that I was ever in Valle Nacional," he said, "Don Pedro ain't the only man that ever escaped from that place."

"One in ten thousand get away," said Lanky. "And it would be a funny thing, Carter, if you and Don Pedro just *happened* to've been there together, and just *happened* to join up for crooked work."

"You got a theory," said Carter solemnly; "and theories are mostly wrong, Lanky. Now don't forget that."

"That back of yours is going to hang you, brother," said Lanky. "And that's good enough for me."

"You mean police, eh, and jail?" said Carter.

Lanky nodded.

"Murder ain't my middle name, like it is yours," he said. "If the law didn't have a hold on you, Carter, I suppose that I'd have to turn you loose and give you a fair chance with your gun to get me. But this way, I don't have to run the risk. I guess the law will sink its teeth right into you, Carter, and swaller you pretty nigh whole."

"Sooner than that," said Carter, "suppose that I tackle you bare-handed—d'you think that you'd live to get out of the house?"

"You ain't going to do that," said Lanky.

"Why not?" asked Carter. "Tell me why I ain't?"

"If you made us shoot you, brother, by letting out a few yells," said Lanky, "that would put out your chances. But if you go to jail, there's the chance of breaking out of jail. Or there's the chance of hiring a lawyer that'll talk you free. Or even if you are found guilty, maybe the sentence would be life, and not the rope, and you might get out of prison, in time. Hope works in a gent like you like a mole under ground. And you'd have hope all the time. But you know that if you make a wrong move while this gun of mine is looking at you, you're as good as dead!"

Carter suddenly grinned. He wasn't human; I could see that as he smiled.

"Well," he said, "you got a logical head on your shoulders, brother. I'll say that for you. But this house is guarded. How you going to get me out of it?"

"I'm going to walk you out," said Lanky, "and when we come to one of your guards, you're going to tell him to back up and leave you alone. Understand?"

Carter nodded. "That sounds all right," he said.

As he spoke, the door of the room was flung open, and the black-bearded fellow excitedly appeared.

"Slim Jake Harlowe's just come in," he said, "with news that Mays has taken to the hills and—"

"Get out of the room!" exclaimed Carter. "Get out and stay out. The next time that you bust in on me without knocking at the door, I'll have your hide for it. Where was you raised? In a barn?"

The man withdrew in haste.

Carter went on: "Manners is something that's gotta be born into the blood. That fellow, he don't know what they mean. Manners is better than money, I always say."

I listened to him in a half trance. It was the smugness of that human devil that fascinated me—the smugness, and the devilish evil in him combined. His sense of humor stopped with himself.

"Suppose that Loren Mays is on the track of the gang?" I said.

"Well, what of it?" retorted Carter. "If I have to go to jail, let the rest of them go to the devil. It's where they belong, so let 'em go!"

"All right," Lanky said. "Maybe that's the best way. Now we're going to start out of the house, Carter. You'll walk first with Nelly Grey, and I'll walk behind you, because I ain't so important. But remember all the time that I got my hand in my pocket, and the forefinger is around a trigger. Watch your step, and if there's a need of talk, you talk up bright and smooth. Come on, boys; we start!"

39

THE GET-AWAY

As we got to the door, I remember that Carter turned and said to Lanky, who was already walking behind us, on guard:

"What made you talk about Blondy, that way?"

"I thought you might 'a' been listening in," said Lanky.

Carter actually chuckled. "Yeah, you're bright," he said. "You're pretty bright, son. You could be useful, some place, to somebody."

I opened the door, and he walked out into the dark of the hall with me. I was carrying the lantern. The shadows struck out by my legs walked enormously along the wall beside us, but strangely failed to gain any distance on us.

We walked down the stairs and came into the big hall where we had had supper. The fire was dying down, but the huge coals were so strong that their light stained everything red. It seemed to me a gloomy and proper prognostication, because certainly before the day came, there was likely to be bloodshed!

It would not have done me any good to know that my feeling made up a good prophecy.

We crossed from the hall to the front door—if that's what you'd call a door opening onto the patio.

Somebody demanded, out of the shadows in the patio:

"Who's that?"

"Me," said Carter.

It was our old friend, the black-bearded fellow. He went on:

"You're always talking about laying low at night, chief. How come this here, with the two strangers?"

"Aw, shut up," said Carter, in anger. "Leave me alone, man. Don't talk back to your elders, is a good rule in any game, but specially in *my* games."

"All right," said the other. "It's your funeral."

I almost laughed as I heard this, nervous and tense as I was.

We walked across the patio, and when we came to the archway that opened out toward the forest, I asked:

"Is the barn out this way?"

"No," said Carter.

"Why didn't you say so before?" I asked him.

"Why should I help you to cut my throat?" asked Carter, with a good deal of reason in his viewpoint.

Well, we had to turn back across the patio, and then we pushed back a big double door that led in on the smell of hay, and the sound of the munching of it.

I was pleased by that. There is nothing in the world that seems so secure and pleasant, and generally all-around lazy and contented as the smell of hay in a barn, and the noise of animals munching and stamping.

Lanky was closing the door behind us, when I heard the black-bearded man sing out:

"Hey, don't take a lantern in there with all that hay. There's enough light from the moon through the windows."

That might have been true. We paid no attention, though, and as I hung up the lantern on a nail, I heard the voice of Blondy saying:

"It's all right. I've got 'em picked out."

He brought out a horse on the lead as he spoke, and coming close to Carter, he exclaimed:

"They've got you, eh?"

"You sneaking traitor!" said Carter. "You dirty, worthless hound!"

"I'm not a traitor, and I'm not a hound," said Blondy, bucking up his head to make the answer.

"All right, all right," said Carter. "I know what you are. You let in the wolves on me. But the trail ain't over, yet, and the world ain't come to an end. I'll get the bunch of you yet. You think it's hanging for me, but—"

Right into the middle of that sentence came a gasping exclamation from the door, and I recognized the voice of the black-bearded man. He had followed, and he had heard enough to let him know that his chief was being rounded up by us.

Lanky understood the same thing, of course, even more clearly than I did. He leaped for the door, thrust it open, and his gun spoke—then barked twice afterward.

He stepped back.

"Only winged him. This means fast riding, boys. Get the four hosses and streak it, I'd say."

We climbed onto the first four horses, as Blondy let them loose from the stalls to which they were tied. They were good horses. I had my pinto, Lanky had his gray, stolen from Tom Acker, and Blondy and the chief were both well mounted. Blondy went through the door first; I was behind him, with Carter's horse next, and last of all was Lanky.

We charged across that patio on the dead run, and behind us, as we went, we heard the house waking up with a roar. A gun went off, the sound muffled by the wall of the house. It was as though guns, like eager dogs, were giving tongue and ready to get at us.

And just after the tail of my horse swished through the outer gate, two rifles opened fire, as fast as possible.

As I got into the open, I looked back, and was glad to see that both Lanky and Carter were riding hard after me. The horses might be hurt, but the riders were intact, and that was the great thing, for the moment.

Then the dark of the woods swallowed us, and the noise of the hoof-beats turned into a soft, heavy pounding. I heard Lanky sing out loudly:

"Blondy?"

"Aye," said Blondy.

"We've got the jump on 'em," said Lanky. "Is there any place where we could pull up and let 'em go by us?"

"The woods are too open!" shouted Blondy in return. "You can't hide four men in this sort of timber."

It was true.

We dipped into a hollow, came out on the farther side, and went like fury down a long, easy slope that lengthened the strides of the horses. At that time, I felt that nothing in the world could stop us.

"Where do we aim to go?" yelled Blondy, still in the lead and playing the part of guide, because naturally he knew this ground better than we did.

"Cat Hill!" shouted Lanky in answer.

My heart sank. I could hardly believe my ears, but then I

realized that Lanky had not been able to resist the chance to make a great, sensational entry, in which the prisoner returned to the jail, bringing with him the recent leader of the riot, with enough charges against him to hang the rioter!

It was a good idea, I suppose. But it left me weak in the knees.

We streaked along out of the woods and into more open country, and now Blondy pulled back the horses to an easier gait. He ranged back beside Lanky and me with Carter riding a little in the lead.

He was free of hand and free of foot, but he never tried any tricks, because he knew that Lanky was always with him, and always had an eye on him. That was a perfectly good reason for going slowly, I can tell you!

Blondy wanted to know what course Lanky would like to take, and he suggested that we should head a little south, as though aiming at the town of Orange, and then, at the last moment, we could turn through Orange Canyon and aim straight toward Cat Hill. In that way, the crooks would not know quite which way to jump.

"Suppose they read our minds, they could aim straight for the mouth of the canyon and cut us off," Lanky said.

"They could," said Blondy. "It would just be a gambler's chance."

"Have we got the best of the horses?" asked Lanky.

"We have," said Blondy, "but the whole crowd of horses are good; mighty good. We won't gain much on 'em. Besides, they can get remounts where they want 'em."

"Where can they get 'em?" snapped Lanky.

"At the Tomlinson ranch, or the Gilbert place," said Blondy

"Couldn't we go there and do the same, then?" asked Lanky

"Listen!" said Blondy.

He held up a hand, and from far behind us, I could hear the noise of hoofs thrumming on the ground, and the faint crackling of brush.

"They're already after us," said Blondy. "By the time we'e changed horses wouldn't they just about be swarming all over us?"

"True," said Lanky, "and that's where they're in the luck They can stop to change, and then make up the lost time while our hosses fag out, but we've got to keep to the same nags."

He groaned aloud, as he said it.

"However," he added, "we've had a pile of luck, so far, and we're going to keep our luck with us. Come on, boys. We'll take the advice of Blondy. He has a head on his shoulders. If we head

toward Orange, they'll keep on that trail, most likely, and we
might shed 'em by the switch towards Cat Hill."

That was plain enough.

In other words, we ought to have a chance of two out of three
to get well ahead of them, by burning up our horses at a rapid
rate. Then, when we were well out in front, we could swing
suddenly aside toward Cat Hill. Even if they changed to fresh
horses on the way, they probably would have to lose some time
working out the trail problem, at the point where we branched
off, and then we would be into Orange Canyon, and bearing
rapidly down upon Cat Hill.

It was a good scheme. My heart stopped racing in a panic,
and it began to seem to me that nothing could beat us.

We reached the creek, folded it, and then turned straight
down along its bank, toward Orange.

The stars burned here and there in the black, smooth side
waters of the creek, and the trees seemed to go by us with a swish,
we were galloping so hard. I was heartened a good deal by seeing
the way that pinto stretched its legs and kept up with the rest. It
never had been backward, after the first mile!

We got down to a dense growth of trees, and turned sharply
to the right, through them.

"We've dropped 'em below the sky line," said Blondy,
exulting. "There's not a sound behind us!"

And there was not!

We rode on through the trees, came to open, rolling land, and
then before us I saw the mouth of Orange Canyon, black as the
muzzle of a gun. At the same time, over the hills to our right,
broke a line of galloping riders!

40

ODD MAN

Hope dies slowly, even in a lost cause. It was a second or so before I could realize what had happened. We had ridden our horses out—they were worn to a stagger, in the execution of a perfectly good plan. But we were beaten! There was no slightest doubt about that! Those riders on our right were sweeping along at a tremendous rate, and their horses were not merely cantering. They were bounding, like deer—the way a horse will do when it is fresh and has a spur working at its flank.

Yes, they had changed horses, and staking everything on the chance that we *would* go for Cat Hill, they had cut across country, and now had the knife at our throats!

I ground my teeth together. It seemed to me that sparks flew out of my eyes—sparks of exasperation and fear mingled. And I heard the voice of Carter laughing, as he rode behind me.

I yelled back to him, as we flogged our horses forward:

"Don't laugh, Carter. Whatever happens, *you* die!"

But he kept on laughing, and yelled, as he rode: "Ride 'em, cowboys!"

Why, as a matter of fact, I suppose that he hardly cared whether he lived or died, so long as plenty of other people would die around him. Blood was what he wanted, now that his temper was up.

We would make the mouth of the canyon, and that was clear. Once there, might we not turn and hold them at bay with our rifles? Yes, that seemed a possibility. But as we came closer, the fatally clear moonlight, that made all clever little maneuvers of deception an impossibility, showed me that on either hand the walls of the canyon went up like specially arranged and cut steps!

No, the instant that we made a stand, they would send a man or two up on the sides of the canyon, and following along as we retreated, they could easily drive us out of any cover that we found below.

There would be no chance of making a series of rear-guard actions. It would all be a matter of bolting through and trusting to the heels of our horses.

But there again we had no chance. We had burned out our mounts in taking a chance that had gone all wrong, and that was all there was to that!

A very sick man was I, as I thought of this.

Then another idea came to me.

Suppose that one man held the throat of the gap, while the others rushed on toward Cat Hill—after all, the distance was not great, only a matter of two or three miles, and galloping horses, even though weary, might cover it quickly enough.

In the meantime, the one man, the forlorn hope in the throat of the canyon, would be giving up his life, perhaps, but he might be the saving of the rest of us.

As I thought the thing out, I remember that a band of ice closed around my forehead and gripped me to the brain. Suppose that the chance fell upon me to remain behind?

Or should I suggest it?

Then I heard Carter saying, and laughing as he spoke:

"One of you boys can plug the gap, Lanky, and the rest of you can ride on to put me in hell. Now lemme see the brave boy that'll be a pillar of the law and society and throw himself away like that!"

He laughed, as he spoke, once more.

"It's a true thing," said Lanky. "Even the worst kind of a hound can bark at the right time. Yell out your choices, boys, and the odd man sticks in the mouth of the gulley!"

And he yelled again: "Now!"

Why, it seemed a foolish thing, but I suppose every puncher is used to it, from the many times that a gang, riding home, makes choice in a similar manner of the unlucky one who is to take all the horses to water, and then unsaddle and unbridle them, and turn them into the barn or the pasture.

So we shouted, Lanky and Blondy and I, all at once.

"Heads!" I called, for that was always my luck,

And like the chime of a bell, I heard their voices sounding together with mine:

"Tails!"

The ice band locked harder around my forehead. It was the end of me. I would cork the bottle for a minute or two, enough to make the others safe, and then—

Through the mist of my cold agony, I heard the voice of Lanky exclaiming:

"It's my turn, Nelly. I've got a scheme in my head that'll keep them howling up the wrong tree for hours. You two ride on like the devil for Cat Hill. If the sheriff's in town, turn over this catamount to him, and nobody else. If he ain't take him to the jail, and call up the men of the town. Then head back here with all the fighting men that you can get. You'll find me still alive, and two thirds of the way back to Cat Hill, by that time. Because, son, this is my lucky night!"

As he spoke, it became clear to the racing men of the Don Pedro gang, that they never could cut us off from the canyon mouth just by sheer riding, and as a result, they turned loose with a shower of bullets, and yelled like so many Comanches.

We were not hit. They could not possibly hit us with anything other than a chance bullet riding at the pace they were holding.

I turned to big Lanky and waved him off.

I tried my voice once or twice, before it would come. Then it came out in a ridiculous squeak.

"It's my job, and I'll take it," I said to him.

But all the time, my rotten weak heart was saying to me: "Why shouldn't he stay in your place? Why shouldn't he cork the canyon for a while? He's full of a million devices. He's a dead shot. He might be able to hold the place, whereas you're sure to go down quickly. Besides, he's older—he's lived more than half his life, and you've got all in front of you!"

I have to admit that those thoughts were going through my mind. As for the protest I made, it was only because I had some shame.

Shame of what? I asked myself that. There were only three to hear, and one was a worthless crook.

And yet I felt shame. I have heard men laugh at conscience, but after that night I know it's a giant and a tyrant.

Lanky did not argue. But he reached out his hand, and gripped mine.

"I know that I ain't got a chance to talk you out of it," he said. "God bless you, son. You're a white man. If they get you, I'll never leave the trail till I get all of 'em, one by one. Good-by!"

And back came young Blondy, his face drawn, and looking silver-gilt in the moonlight.

He grabbed my hand, also, swinging far out from his galloping horse as he did so.

"By rights it ought to be me," said Blondy. "But you're the kind that lives through the fire, and the world never forgets!"

He meant what he said. As for me, I had a crazy desire to laugh, when I thought of all that had happened to foist me into a false position as a gunman and a hero.

A weak-kneed hero was I, as big Reginald Channing Carter leaned from *his* horse, in turn, and showed me a face twisted horribly.

"The minute I seen you," he said, "I knew that you was fodder for the guns, and now they'll get you and eat you—you fool!"

We rushed into the shadow of the end wall of the canyon, at this moment, and I jerked Pinto around, while the others went cantering on. I saw the stagger of their tired horses. They were only going a snail's pace, and at that rate, how long would it be before they covered the few miles to Cat Hill? And how long would it be before they came back with the help that I needed?

There was not much chance to think about that.

As I dived out of the saddle to the ground, I gave the reins a jerk, and shouted a command that brought Pinto to his knees, and then to the ground beside me. And looking back, I saw the bandits coming on the run into the funnel-like mouth of the canyon.

I jerked my rifle butt into the hollow of my shoulder and opened fire. I was half blind. It seemed to me that those riders were larger than human, and they were coming as fast as hawks swoop out of the upper sky.

I knew, somehow, that I could never check that rush. They would sweep over me, and smash me to the earth with flying lead, and then they would go on to destroy Lanky and Blondy.

I fired four or five times as fast as I could, aiming into a mist. Then I managed to look out clearly, and see that every man had disappeared.

41

ONE AGAINST MANY

Well, I was in, and I knew that they were going to come for me like devils, now, because like so many devils they were yelling and raging as they saw that the canyon was corked, and that before that cork could be drawn to let them through, their chief would be lodged in the Cat Hill jail!

It meant the break-up of their gang. It meant the end of a lot of things to them. I don't suppose that there was one of the lot— perhaps excepting Tom Acker—who realized that Carter was Don Pedro, in fact, but the others at least knew that Carter was a tremendously important factor in the crowd. And I suppose that they expected that Don Pedro would have their scalps for letting Carter be run away.

More than all that, they had been checked when their teeth were about to close on the game, and that is why, I suppose, that they yelled like wild Indians among the big rocks that were scattered at the mouth of the canyon.

Their yelling quieted down. That meant that they were taking counsel. And presently two men started up the steep slope toward the top of the ravine wall at my left, carefully dodging back and forth among the rocks.

I drew a steady bead, waited for them to cross a gap between two rocks, and fired.

I saw my man leap into the air, with a yell that rang in my ears. But he jumped all the more agilely to cover, and I knew that I had merely put a spur into him, not disabled him at all.

I looked to the right, and made out a glimpse of one man climbing in a similar manner among the rocks, then of another.

I supposed that there were ten or eleven in the whole band. They were putting out these flankers to pot me from the top of the cliffs, and when I was done for, they would simply turn around and work back toward the mountains; they would never strive to press on, after this loss of time, to recapture their lost leader.

For all of that, I was not much happier. My friends were free, but I was certain to be snagged.

I began to shake so that when I twice tried for the men who were climbing to my right, I knew, as I pulled the trigger, that the trembling of my hand was sending the bullets awry.

A sort of passion of impatience came over me. I lifted the barrel of the gun and let it drop heavily, smashing my left hand against the top of the boulder which I was using as a rest.

That hand went numb. It became perfectly steady, after that, perhaps simply because there was no feeling in it.

And now I saw a fellow make a flying leap between two rocks, and tried for him with a snap shot.

He struck the farther stone, recoiled, and pitched down onto the ground.

I saw him writhe into a knot, and felt a sympathetic pain shoot through my vitals. I had not the heart to fire at the figure which streaked past the fallen man and got to safety among the boulders near the top of the canyon wall.

They had me now. The best that I could do was to wriggle in between a pair of the biggest stones that I could find, and lie there, keeping my eye peeled to either side for a sight of marksmen on the top of the cliffs—one on my right, and two on my left. But I had to have my face toward the mouth of the canyon, for at any moment, I knew that the rest of them might make a rush that would swallow me up.

As for the second man on the right, he was no longer trying to climb. He was crawling down on hands and knees, and I saw him repeatedly among the rocks. For he took little pains to conceal himself, and though I could have knocked him over a dozen times, I had not the heart to fire again.

Even then, I wanted to stop them, not to kill them. For the sight of Josh Acker falling was never out of my mind's eye.

As I kept a good lookout, I cursed the brightness of the very moon that enabled me to see so clearly. All of you who have been among Western mountains know how clear the stars are, and how the moon is like a ghostly silver sun for brightness, throwing deep, charcoal-black shadows.

Well, the moon that night seemed to me ten times brighter than it ever had been before in all my life of looking at it, and admiring it. From that day to this, a full, bright, round moon, in the middle of the sky, gives me the creeps. I cover my eyes while other people praise it!

For it was giving the same fine, clear light to those fellows who were on the edges of the cliffs on my right and my left, and all I could do was to snuggle there among the rocks, and hope that they would not locate me.

If I had had around me stones big enough, stones like those at the mouth of the ravine, I would have been able to find a fairly secure refuge. But as it was, the rocks were so shallow that I knew my enemies could easily angle their shots down into my body. I was hoping against hope, in the position that I held, then, and knowing that every hope was no good!

Then a gun spoke twice, in rapid succession, close before me, and behind a rock, a voice—the voice of Tom Acker—sang out:

"Who's there? Whoever's there, we'll let you stand by while we ride through. Understand? We'll let you stand by, safe and sound, and so help us God!"

I thought, my eyes squinting at the idea.

Had the three riders gone a great enough distance on the road to Cat Hill?

No, I remembered how their fagged horses had staggered, and I remembered how the horses of the Don Pedro gang had been bounding over the ground, fresh as antelope. They might still overtake Lanky and his cargo.

"Acker, go to the devil. I won't stand aside," I said.

"Hey," said Tom Acker. "It's the kid, is it? Is that you, Grey?"

"I'm here," said I.

"Listen to me, Grey," said he, "and I mean it. I'll bury the grudge that I've got against you. Maybe that was a fair fight between you and Josh. I've always thought that it was, for my part. I'll bury the knife. You stand back, kid, and you won't be hurt. But if you don't move, we're going to shoot you full of holes."

"Go ahead and shoot," said I.

My throat was very dry as I spoke, and the words came out with a rasp.

Dan Porson—he ought to be here, if there were a just

Providence. He ought to be lying under the fire of the other rifles, where I was lying at that moment!

I groaned, as that thought went home in me like a knife—a stabbing knife that is twisted around in the wound.

"You poor fool!" yelled Tom Acker. "I'm offering you your life. You're nothing to us, compared to what we're riding for. I'm offering you your life. Understand?"

"I know what you're riding for," I yelled back. "You're riding to save Don Pedro, but I'm going to make you too late. Understand *that*?"

I heard him curse, softly, deeply, like a man to whom even the curses are a feeble mode of expression. Then he said, not loudly, for he was very near:

"Then take what's coming to you, you half-wit!"

His voice was raised, running high up the scale in a long, wavering call, the sort of a voice that every mountaineer learns to use, when he has to make his voice cut through a distance.

"Hai, Jerry!"

And back from the ravine wall on my left came a voice that faintly answered: "Hai, Tom!"

"He's here!" yelled Tom Acker. "He's here close before me, between the two low black rocks. Blast the lead into him, the fool! Kill him, Jerry!"

I squirmed lower into the ground. It seemed to me that I reduced the thickness of my body by half, and twisting my head about, I looked back at other rocks, farther down the ravine.

Every one of them seemed to be ranged as a member of a pair, and every one of them seemed bigger and better than the rocks I had chosen as a natural fort.

Then it occurred to me that I could have tried to lift up heavy stones, and put them one on top of the other and so I could have made a better fort for myself. But there was little chance of that maneuver now, for expert riflemen were looking down upon me, and ready to shoot at the slightest move.

By my idiocy in answering the questions of Tom Acker, I had enabled them to locate me, a thing which otherwise might have held them up for an hour. Now they knew where to look, and their keen eyes could not be long delayed.

As I thought of that, something hit the rock on my right a sharp blow, and a long splinter of rock fell down against my face.

Well, they had me, after that, and they would pay me out, before long. It was Jerry's rifle—Jerry's rifle shooting from the left that was probably doing the mischief.

The report of the rifle clanged loudly in my ears, and then was dissipated slowly in echoes, that flew off on heavy wings down the ravine.

Where were Lanky and the others, on their staggering horses? How far had they gone on the way to Cat Hill? Just how long was I to stay here?

Well, time hardly mattered. A few minutes would be all that I could last.

I was not very much afraid, by this time. I think that the pain of the bullets, striking into my flesh, was what I was chiefly concerned about.

And first I told myself that I would be able to stand it. And then I remembered how the man to my right had screamed out when the bullet struck his body.

No doubt he was as resolute as the rest of them, far bigger and bolder than I. But still the terrible sense of the lead ripping through his body had been enough to unman him! What could I hope to do except to yell like a cur that's been kicked! The great Don Pedro—had he not been forced by pain to crawl on his hands and knees and lick the hand of the man who had flogged him?

I broke into a sweat.

Then a smart blow struck me on the left leg, and with it went a long, twisting, red-hot pang of agony. Afterward, the report of the rifle followed, clanging in my ears.

It was the man on the right-hand cliff who had fired that bullet. And all that I could feel, if you'll believe it, was a strange sense of gratitude to the Maker that the pain was not greater and that I could bear it so easily.

It was bad. It was a very bad pain. But I had endured worse. Once I knocked my knees together jumping down off a high bank. That was worse, for instance!

Now I went on thinking that if I lay still, perhaps they would not be able to make out that I was really there. If they kept on firing and firing, without really making me out through the shadow of the rocks—if they simply were firing blindly into the gap between the two rocks, perhaps before long they would give it up, and swear that I had gone to some other place.

That pain, which I had been congratulating myself about because it had been so small, suddenly assumed immense proportions.

It struck me like a tidal wave, and passed through every nerve in my body. The first shock had partly numbed the nerves. Now every one of them that had been torn in two, cried out at once. I wanted to yell. I felt my tongue stiffen against the roof of my mouth.

Suppose that I offered to let them through now? Would they take the offer?

I think I should have proposed it to them, but it seemed to me that a whole hour had passed since Tom Acker made his first proposal. Now they would know that it was too late!

I had been neglecting the approaches to the canyon walls, on either side. Now I saw another man running up on the right hand, toward the top of the cliff. I tried a second snap shot, and by a strange grace of luck I saw this fellow double up exactly as the first one had done—exactly as a hurt caterpillar does!

42

CLOSING IN

I disregarded that man for a moment. Then I saw him rolling toward cover, and I followed him in the sights for an instant. I was to die. It was right that some of the rest of them should die also.

A voice yelled, somewhere: "Hey, Tom!"

And from the right, where the wounded man had just disappeared from my sight behind a stone, a voice called, not too strongly:

"Help!"

I heard a man just in front of me exclaim:

"By thunder, Tom's gone."

"He's down, but he ain't gone," said another voice. "Get up there and bear him a hand."

"Bear him a hand yourself," said the first speaker. "You see how Grey can shoot?"

I could have laughed at that; but all desire for laughter was wiped out of me by a rattling fire that began to hammer on the rocks around me. If they had been in any doubt about my hiding place, they were reassured now, after I had fired that shot. They kept up a continual stream of bullets from either edge of the cliffs.

And now, with a hammer blow, I was struck on the right

shoulder. It spread a wave of numbness down to my finger tips, and inside me to the very heart.

The right shoulder—the gun arm!

I had to get out of there—but how could I get out, when I was shot through the leg?

I counted six shots in rapid succession, from either cliff; none of them hit me.

The numbness left my body, and in its place, terrible pain began to shoot through me. The wound in the leg and the wound in the shoulder joined hands and—gripped hard. What agony!

A fresh hail of bullets commenced from the cliffs, and now through a haze of pain, I saw half a dozen figures start up from the rocks in front of me and to either side. They came running in, screeching.

I jerked myself to my knees, and fired at a man right in front of me.

He leaped to the side like a gigantic jumping jack, and landed on his side, on a rock, and I heard the breath go out of him with a grunt.

The other dark forms had disappeared at the same instant, and now that I was up on my knee, I stood up and started to run back down the ravine.

Well, that may sound like a strange thing, but all that I felt in my wounded leg was a sort of jellylike weakness, so that the muscles were slow in responding to my will, and I had to think specially hard about the dragging strides that I made with that foot.

I found another pair of boulders, where the neck of the ravine narrowed a little, and as I was dropping in between them, a red-hot knife ripped across my back. Yes, "rip" is right. Imagine a red-hot knife with a ragged edge, cutting the flesh, but tearing more than it cuts! That was how I felt!

But there I was, lying writhing with the agony, in the shelter of the rocks. I was right. They were higher than the first pair. There was a bit of gravel in between them, too, several inches of it, and as I scuffed this out, I was able to get still lower, still closer to the ground.

They knew they had me, oh, how well they knew it.

"He's gone!" screeched the man on the left-hand cliff. "Close in! Close in! He's gone! I put a slug right through him."

You don't feel fear, at a time like that. At least, not when you know for certain that you are going to die—when you're actually dying, as I felt sure that I was, at that moment.

No, what you want is to get back at the fellows who have sunk your ship, and when I saw that devil on the cliff leap out and dance beside a boulder on the one hand and a shrub on the other, I took my sound left hand and with it I arranged my useless right arm, and tucked the rifle well back into the hollow of the shoulder, and made my numb right hand close around the trigger.

I wanted to get in one more good shot—and then I wouldn't care what happened.

So I took a careful bead, and as I took it, I felt the blood trickling down my back, and over my chest, and the blood on my leg was flowing also. That sense of bleeding was a queer thing— water running from a spring that is soon dry!

And so I got the jumping jack in the middle of the sights.

I could hear other men shouting and yelling in jubilation toward the mouth of the valley, and I could see, from the corner of my eye, their shadows as they ran toward me.

I was pleased, if only that right hand of mine had strength enough in it to pull the trigger.

Gradually that right hand began to contract. The jumping jack on the top of the cliff was still prancing, still yelling. And then, surprising me, the rifle exploded against my wounded shoulder and sent a thrill of the most exquisite agony through my entire body.

The jumping jack stopped his dancing and prancing. And, like one about to make a long and beautifully graceful high dive, he leaned out from the brow of the cliff and shot downward, and went into the shadowy blackness under the brow of the rock like a diver entering water, without a ripple, without a splash.

I laughed a little, as I watched him fall. There was one life gone, at least—one full life, to pay for mine. And I felt no twinge of conscience, but only a great relief. It seemed to me that dying would now become an easy thing.

I looked ahead of me, expecting to see the gang about to close in on me, and knowing well that I could not get the rifle into position again for a quick shot.

But they had disappeared. There was only a brandishing pair of legs as one fellow dived for cover behind a rock.

I heard their startled voices, as they exclaimed to one another. One of the men shouted out, with wild tones of rage:

"Is one damned brat going to stop the whole of us? Get him out, and eat him raw!"

And from the valley floor a long, wavering cry came:

"You do the eating! I ain't got any appetite left."

At that, I heard laughter, all around me, as it seemed—shouts and hoots and roar of laughter, far and near. And a moment later, I found that my own voice had joined in the mirth hysterically. My own voice!

The laughter ceased, and the echoes of it flew for a moment up and down the ravine.

Rifles began again, from the cliffs on either side. Another bullet nipped me, somewhere, but just where, I could not be sure.

I was going to sleep.

That, I knew, was the forerunner of death. Just as sleepy numbness is dreaded by the man in the snowy Arctic, so I knew that the loss of blood will make the brain dizzy. And so it was that I was passing out of my senses.

What did I think of then?

Well, I thought mostly about Dan Porson, I'm ashamed to say. I dare say that there were heroes in the world who would almost have relished a position such as mine, and who would have been glad to die, so that one crook could be brought to justice, and two good men saved.

But I don't pretend to be a hero of that stature. Mostly, as I say, I was thinking about Dan Porson, and wishing that he could lie where I was lying, and feel the blood trickling down over his body, and feel the lightning twists of agony that ran through me.

Why didn't they rush in on me, as I lay there half insensible?

Well, I suppose the picture of the fellow leaning off the brow of the cliff was still too brilliantly imprinted in their minds.

If only Dan Porson could be made to lie there where I was lying, and if only I could be sitting, somewhere, in the broad honest warmth of the sun, talking to Bobbie Meade, and telling her about a dimly dreadful moment in my past, when I lay in the bottom of a wild ravine, whose one wall was white with the moonshine, and whose other wall was covered with the most jet darkness of the night!

The thought of Dan Porson ended in me.

I found that I *was* sitting with Bobbie Meade on her own veranda, and I was telling her about that very moment in the valley. I was talking to her, and in the distance, somewhere far in the distance, rifles were firing, as men stupidly kept up some sort of a target practice!

A nearer noise burst in upon my brain.

Instantly, I was snatched from the side of smiling Bobbie, and found myself lying once more in the rough gravel between the two boulders, in that horrible, cold valley, with the slow oozing of the blood from my body, and with a brain lighter and lighter with every moment.

I lay there, and before me, I heard men shouting wildly, and heard their feet running, stamping on rocks, stamping on gravel.

Another sound came up the valley in a smoothly increasing roar. It was like the noise of water. I wondered if a great freshet had started down the ravine, and if the water would overwhelm me, and with so much blood out of my body, if I would not be as light as a cork, dancing on the waves.

Then I realized that it was not the sound of rushing water, but the thundering of hoofs, out of which men's voices arose.

The men from Cat Hill—Lanky—Blondy!

I forgot my wounds and my weakness for that moment.

There was still some strength in my left hand, and with that I gripped the edge of the boulder at one side, and pulled myself up, and sat on the stone, and as I did that, around the curve of the ravine came pouring a whole wave and battle front of galloping horsemen. It was the finest sight that God ever placed upon this earth for mortal eyes to see.

And it seemed to me that from the rocks in the mouth of the ravine I heard screeching voices, as from human rats already underfoot.

43

THROUGH A FOG

There was no fainting done. I dropped into a mental mist, but the light never went entirely out. I remember everything. I remember particularly how Lanky picked me up in his amazingly strong arms, and carried me to the side of the ravine, and how I was laid down there on blankets that were spread on top of a pile of pine boughs.

I remember that one fellow said: "That's going to be the spoiling of a lot of dog-gone good hoss blankets—"

Then he caught himself and added: "I didn't mean that."

"You cheap fool!" snarled some one at him.

They had a doctor with them, not on purpose, but by accident. He was the sort of a doctor who would get into a fight for the fun of it, and therefore he was a good doctor—which is the main reason that I'm now writing down these words, and still wondering a good deal as I see that my right hand is pushing the pen, and not the hand of a ghost.

He started working over me. Then he barked out some orders. He was ordering medicines and stuff to be brought out from Cat Hill, and the men departed with their horses on the dead run.

"Not much use," said the doctor, "but we'll give the youngster every chance we can."

A big hand pushed the hair back from my eyes. It was Lanky, who said:

"You fix him, doc. I'll spend the rest of my life paying you back."

"Oh, damn the money," said the doctor. "What a lark *this* kid has had before he cashed in."

"Shut up!" said Lanky. "He can hear you."

He leaned closer to me.

"Say what you want!" he said.

"Water!" said I.

"You've drunk a gallon," said Lanky. "Is it all right, doc?"

"Make him happy," said the doctor.

I got the water, with Lanky's hand under my head while I drank it.

The bandaging was still going on. My body felt like a loose sack. Almost all of the pain had ended.

"What else?" Lanky asked.

"I'd like to see Bobbie Meade," said I. "If she feels like riding this far."

"She's been sent for," said Lanky.

"Has she?" said I. "You always think of everything, Lanky."

I felt sleepy. Then I heard Lanky telling me to hang on like hell. I opened my eyes and asked him what I should hang on to.

"Here!" said Lanky. "Hang on to Bobbie's hand. Bobbie, for Heaven's sake, pull him through!"

I made out Bobbie's face against the dawn.

"Why, he's all right," she said calmly. "You're all right, Nels. We're going to pull you through like nothing at all."

"Sure I'll pull through," said I, "but I'm sleepy, or something. I don't seem to see you very well."

"It's a mighty foggy morning," said the voice of Blondy. "I can't see very well myself."

"Nobody can," said Lanky. "It's just a damned foggy morning, is all. There's nothing the matter with you, kid."

"Sure there isn't," said I.

I asked about the gang.

"Four of them got away—for the time being," said Lanky. "And Acker has just died. You got three of them, son, and you crippled some more. It was a grand fight."

"It was a *great* fight," said the heavy, solemn voice of Robert Meade.

"Was it?" said I. "Are you there, Mr. Meade?"

"I'm here, my boy," he said.

"I can't make you out—account of the fog," said I.

"Neither can I see you very well," he said, very quickly. "It's just the fog."

"That's it," said I.

"You're coming around," said Robert Meade. "We need you, and that's one reason that you're going to come around."

"Are you going to cry, like a fool!" said the whisper of Lanky.

"I'm not crying," whispered Bobbie, in return. "It was only the flash of the sun that sort of brought water to my eyes."

I wondered, vaguely, how the flash of the sun could be so bright on a morning that was so desperately foggy.

"That fellow Carter is in for the rope," said Lanky. "Acker lived long enough to confess everything about the gang, and how he and Carter ran it, and Don Pedro was a harmless Mexican ghost behind the whole idea."

"Can I speak to him now?" said a voice that I knew.

"You keep back and be damned," said the doctor briskly.

"I'm damned already," said the voice.

"Hello, Dan," said I. "Where are you?"

"I'm here, partner," he said. "Look, where I'm here beside you. Can you see me, Nels?"

"Sure I can," said I. "But the damned fog gets between. It's all right, Dan."

"It would do me a lot of good," said Dan Porson, "if you'd tell me a couple of times what a skunk I am. Everybody else in the world knows what I am—but I'd like to hear it straight from you."

"You're all right, Dan," said I, suddenly seeing with my mind more clearly than I could see with my eyes—more clearly by far. "You had the wrong steer, that was all. Your father gave you the wrong steer, and after you started the wrong way, you kept on. It's all right."

"You forgive me, Nels?" he said.

"I do," said I.

"My Heaven," said Dan. "You're a man!"

"You blubbering jackass, get out of here," said Lanky. "You talk as though something were going to happen. Nothing's going to happen except that he'll pull through."

"Why, sure I'll pull through," said I.

It was hard to breathe.

"Bobbie," said I.

"Here I am," she said, in a faint voice.

"Bobbie," said I, "take a good grip, I'm sort of sinking."

"Look," she said. "I'm holding with all the strength of my soul."

My eyes opened, and I saw her face with perfect clarity. And I saw the great, wild golden flush of the morning, and that her eyes were wet and red, but that she was smiling, as though she had been crying from happiness. And a warmth went through me, in a miraculous way.

After that, I fell asleep.

I should, of course, have died. The doctor agrees, in that. He says that I had no chance in the world to recover, and that he knew it from the first, and that he was willing to stake his whole reputation on the fact that I would die, and immediately.

However, Lanky said that Bobbie had too hard a grip and wouldn't let me get away.

And Bobbie says that Lanky saved me, because when I came back to life enough to start raving, in a feeble way, he started in and told me a story that had no sense at all. But it seemed to please me, and I went to sleep again, and woke up with an eyelash grip on life.

That was all there was to it.

Carter?

Carter amazed the world by refusing to have a lawyer and defending himself, and somehow or other, he talked himself into a sentence of merely life! And I suppose, in time, that he will talk himself out of prison, too.

However, I don't mind that. I don't mind anything, and for these years, I've never been able to wish anybody bad luck—not with my own pockets so chuck full of happiness.

Bobbie, however, seems to bear a little malice, and she speaks with a good deal of disgust of the reports that Carter is doing a great deal of good, saving the souls of the other prisoners in the penitentiary.

Well, he always had a wonderful flow of words.

As for Lanky, he won't spend a great deal of time with us. He finds life on the ranch rather dull. We never know when he'll be gone. We never know when he'll come back. But it's never a bad day when he arrives and stretches his long legs under the table, and says:

"Why, Bobbie, that reminds me of a time when I was with a gent up in Colorado, and—"

ZANE GREY'S
GREAT
WESTERNS

_____ 80451 **ARIZONA AMES** $1.50

_____ 81434 **BOULDER DAM** $1.50

_____ 81326 **FORLORN RIVER** $1.50

_____ 81017 **KNIGHTS OF THE RANGE** $1.50

_____ 81136 **LIGHT OF WESTERN STARS** $1.50

_____ 81321 **LONE STAR RANGER** $1.50

_____ 81325 **LOST PUEBLO** $1.50

_____ 81275 **MAN OF THE FOREST** $1.50

_____ 80454 **MYSTERIOUS RIDER** $1.50

_____ 80453 **RAINBOW TRAIL** $1.50

_____ 81374 **ROBBERS' ROOST** $1.50

Available at bookstores everywhere, or order direct from publisher. ZGA

POCKET BOOKS
Department ZGA
1230 Avenue of the Americas
New York, N.Y. 10020

Please send me the books I have checked above. I am enclosing
$ _____ (please add 50¢ to cover postage and handling). Send check
or money order—no cash or C.O.D.'s please.

NAME _____

ADDRESS _____

CITY _____ STATE/ZIP _____

POCKET BOOKS

ZGA

ZANE GREY'S
GREAT
WESTERNS

_____ 81228 SHADOW ON THE TRAIL $1.50

_____ 80522 SUNSET PASS $1.50

_____ 81322 TRAIL DRIVER $1.50

_____ 80701 TO THE LAST MAN $1.50

_____ 80447 TWIN SOMBREROS $1.50

_____ 80456 U.P. TRAIL $1.50

_____ 80450 VALLEY OF WILD HORSES $1.50

_____ 80728 WEST OF THE PECOS $1.50

_____ 80523 WESTERN UNION $1.50

_____ 81323 WILDERNESS TREK $1.50

_____ 80317 WILDFIRE! $1.50

Available at bookstores everywhere, or order direct from publisher.   ZGB